PRAISE FOR JO

Praise for *Dove Season:* A Jimmy Veeder Fiasco

Winner of the 2012 Spotted Owl Award for Debut Mystery

"[Johnny Shaw] is excellent at creating a sense of place with a few deft strokes . . . He moves effortlessly between dark comedy and moments that pack a real emotional punch, and he's got a knack for off-kilter characters who are completely at home in their own personal corners of oddballdom."

—TANA FRENCH, author of *The Trespasser*

"Johnny Shaw calls *Dove Season* a Jimmy Veeder Fiasco, but I call it a whole new ball game; I enjoyed this damn book more than anything else I read this year!"

—CRAIG JOHNSON, author of the Walt Longmire Mystery series

"*Dove Season* is dark and funny, graceful and profane, with beating-heart characters and a setting as vivid as a scorpion sting on a dusty wrist. Debut author Johnny Shaw is a welcome new voice. I'm already looking forward to Jimmy Veeder's next fiasco."

—SEAN DOOLITTLE, Thriller Award–winning author of *Lake Country*

Praise for *Big Maria*

Winner of the 2013 Anthony Award for Best Paperback Original

"Comic thrillerdom has a new star."

—*Booklist Online* (starred review)

THE UPPER HAND

ALSO BY JOHNNY SHAW

The Jimmy Veeder Fiascos

Dove Season
Plaster City
Imperial Valley

Stand-Alone Novels

Big Maria
Floodgate

THE UPPER HAND

JOHNNY SHAW

THOMAS & MERCER

Published by Thomas & Mercer, Seattle

www.apub.com

Amazon, the Amazon logo, and Thomas & Mercer are trademarks of Amazon.com, Inc., or its affiliates.

ISBN-13: 9781503900738
ISBN-10: 1503900738

Cover design by Ed Bettison

Printed in the United States of America

For David Downing

Thank you

PART ONE

CHAPTER 1

Call him sentimental, but when Axel Ucker planned a robbery, he thought about his old man. Larceny had been one of the few things they had in common.

Sitting outside at the Mexican restaurant El Rey de Los Chingones, Axel put down his well-worn copy of *Emotional Alcatraz: Breaking Out of the Prison of Your Past* and again turned his attention to the other side of the street. He'd read the Tony Rogers book twice and knew passages by heart. At present, the book acted as a prop to appear inconspicuous. A man reading a self-help book was as threatening as a three-legged kitten.

He spooned more guacamole onto his plate and made notes in his pad. Decked out in his Wilke Rodriguez suit, Axel blended in with the downtown lunch crowd. No one would suspect that he was casing the Little Grass Shack across the street as he dined luxuriously on his carnitas burrito and mandarin Jarritos.

The medical-marijuana dispensary did brisk lunchtime business. Because the Little Grass Shack was a cash-only enterprise, Axel considered it an upside-plus target. According to the May issue of *High Times*, it was one of the top three dispensaries in the San Diego metropolitan area. Five cannabis leaves out of a possible five. Only Global Chillage and Planet Hollyweed ranked higher.

Well fortified with the same precautions as a pawn shop in a lousy neighborhood, the Little Grass Shack stood prepped for attack. Barred windows, razor wire on the roof, and security cameras where you would expect them: two in front, two in back, and six inside. No security guard, but there would be firepower under the counter. Marijuana dispensaries drew mostly amateurs. The robberies that Axel had read about were uncreative smash-and-grabs that lacked finesse. A good thief knew a gun was a precaution, not a plan.

Axel ate more chips and went over his calculations. Carrying out the robbery on a Friday would increase the odds of success by thirty-two percent. Closer to thirty-eight if it was a three-day weekend. Plus or minus three percent depending on downtown traffic. Plus or minus two percent depending on the weather.

Jackson Armored made its pickups on Mondays and Fridays. The money from weekend business would be larger—maybe by double—but the size of the haul wasn't nearly as important as the not-going-to-prison part of Axel's plan. The armored car drivers on Monday were police-academy rejects who took their jobs too seriously, gun range bros with trigger fingers itching for something other than paper targets.

A good plan hinged on finding the weakness in the security measures: a low-quality safe, an outdated alarm system, a disgruntled employee. No matter how seemingly impenetrable a wall, a patient thief could find the fissure. In the case of the Little Grass Shack job, that crack was ten feet wide with a "Take All the Money" sign at the entrance. That crack went by the names of Stanley Pruitt and Steven McCrary.

"Hello, boys," Axel said as the banged-up GMC Griffin armored truck pulled up to the loading zone in front of the Little Grass Shack. One wheel went over the curb, the truck bouncing when it came off the sidewalk.

The two Jackson Armored drivers never showed up on time and looked stoned when they finally arrived. For a month, Axel had witnessed the pair leave one of the car doors open, get in a shoving match over whose turn it was to drive, and almost forget a bag of cash on the curb. Stanley was the senior employee of the two. In his mid-forties, he walked like his ass hurt. An otherwise thin man with a tight beer belly that made him look like a boa constrictor digesting a globe. Steven's bodybuilder physique made his arms float at his sides like a marionette's. He looked like everything confused him, and he never managed to tuck in his shirt all the way.

Exiting the armored car, Steven—true to form—tripped on the sidewalk. Stanley called him a "butt collector" and farted loud enough for Axel to hear across the street. The sound made a passing French bulldog bark uncontrollably.

"Unbelievable," Axel said.

Even if these two couldn't be coerced into abetting—which he was confident they could be—their incompetence would be enough to create a workaround.

Stanley buzzed the intercom outside the Little Grass Shack. Steven pushed on the door, but it didn't budge. Stanley shook his head and pulled the door open, pointing at the "Pull" sign.

Axel flipped through the thirty pages of notes in his pad. Calculations, timelines, drawings, questions. For weeks, he had spent hours on research—background information about the dispensary employees, sketches of the armored car route, three trips to the county planning office for building specs, analysis of traffic patterns. He had monitored both armored car drivers over the last week to finalize the plan.

There wasn't any more research or planning left to do.

Axel finished his orange soda, paid the bill, double-checked his tip, added another dollar, and walked onto the sidewalk. He stared at the

Little Grass Shack and nodded to himself, satisfied that he had thought of everything.

It was time.

He wrapped a thick rubber band twice around the notebook and dropped it in his bag. He would put it with the other robbery notebooks that he had written over the years. Hundreds of robberies that no one would ever perform. Knowing that he could successfully rob a place was victory enough.

What didn't make sense to him was why he was planning yet another robbery. He usually only did it as an outlet for stress, but everything was going well in his life. He had an incredible girlfriend, a new house, and an upcoming promotion. The only plan that mattered was the plan he had made for his life.

Axel turned the corner, looked up at the thirty-story building, and walked through the big glass doors. Working in the skyscraper made him feel like a grown-up. He pressed the call button and waited for the elevator. He had broken loose from his hometown, his past, and the stigma attached to his family. Nobody treated him like he didn't belong. He no longer looked like he owned a pair of camouflage pants.

But if he was going to really move on, Axel needed a new hobby. Regular people didn't case joints and do background checks on strangers. They didn't sit in their cars in front of armored car drivers' homes, pissing in Gatorade bottles. They did other things. They went to the gym. They played fantasy football. They were alcoholics.

Axel decided to buy a crossword puzzle magazine on the way home from work. Or maybe sudoku.

The Little Grass Shack would be his last hypothetical robbery. His days of thinking like a thief were over. To commit to the future, he had to let go of the past—which not coincidentally was the verbatim ad copy on the cover of the Tony Rogers book in his bag. It had been staring him in the face all along.

CHAPTER 2

Axel might have been the brains of the family, but Axel's sister, Gretchen, had the balls.

When they were teenagers, she found his notebooks full of elaborate schemes. She had used one of the plans, without his knowledge, to steal a box of *Playboy* magazines from Mr. Hernandez's garage. The "Women of Mensa" issue had been integral in the discovery of her sexual identity. That first burglary had catapulted her onto her current career path.

Gretchen Beetner fancied herself a second-story man, but due to her sex and the preponderance of ranch houses in the San Diego area, she was more of a sliding-glass-door gal.

She looked at the list of names and addresses that she had culled from her other brother's computer, all the nerds that shared his love for role-playing games.

Disappointment followed. No danger or thrills today. Run-of-the-mill thievery. No laser tripwires or Indiana Jones–style booby traps. None of them even owned dogs, due to allergies and/or asthma.

The scores were lucrative, but Gretchen needed to reevaluate the long-term potential of stealing comic books. It was just too damn boring. She wanted to feel like a Viking warrior plundering a city for its spoils, not a petty thief stealing funny books from geeks.

With Comic-Con in full swing and the entire nerdiverse in attendance, there were a lot of empty houses waiting to get hit. This was her third burglary of the day, and it wasn't even eleven o'clock. If she got to all the addresses on her list, it would be a new one-day record.

The next name on the list was Chandler Price, a.k.a. mrawarrior6969 on 4chan, a.k.a. @redpillpopping on Twitter.

Gretchen sat in her Honda Civic in front of Chandler's parents' house at the end of the cul-de-sac in La Jolla. Huge house, huge yard, huge view. She wondered if Chandler got an allowance to mow the lawn or if that stopped after he turned thirty. Who was she kidding? Residents of La Jolla didn't mow their own lawns. Mexican people did.

Chandler's father was performing root canals. Chandler's mom would be at her yoga class after dropping her son off at the convention center. The house would be empty.

Gretchen got out of the car, put on her backpack, and walked straight for the house. She held a flyer that she had pulled from a nearby telephone pole. If anyone stopped her, she was looking for Rascal, a missing calico cat.

Most sliding glass doors came standard with bolt locks. But locks didn't do any good if homeowners didn't engage them. In less than ten seconds, Gretchen had the back door open. Nobody would ever know she'd been in the house.

At the end of a long hallway, she found the door to the "comic book room." It wasn't difficult. A life-size poster of Deadpool greeted her with "Keep the Fuck Out" in a word balloon. Not heeding the sign, Gretchen walked the fuck in.

She stepped into the grand hall of the Museum of Stunted Maturity. Action figures and small statues of superheroes and monsters lined the shelves. At the center of the room sat rows of folding tables with long cardboard boxes on top and underneath, each of them full of clear plastic bags and titled dividers like you would find in a record store: Action Comics, Adam Strange, Adventure Comics, and so on. A dehumidifier hummed in the corner.

Posters adorned the walls, either of women with impossibly huge tits and eternally erect nipples, or of men with muscles where muscles didn't exist bulging beneath skintight primary colors. Overcompensation at war with homoeroticism. Except for Evel Knievel and Prince, few straight men could pull off a cape. Not even Samuel L. Jackson on a good day.

De rigueur for any collector, the comic books were organized first by publisher, then alphabetical by title, and finally chronologically by issue number, with annuals and special issues in back. It was like looking for a needle in a clearly labeled package of needles. It would take Gretchen less than ten minutes to find the issues on her list, throw them in her backpack, and be in her car on the way to the next house.

Her comics du jour were bronze age Marvel, a stable commodity with good resale. The titles were familiar to her. *The Amazing Spider-Man* #129, *Daredevil* #158, *The Incredible Hulk* #181, *Marvel Spotlight* #5, *The Tomb of Dracula* #10, and *The Uncanny X-Men* #94 were the biggies, but there were plenty of second-tier books that fetched good coin. Chandler wouldn't own all of them, but all serious collectors had a few key issues.

Wasting no time, she flipped through the comics and pulled out *Iron Fist* #14—a 9.4 CGC copy that could fetch as much as five hundred bucks.

A car pulled up outside. Without rushing, she stowed the comic in her backpack and moved to the window. A middle-aged woman and a well-built young man with a man-bun and Capris got out of a Ford Explorer. They grabbed their yoga mats and headed to the house.

Gretchen remained calm and went back to quietly flipping through comics, no doubt in her mind that Chandler forbade his mother from entering his sanctum sanctorum—which was definitely what he referred to the room as. A few minutes later, she had found fourteen of the comics on the list. Nobody had discovered her presence or tried the door, but she still had to get out of the house.

Sometimes you have to win ugly. She walked to the window. There was enough foliage between the house and the street that even if a nosy neighbor was snooping, she could exit unseen.

With maximum effort and a sharp pain in her lower back, she jammed the window up a quarter inch, making far more noise than she intended. Paint chips scattered over the carpet. Gretchen mouthed a few choice swears at the painted-shut window. She stared at the door, expecting it to open at any moment. After twenty long seconds, she exhaled. She dusted the paint chips from the floor and put them in her pocket.

She would have to go through the house. Gretchen moved to the door, closed her eyes, and listened. Nothing. She felt her heart beating in her head. She turned the knob and opened the door a crack. Enough to get a view down the hallway. Still nothing. They could be anywhere.

She found her just-in-case balaclava in the bag and put it on. One last big breath and she stepped into the hallway. Moving quickly but quietly, she took big, cautious steps. Then she heard Chandler's mom.

The moans and heavy breathing from the bedroom weren't loud, but they were distinct. Peppered with detailed instructions concerning pace and pressure, the conversation left no doubt what was happening behind the bedroom door. And it wasn't yoga—at least not in the traditional sense.

"Don't get fancy. That's it. Keep it simple. Like eating soft serve. Eat that froyo, Alchemy."

Good for Chandler's mom. She knew what she wanted. And she wanted a guy named Alchemy to eat her froyo.

Taking off the balaclava and throwing the backpack over her shoulder, Gretchen strode down the hallway and out of the house. She put the flyer for the missing cat underneath the windshield wiper of the Explorer and walked to her car. Before she went to the next house, she would need to find a Dairy Queen. Suddenly, she was in the mood for an ice cream cone.

CHAPTER 3

Kurt Ucker pushed away from his desk and walk-rolled his chair over to the mini-fridge. He grabbed a Snickers from the freezer. The first bite deliciously hurt his teeth. With the phone cradled in his neck, he talked through caramel lockjaw. "Wow, that sounds like a score."

"Yeah, I couldn't believe it," Gretchen said on the other end. "It was like the guy didn't know what they were worth. You're sure you don't mind helping me sell some of them?"

"Not at all. I'll put them in the stack with the others."

"You're the best, Kurty. I'll come by tonight. When does band practice end?"

"Around nine."

"If I get in early, I'll meet you over at Louder's."

"And you know, around Mom, it's not band practice. It's Bible study."

"You're still lying to her? You're an adult."

"It's not her kind of music," Kurt said. "Did I tell you? Some rando on the internet called the Skinripper song 'Kokytus: River of Lamentation'—and I quote—'sort of okay basic doom metal if you're into that kind of thing.'"

"You should needlepoint that onto a pillow."

Kurt loved that comic books had brought him and his sister together. Gretchen was the bad girl in the family. Sometimes Kurt wished he were more of a bad girl. They ended the call. Kurt returned to the eBay auction he was listing: a CGC 9.2 copy of *Giant-Size X-Men* #1 that Gretchen had scored a few weeks back.

Kurt glanced at the clock in the corner of the screen. Lunchtime. He posted the listing and lifted his large frame from the chair. His back and legs ached. He leaned on the desk, suddenly light-headed. He hadn't stood in three hours. He needed to stand more. He'd read an internet article that said sitting too long led to a shorter life. It was time to get a standing desk or a Fitbit or to stop reading internet articles.

He opened the basement door to the kitchen, and the familiar voice of a bloviating preacher blasted from the other room. Kurt recognized the baritone of Brother Tobin Floom, his mom's longtime preacher crush. She never missed his *Health, Wealth, and Salvation* broadcast. Three jam-packed hours of charismatic evangelism and bad music.

Kurt smiled every time he heard the *HWS* slogan, "Heaven is a phone call away." It was the same phrase used by an old phone sex ad that once played on late-night TV. Some adman had gotten a lot of mileage out of that line.

In the living room, Bertha Ucker sat in her vintage Barcalounger. A cigarette emitted a thin line of smoke from the ashtray next to her. Kurt's mother rarely took more than a few puffs nowadays but liked to have a butt burning. The smoke in the room was thicker than an after-hours jazz club in Winston-Salem. The white curtains had turned the color of flypaper years ago.

Kurt leaned against the doorframe and watched Brother Floom do his thing. The early-seventyish man with a majestic white pompadour wiped sweat from his brow with a gold handkerchief. A large gold cross around his neck complemented his chunky gold watch and gold rings.

THE UPPER HAND

Stalking the stage like a caged albino panther, he looked out to the hundreds of members of his congregation.

"When I look out into this sea of Christian faces, do you know what I see?" Brother Floom smiled. "I see the beauty of Christ Jesus. I see the faith inside each and every one of you. In your eyes and in your hope. Anointed in the blood of our Lord and Savior. Praise Jesus."

Kurt walked to the TV.

"I'm watching that," Bertha said.

"But I also see doubt," Brother Floom said before Kurt turned down the volume.

Bertha searched for the remote as Kurt quickly asked, "Is tomato soup and a turkey sandwich okay? That's all I need to know."

"Is that all we got?"

"I had planned a menu of oysters Rockefeller to start, halibut poached in truffle oil with ramps and shallots for the main, and an individual baked Alaska for dessert, but then I remembered I don't know how to make any of that."

"Is the turkey that low-sodium garbage?"

"We have ham, but it's low-sodium-garbage ham. Or unsalted-garbage peanut butter. Pretty much anything in the low-salt-garbage sandwich pantheon."

"Tastes like wet paper," she said. "Don't matter. I'm missing my show."

"How much new material can Brother Floom have? He quotes from one book."

"Don't blaspheme," Bertha snapped. "Show some respect."

Kurt had grown up with a Bible in every room and mandatory church on Sunday. After Kurt's father's death when he was six, Bertha ramped things up. Kurt attended sermons three days a week, after-school Christian clubs, and Bible camp in the summer. He avoided home-schooling only because Bertha was so focused on her own devotion.

Kurt prepared the food and set a TV tray in front of Bertha.

13

"You need anything else?" Kurt asked.

She glanced at the food and shook her head. "You going to sit with me?"

"Of course." Kurt took a seat on the couch.

Bertha ate as the two of them watched Brother Floom clap along to a performance by the Young Lions, a three-person boy band in hoodies singing a song called "The Coin in the Fish's Mouth." Kurt ground his teeth at the saccharine pop. Rock and roll used to be considered evil, but now it was okay—so long as it was performed by pretty white people and was awful.

> *He told them homies he could trust in thee.*
> *He told them, dawg, cast your rod to the sea.*
> *When you look in the mouth of the fish you caught,*
> *There be a coin. Son, you been taught.*
>
> *This ain't a story. We ain't satirical.*
> *Jesus was real, yo. That coin is a miracle.*

Bertha picked up the remote, lowered the volume, and turned to Kurt. "I miss the old hymns. Be a good boy and get me a pickle."

"Sodium."

"If I'm killed by a dill pickle, I absolve you of all guilt."

"The smallest one in the jar."

Brother Floom's voice reverberated as Kurt pushed the dills around the jar with a knife. "That fancy car you always wanted. That big house on the hill. The finest clothes and jewelries. Do you think God gives those things to everyone? Hands them out willy-nilly? No, he does not. He provides to those with faith. Those that show the faith of sacrifice. I want you to pledge your faith today.

"If a millionaire gives one hundred dollars, is that generous? Is that sacrifice? Chump change. Is our Lord a chump? No, he is not. Can I get an amen? You've heard people say, 'Give 'til it hurts.' That's what God wants, what he deserves, what he demands. He wants you to give 'til it hurts. If you have fifty dollars, he wants you to give twenty. If you have a thousand dollars, he wants you to give five hundred. Because those that put their true faith in our Lord, they will be rewarded for that pledge tenfold. Both here on earth and in the eternity of heaven.

"Take out your Bibles and your checkbooks."

CHAPTER 4

Axel, briefcase in hand, stood on the sidewalk in front of his new Spanish-style house with its manicured lawn and the square hedges. It was a Jimmy Stewart moment, the epitome of suburban life. The American Dream was alive and well in Encinitas at 148 Xanadu Lane.

He called the house "his," but it was really his and Priscilla's. And the bank's. Mostly the bank's, but the bank couldn't have felt the same as he did. Financial institutions were considerably less sentimental about their possessions.

It was more house than he and Priscilla needed, but the extra bedrooms created the incentive to start thinking about children—something he thought he'd never consider. Priscilla made Axel a better man. She inspired him to action. Not just making plans, but following through.

As a real estate agent, Priscilla had used her knowledge not only to find their four-bedroom castle, but to negotiate the deal, too. She knew just the right amount to bid above the asking price. She had even helped Axel secure the bank loan. Every penny of his savings had gone into the down payment. Ten years of pinching pennies, but you couldn't put a price on a dream.

It made his promotion at work that much more essential. Six years at an entry-level position, watching employee after employee leapfrog over him. It didn't matter if he was smarter, better read, and more experienced. If you were dumb on paper, that's what they saw.

On Priscilla's urging, Axel had marched into Mr. Stringer's office and demanded the recently open financial consultant position. The confidence that she had in him was contagious. It made him strong. Mr. Stringer saw that strength and gave him the job right then and there. On a trial basis with no bump in salary but a modest commission.

In the foyer he dropped his keys in the bowl and set down his briefcase. He smiled at the thought of having a foyer, ninety-nine percent sure he was pronouncing the word wrong in his head. He pronounced it the other way, and it still sounded wrong.

Axel thumbed through the mail. Mostly junk, a couple of bills, and a DVD of *The Flim-Flam Man* he had ordered online. He bunched up the junk mail to chuck in the recycling bin and threw the bills and DVD on the table.

That's when he saw Priscilla's note.

It wasn't a pick-up-some-milk-and-eggs-at-the-store note. Those weren't written on three lined pieces of paper. They also weren't adorned with frowny faces every third sentence. Those didn't have the house keys sitting on top of them.

Priscilla's handwriting looked like the calligraphy on a wedding announcement, the loops and lines so perfect they appeared computer generated. Against his better judgment, he read the first few sentences.

"My dearest Axel, I almost texted you this afternoon, but a text felt like an impersonal and heartless way to break up. (frowny face) I read an article online that said handwritten letters were a lost art. It made me want to write you a letter, not only to connect personally but to do my part in keeping the art alive. I'll send you the link to the article. (smiley face)"

Axel set the sheet of paper back on the table and walked into the kitchen. He dropped the junk mail into the recycling bin, kicked the recycling bin several times, found some duct tape in the junk drawer, duct-taped the hole in the side of the recycling bin, kicked the everloving shit out of the recycling bin again, retaped the recycling bin, and returned the duct tape to the junk drawer.

The only hard liquor in the kitchen was a half-full bottle of Smirnoff Fluffed Marshmallow vodka that someone had brought to the housewarming party to make a drink called the "S'More Drunk Than You."

Axel poured himself a tall glass. It smelled like aftershave that a circus clown would wear. He took a big swig. It tasted like poison that a circus clown would try to kill you with. He took another gulp, refilled his glass, and walked back into the foyer. He now hated the word *foyer*.

He stared back at the note. In that moment, Axel understood. He saw it. He saw the whole thing.

"It's beautiful," he said. "It's awful, but beautiful."

"Uncage Your Inner Tiger and Learn to Tame Your Supreme Dragon."

That was the name of the Tony Rogers retreat where he and Priscilla—if that was even her real name—had met. Despite the unwieldy acronym, UYITALTTYSD (pronounced *You-Ital-Ti-Sed*) was her sixth Rogers event that year alone. She had the vocab down, more confidence than a drunk bodybuilder, and a stare that made him three-quarters erect. She had five- and ten-year plans, an ambitious career path, and an exercise regime that kept her body stare-worthy. She grabbed hold of whatever she wanted and made it hers.

Apparently she discarded things as quickly. But this wasn't really a breakup. This was the icing on a four-month con game that Priscilla had played on Axel. That moment their eyes met hadn't been love. She had found a mark.

How much had she made? The commission on the listing was substantial—maybe fifty grand. If he dug, he would probably find that she had owned the house through some shell. He had bid well above the asking price—on her recommendation. A hundred-grand profit, maybe two, depending on what she had bought the house for. Not bad for four months' work. A straightforward Gold Brick Scam. If the house went into foreclosure, she could even rebuy it and stiff another sucker.

Axel drank more circus vodka. "Screw her. I can make this work. I still have my promotion. Nice guys don't finish last."

He picked up his briefcase, plopped down on the couch, and cracked open the reading materials that Mr. Stringer had given him. Priscilla and her frowny note could go to hell. He would fully devote himself to his new job. He'd become the best personal financial consultant on the West Coast.

Fifteen minutes of reading was all it took to burst his bubble. To burst his bubble and then take a shit on the soapy residue of that same bubble. Fifteen minutes was all Axel needed to recognize a con game—a totally different con game, but a con game nonetheless. The bank had just promoted him to be their lead huckster.

A personal financial consultant's job, apparently, was to advise clients to invest in predesigned company funds while assuring them that those funds were the best option, regardless of whether or not there were better options or if the funds were bad options. At the same time charging consultant fees up the wazoo along with a slew of additional hidden costs. He wouldn't be doing any analysis or research. He would be selling trust and, in return, giving his customers a knowingly inferior product. The definition of a confidence game.

He read the documents twice, shocked at their unambiguousness. They read like straight-up fraud, some of the tactics derived from classic boiler room scams. Axel immediately recognized common cons like the Budapest Shuffle, the Fried Liver Attack, and the Malachi Crunch.

He took another drink, looked toward the kitchen, and considered giving the recycling bin a few more kicks.

"This demands fire!" he shouted.

He got up and tripped over the coffee table. Back on his feet, he chucked the work papers into the empty fireplace, filled his mouth with vodka, spit-sprayed it onto the papers, and lit them with a fancy long match.

He stumbled into the foyer—seriously, fuck that word—and picked up Priscilla's note. He spotted her jacket on the coat rack and grabbed that, too. They both went into the fireplace.

"Her gluten-free crap!" Axel shouted.

He went into the kitchen, opened the fridge, and pulled out the bread, some muffins, and all the other gluten-free swindle-food that Priscilla had demanded he buy.

The sound of the smoke detectors and the smell of burning synthetic leather alerted Axel that the flue was closed. With the burnt-pleather fumes searing his eyes, Axel navigated the smoke-filled room, opened the flue, and continued the immolation of the physical evidence of Priscilla's existence—one inedible muffin at a time. Mostly sawdust, they burned well.

Watching the burning baked goods, he had a moment of clarity—as clear as one's thinking could be when clown-drunk and arson-raged. He knew what he needed.

CHAPTER 5

Gretchen hated Warm Springs.

With a name that evoked the part of the public pool where someone had recently peed, Warm Springs hit the shit-hole trifecta: a desert town, a border town, and a prison town all rolled into one sweltering turd town. Everything in Warm Springs was second-rate. During World War II, it had a camp that housed Italian prisoners of war. It couldn't even get Nazis. The current prison was second-rate, too. Not a prison at all, in fact, but a juvenile ranch facility—the junior varsity of the penal system.

To call it a town was a kindness. The downtown was a three-block stretch that had a mediocre Mexican restaurant, a hardware/feed store, a Dairy Queen, and a grocery store with overpriced toilet paper.

Gretchen parked in front of her childhood home. The house wasn't much to look at, but it was home. She walked the three blocks to the Laudens' house. As she approached, she felt the vibrations of heavy bass through the soles of her shoes. When no one answered the door, she picked the lock and let herself inside.

The weighty sound of Skinripper's doom metal rose from the basement. The slow, tuned-down heaviness shook the floorboards. Gretchen couldn't make out all the growled lyrics, but she made out the word "crepuscular." No idea what it meant, but damn if that wasn't the metal-est word she'd ever heard.

She walked into the kitchen, ripped some paper towel off the roll, stuck it in her ears, and opened the door to the basement. The power of the big arena sound almost knocked her backward.

Skinripper was a power trio. Amanda "Louder" Lauden on drums. Jose "Pepe" Marrero on bass. Which left Gretchen's brother Kurt "No Nickname" Ucker on guitar and vocals. One hundred decibels of plodding dread that sounded like Chewbacca in a suit of armor slowly falling down a staircase. In a good way.

Gretchen sat down on the bottom step and watched them play. Kurt strummed, stomped his foot, and wailed.

> *A journey of terror.*
> *Gauntlet of an iron hand.*
> *Crushing the peasants.*
> *More than one man can stand.*
>
> *Visigoth nightmare.*
> *A wizard's pox on the land.*
> *Horror and violence.*
> *The womb of the cursed child be damned.*

On "damned," Kurt let out a sustained scream for twenty seconds. His neck muscles bulged, and his face was beet red. Big drum flourish, cymbal crash, then silence.

Gretchen stood and clapped. "You guys sound good. Ass has been kicked."

"I don't know," Kurt said, breathing heavily. "The basement's got strong acoustics."

"He's being modest," Louder said. "Of course we're awesome."

"You staying the night?" Kurt asked.

"Yeah," Gretchen said. "I'm going to say hi to Mom. We can chat when you get home."

"Awesome. Looking forward to seeing those comics."

Gretchen went back up the stairs, turned, and waved. "Good to see you guys, too."

Pepe waved. Louder shot her some finger guns.

Kurt turned to them. "We crushed 'Berzerker Bloodquest.' Let's see if we can get through 'Chaotic Evil (Horak's Journey).'"

At her mom's house, Gretchen stopped in front of the fifteen-year-old Sears family portrait of her parents and siblings. She had often found herself examining the photo, trying to find its secrets.

At first glance, she saw their normalcy. Opening presents on Christmas mornings. Summer camping trips to Kitchen Creek. Fishing trips to Lake Morena. Dove hunting in the Imperial Valley. The events and images that filled a photo album.

Three months after the photo was taken, they found Henry Ucker's body in the desert. Twelve when he died, Gretchen remembered him as a child does, no longer sure whether the memories were real or manufactured from the sparse photographs and video.

According to multiple newspaper accounts, two off-roaders had found the lifeless body of Henry Ucker approximately nine miles south of Highway 8 in the Yuha Desert between San Diego and El Centro. The cause of death: a single gunshot wound to the chest.

Three days after the discovery of the body, video surveillance surfaced of Henry Ucker and an unidentified male accomplice burglarizing Haskell Diamonds in San Diego. Gretchen's father's face was clearly visible. According to the insurance company report, an estimated three hundred thousand dollars' worth of diamonds, gold, and precious gems were stolen.

The police questioned Gretchen's mother relentlessly, never treating her like a widow, but always as a potential accomplice. Rude, aggressive, and unnecessarily cruel. They searched the house multiple times, flashing warrants and breaking items without apology. They threatened house seizure, foster care, and forfeiture. Innocent until proven guilty didn't apply to the family of criminals.

Warm Springs had a decision to make: have the Uckers' backs, or turn their own backs. Martha Ramirez summed up the sentiment of the town in her statement to the papers: "I'm never going to feel completely safe knowing there had been a criminal next door. Until my husband is released from prison next year, these doors stay locked."

At the conclusion of a yearlong investigation, fifteen individual thefts spanning a year were attributed to Henry Ucker. In most of the cases, there was little doubt of his participation. A few cases appeared dubious, tossed in to clear an open case. The fact remained: Gretchen's father had been a professional thief.

The unidentified male accomplice at the Haskell Diamonds theft was never identified.

The Imperial Valley Sheriff's Department investigation into the murder of Henry Ucker remained open.

Not a single suspect was named in his murder.

Not a single item of the stolen merchandise was ever recovered. In total, over two million dollars' worth of stolen cash, jewelry, bearer bonds, coins, and stamps was attributed to Henry Ucker.

Everyone in Warm Springs focused on the revelation that Gretchen's father was a thief. Nobody showed compassion for the kids who lost their dad. After all, the children were probably thieves, too. Bad blood and all that. Friends were no longer allowed to play with them. They became the town scapegoats. When something went missing at school, they were accused of the crime. They became "those Ucker kids." The year her father died was the same year Gretchen learned how to fight.

She kissed her hand and pressed it to the image of her father.

Gretchen knocked on the door and entered her mother's bedroom. "Mom? You up? It's Gretch."

"Come in. Come in," Bertha said, setting down the book she was reading and sitting up in bed.

Gretchen sat on the edge of the mattress. She knew that her mother hated to be asked how she was feeling, so she asked, "How are you feeling?"

Bertha shook off the question. "You're the one that's too thin. Are you eating? Taking care of yourself? Is that another tattoo?" She pointed to the stick figure with a halo on Gretchen's arm.

Gretchen wondered if her mother recognized the image as the calling card for gentleman thief Simon Templar, the Saint.

"Your angel doesn't have any wings," Bertha said. "Why do you mark your body up like that? You staying out of trouble?"

Gretchen winked. "It isn't trouble if you don't get caught."

"What about the new job?" Bertha asked. "What was it? Sales trainee?"

"Sales associate." Gretchen was offended that her mother had diminished her pretend job title.

"Are you seeing anyone?" Bertha asked.

"You're burning through the questions tonight. I've sworn off men for a while." Gretchen had dated a few women in the last six months, but she didn't want to have that conversation again.

"Don't give up," Bertha said. "You were too young when you married Richard. There's a good man out there. If you went to church, you might find him."

"Speaking of something completely different, I was looking at the family portrait in the hall. The one with all of us together. With Dad."

"You can almost see Henry's secrets in that photo."

"I thought we were happy," Gretchen said. "But when I look at our smiles, I only see teeth."

"There's more under the surface."

"I wish I had known Dad better."

"You and me both." Bertha reached for her cigarettes. "When you leave, take that picture with you. I don't want it in this house anymore."

"Okay."

"Your father was an Ucker. People warned me. People that knew that family. They told me not to marry Henry. Not to marry an Ucker. We always trust the wrong people."

"Do we still have family out there?"

Bertha dug out a cigarette from the pack, lit it, took a deep drag, and hacked a cough that sounded like crinkled plastic wrap. "You don't want anything to do with those people. Liars and cheats. Thieves and sinners."

"It's not up to you whether or not we meet them. We should know."

"'Watch ye and pray, lest ye enter into temptation,'" Bertha said.

"Don't try to Bible your way out of this," Gretchen said. "How do I find them?"

Bertha coughed uncontrollably for twenty seconds. She stubbed out the cigarette. "You want a grilled cheese?"

"Are you serious?" Gretchen asked. "I'm not going to let this go."

"It's for your own good," Bertha said. "Ask your brother to make you a grilled cheese. He makes the best ones."

CHAPTER 6

Kurt, Pepe, and Louder loaded the last of the equipment into the back of the Skinrippermobile. Kurt shut the sliding door of the van and sat down on the bumper next to Louder. The Skinripper logo and their mascot, Bloodface, adorned the side of the van. Bloodface was a badass, zombie-like creature with red, bloody scratches from forehead to chin.

Pepe found a joint in his shirt pocket, lit it, and took a huge hit.

"A few steps back, Pep," Kurt said. "I don't want Mom to smell pot on me."

Pepe nodded and backed up.

"I might have got us a gig," Kurt said.

"Not another wedding?" Louder said. "You made me learn 'YMCA' and 'Celebration.' I had to wear a dress."

"We played the 'Macarena,'" Pepe said. "Twice. Love that tune."

"They hated us," Louder said.

"This is a Skinripper gig," Kurt said. "Straight-up rocking. Bringing the Warm Springs metal revolution to the people. La Choperia in Tecate."

"The place we saw Baculum with Queef Jerky?" Louder asked.

"That was badass," Pepe said. "Someone pegged the singer with a full bottle of beer."

"He was unconscious for fifteen minutes," Louder said. "There's no air-conditioning. They're violent."

"The toilet paper roll in the bathroom was on a screwdriver jammed into the wall," Pepe said.

"Now that's just ingenious," Kurt said. "Doing my best. Not a lot of people knocking down our door offering us gigs."

"There's got to be a sweet spot between the chicken dance and aggravated assault," Louder said.

"I can cancel," Kurt said, defeated.

"Screw it," Louder said. "I'm in the back of the stage anyway. You and Pepe can shield me from projectiles."

"Do you guys care about what I think?" Pepe asked.

"Not really," Louder and Kurt said in unison.

"Cool," Pepe said, putting the joint out on his tongue and climbing in the driver's seat. "I'll bring the van back tomorrow. See you later."

Kurt and Louder walked the three blocks to his house. They argued about how bad the Receptionists, their wedding band, had actually been.

"Come on, admit it," Kurt said. "Our reggae cover of 'White Wedding' was inspired. That one dreadlocked dude hippie-danced to the whole thing."

"Whose car is that?" Louder asked, pointing at a fifteen-year-old BMW parked on Kurt's lawn.

"It looks like my brother Axel's," Kurt said.

As if on cue, Kurt's older brother got out of the car. "Got out" was generous. In truth, Axel opened the car door, vomited, and fell out into his own puke. He then closed his eyes, curled into a ball, and squiggled in the glop until he found the sweet spot.

"Yeah, that's all you," Louder said. "I gag too easy. Great rehearsal." She gave Kurt a high five, followed by a big hug.

"What was that for?" Kurt asked.

Louder shrugged and walked back in the direction of her house.

Kurt turned to Axel and kicked the bottom of his foot. "Ax? Get up. You're sleeping in throw up."

Axel opened his eyes and stared at Kurt. Grass blades stuck to the side of Axel's face.

"Did you drive here from SD?" Kurt asked.

"Kurt, little bro!" Axel yelled. "What're you doing here?"

"You're in Warm Springs," Kurt said. "How did you not die driving through the mountains?"

"It's a Christmas miracle."

"It's July."

"It's a Halloween miracle."

"Cheese 'n' rice." Kurt walked to the side of the house. When the cold water from the hose hit Axel, he shot to his feet and ran serpentine around the yard. Kurt chased him until Axel was thoroughly soaked.

"I'm wet," Axel said. "I'm dripping, soaking wet."

"You shouldn't have asked me to spray you with water."

Axel stared at his brother, confused. "Did I?"

"You must have. Why else would I do it?"

Axel nodded. "Thanks, little brother."

It wasn't the first time that Kurt had Obi-Wanned his brother when he was wasted.

"Gretch is here," Kurt said. "It's been forever since we've all been together."

"Hasn't been that long," Axel said.

"Two years, Ax. Over two years, actually. You live fifty miles away. Mom misses you."

"Momma."

"Probably want to save that visit for tomorrow," Kurt said. "Unless you want a lecture about the evils of alcohol spirits."

"Sorry. Meant to visit. My busy is life. House on Xanadu. I got the Inner Tiger. The Supreme Dragon."

"Whatever that means," Kurt said. "Were you at a cookout? You smell like burnt marshmallows."

"S'More Drunk Than You."

"Yes, you are," Kurt said. "You most definitely are."

Axel sat at the kitchen table and sipped black coffee. His hair dripped, but he wore clean, dry clothes. Kurt's sweatpants and shirt were three sizes too big, making Axel look childlike.

Kurt cooked grilled cheese sandwiches one after the other. His secret was to use mayonnaise instead of butter or oil on the outside of the bread. Kurt took his cheesy bread seriously. He spatulaed the last one onto a plate and brought them to the table. One for Gretchen. One for Axel. Two for him. He was a growing boy.

Axel greedily grabbed his sandwich and took a bite. He froze and looked up at Kurt. "This tastes better than other tastes."

"I hope it stays in your stomach and not on the floor," Kurt said. He topped off Axel's coffee.

Gretchen stared at Axel but didn't say anything. Kurt couldn't tell whether it was anger or curiosity. Gretchen wasn't always easy to read. It wasn't glee. He knew that.

"Mom wasn't kidding, Kurty," Gretchen said. "You killed it on this sammie. I could eat like ten of these." She punched Axel's arm. "Why are you here? What do you need?"

"Ow. What's with hitting?" Axel said. "Why do I need something?"

"Because you do," she said. "You wouldn't be here otherwise."

Axel lost a battle with a string of melted cheese that ran from his chin to the plate. He left it there. "I missed everyone. Came to see family, you, Mom. Didn't know what to do. Got burned."

"What's her name?" Gretchen asked.

"Why a woman? Why couldn't it be maybe something else?"

"You only get drunk when you get dumped," Gretchen said. "Don't get me wrong, Drunk Axel is my favorite Axel. You get weird. You're fun to mess with. But come on, it's always a woman."

"It was a woman the last three times," Kurt said.

Axel looked mad for a moment and then drunkenly shrugged. "Priscilla is her. Good, then everything went to bad. Everything. Like in ten minutes. I had it all. And boom, boom, boom, I had shit, shit, shit. I had all the shit."

"You fall in love faster than I can choose pizza toppings," Gretchen said. "You trust the worst people. Bites you in the ass every time."

"Love is trust. That's love. Priscilla fooled me. Conned me. My job? Another con. Nothing I have is what it is. I had answers, then questions, then the wrong answers—then I had fire. I missed you guys."

"Are you talking in slam poetry?" Gretchen said. "You're speaking gibberish."

"I have a plan," Axel said. "We're going to get it back. You and me and you."

He pulled some sheets of paper from his back pocket, unfolded them, and ironed them out with his hand on the table. From Kurt's vantage point, it looked like a serial killer's scrawl alongside children's drawings.

"Whatever you say," Gretchen said.

Kurt washed the pan in the sink. "Let's enjoy the three of us being together. It doesn't happen often enough. Mom's going to be happy to see you. For tonight let's be a normal family. Eat your sandwich."

"Oh, for Christ's sake," Gretchen said. Axel had fallen asleep, using what was left of his sandwich as a pillow. Cheese oozed from between the slices of bread.

"Think he'll remember any of this tomorrow?" Kurt asked.

"Who cares?" Gretchen said. "All I know is that I'm going to eat the rest of his sammie."

CHAPTER 7

Axel was either dreaming or had traveled in time—or he was dreaming about traveling in time. Through some miracle of science or magic, he had been transported back to his childhood bedroom. Tucked into his San Diego Chargers sheets, he half-expected "I Got You Babe" to play on the alarm clock.

The events of the previous evening blurred into focus. Bits and pieces. Fire, vomit, and grilled cheese—which sounded like a short story anthology that Priscilla would make him read.

"Priscilla. Right," Axel said. "So wrong."

The decor of his old bedroom hadn't changed since he left Warm Springs—the National Forensic League speech trophies, the bookshelf stacked with board games, his old notebooks.

Axel got out of bed and took down the Amy Grant poster on the door. Underneath, the *Baywatch*-era Pamela Anderson poster remained. It brought back different memories. Pam stared back at Axel seductively. Many a lonely teenage night had been spent fantasizing about traversing her silicone topography.

What the hell, he thought. He had earned it.

Axel jumped in bed, threw back the sheets, and pushed his underwear to his knees. He set the fantasy in motion, starting at Pam's eyes. He could tell that she'd missed him.

Pulling rope for a half minute, Axel brought out the big guns and concentrated on Pam's cleavage. A line and shadow on paper, but so much more. The road crew finally got together, working in unison to raise the circus tent.

The door swung open. Instead of Pamela Anderson, Gretchen stood in the doorway. Axel froze, dick in hand, then quickly averted his eyes from his sister's chest.

"Get out of here!" Axel ejaculated. Or rather, didn't. He pulled up the sheets and his underwear at the same time but managed to tuck the sheets through the leg of his briefs. Tangled up with one nut poking out, he curled himself into a fetal ball.

"Get up, pervert," Gretchen said. "Mom died. Mom is dead."

"Bad joke, sis."

"Look at my face. She's dead. Kurty's a mess. Drop your wang, and pretend to be his big brother. He needs you." Gretchen slammed the door, leaving Axel by himself.

Pamela Anderson stared at him with shame and pity. It would never be the same between the two of them.

Axel walked into his mother's bedroom. His clothes from the night before were damp and smelled of sick. Between the pounding in his head, the queasiness in his gut, and his slimy exterior, he didn't know if he'd ever felt more awful. On top of his mother being dead, of course.

Bertha Ucker lay on her back, peaceful and still. Her eyes were closed, but there was no mistaking the difference between someone sleeping and someone not living.

This wasn't how Axel had expected this family reunion to play out. He expected his mother to be alive, at the very least.

Gretchen sat on the edge of the bed. She gave a head-tilt toward Kurt, who sat in a chair against the wall. Axel's younger brother wept, staring at Bertha. He softly repeated, "What happens now? What happens now?"

Axel walked to Kurt and put a hand on his shoulder. "It's going to be okay."

"No, it isn't. What happens now?"

"I don't know," Axel said. "We'll come up with a plan. Me and Gretchen, we're here for you. Isn't that right, Gretch?"

"That's right," Gretchen said.

"No, you're not," Kurt said. "You never are. Neither of you. You both leave. You always leave."

"This is different," Axel said. "I'm not going anywhere."

"Me neither," Gretchen said. "We might suck at it, but we're a family."

"That's how I found her," Kurt said. "I tried to wake her up. Her skin was cold. Weird cold. Not normal cold. Dead cold."

"Was she sick?" Axel asked. "Had the cancer come back?"

"Who cares right now?" Gretchen snapped, her voice cracking.

"You're right." Holding out his arms, Axel walked to Gretchen. "Come here, sis. I could use a hug."

"You're slimy and gross, but screw it." Gretchen squeezed Axel, crushing him. She whispered, "What you said, you being here for Kurty. That better not be bullshit."

"I'm going to step up," Axel said.

She gave him a nod, pulled away, and turned to Kurt. "What are you doing sitting there by yourself? Get in on this hug action."

Kurt wiped his tears with his forearm and joined them. He was big enough to hug Axel and Gretchen at the same time.

"I'm going to miss her so much," Kurt said. "I need to make pancakes."

Kurt broke the embrace. At the door, he took one last look at his mother. He shook his head and walked down the hallway.

"We're going to have to take care of Kurty for a while," Gretchen said. "You and me."

"Results may vary. Trying and knowing what I'm doing are two different things."

"Don't pre-apologize for screwing up," Gretchen said. "As long as you don't run, it'll be an improvement."

"Something something about a pot and a kettle and blackness."

"I'm going to try, too," Gretchen said. "It's been just Mom and Kurty for a long while. We lost our mom. Kurt's life has changed completely."

Axel walked to the bed and pulled the sheet over his mother's head. There was nothing particularly disturbing about her dead countenance, but he wanted to remember her alive. He wanted to remember her laughing, even if he couldn't actually remember her laughing.

While Kurt made pancakes in the kitchen, Axel called 9-1-1 and reported the death. They walked him through the procedure, warning him that it might take a few hours to get someone out there. Warm Springs sat on the eastern edge of the county, the nearest medical examiner thirty-five miles away. After that, they'd have to find a funeral home.

After he set the necessary procedures in motion, he called his job. They would be wondering why he hadn't come into work on the first day of his new promotion.

"Axel Ucker for Mr. Stringer . . . Yes, I'll hold . . . Mr. Stringer, hi. It's Axel. I'm not going to be able to come in today. My mother passed away last night, and I have to be with family . . . Thank you, I appreciate that."

Gretchen stepped into the living room with a plate of pancakes. Axel shooed her away, but she didn't budge and shoveled a forkful of flapjack into her mouth.

"Here's the deal, Stringer. I'm not coming back to work. I can't do it. I'm calling to tell you—well, pretty much all of Associated Banking—to fuck all the way off."

"Dang," Gretchen said. "That's one way to do it."

Axel walked away from Gretchen, but she followed while he continued. "If I wanted to run a confidence game on people, I wouldn't need the umbrella of a legitimate company. I bet you don't even bother to rationalize, to pretend like you're doing good. You've always seemed like the kind of Wall Street bro A-hole that laughs at the stupid people you dupe with all the other A-holes in suits. To be clear, I'm not quitting because it's morally or ethically wrong. I'm fluid in those areas. I'm quitting because I can't be part of your mediocrity. You can take my job and recent promotion, form it into a conical shape, and shove it far enough up your ass that it pokes a hole in your liver. Ucker out."

Gretchen set the plate down and slow-clapped.

Axel shook his head. "He hung up when I told him to fuck all the way off, but I needed to get the rest out of my system."

"Quitting jobs is like the best, right?"

"Mom is dead. I have no job. No girlfriend. No money in the bank. A mortgage I can't afford. For a house that isn't worth it. And a responsibility to my family that I've failed at every time I've tried. I'm not ready to celebrate."

"In Chinese, the word for 'crisis' and 'opportunity' is the same," Gretchen said, smirking.

Axel laughed. "That isn't even true. They're two different words. Google Translate would shame that horseshit."

The aroma of pancakes hit Axel and immediately made him hungry. He wandered into the kitchen past Gretchen. A cartoon-size stack of pancakes sat on the table, with a half dozen more on the griddle.

"Smells great, little brother," Axel said, making himself a plate.

"Is it okay if I eat my breakfast with Mom?" Kurt asked. "I want to be with her a little more before things happen. Before they take her. But I don't know the rules about food and dead people and stuff."

"Go ahead, Kurty," Gretchen said. "I'm sure it's fine."

Kurt turned off the griddle, put the remaining pancakes on a plate, grabbed the maple syrup, and left the room.

"Poor guy," Gretchen said.

"He's stronger than we give him credit."

"I hope so."

"Not to be unemotional," Axel said, "but we're going to have to figure out how to pay for the funeral and stuff. I'm broke, and my credit's maxed out. Did Mom have any money saved?"

"I got no idea," Gretchen said. "Tell me how much you need. I got a few things going."

"I don't want to know what that means," Axel said. "Do I want to know what that means?"

"No." Gretchen smiled. "You definitely don't want to know."

CHAPTER 8

Bertha Ucker's funeral was held the following weekend at the Second Christian Reformed Church. Oddly, there was no First Christian church in Warm Springs. Gretchen took it to be another example of Warm Springs' second-bestness.

Gretchen stowed her jeans and T-shirt for the day and donned the one legit church dress she owned. Nothing had made her mom smile more than Gretchen dressing like "a proper lady and not a thug's stripper girlfriend."

People shook hands and side-hugged Gretchen and Axel as they greeted them in the lobby of the church. Old ladies. A few families. A guy with alopecia wearing a fake mustache, crooked eyebrows, and a one-size-too-small toupee. A lady carrying a black cat that may or may not have been alive. A dead ringer for Harry Dean Stanton—although that description fit a third of all desert males. They gave monotone "Sorry for your losses" and "She's with Jesus nows." Fewer than fifty people peppered the pews, hardcore church members and those ladies that really loved a good funeral.

After greeting everyone, Gretchen and Axel stood in the lobby in no hurry to start the proceedings.

"You know what you're going to say?" Gretchen asked.

"I wrote some stuff down. I didn't know Mom that well these last ten years."

"What's there to know? She watched that Floom guy and those other TV preachers all day. Chain smoked and judged her children, tallying their sins."

"Kurt should do it. He knew her. I've never been good at public speaking."

"You're weird all the time," Gretchen said. "I wouldn't mention that you were jerking it when you found out she died, but that's just me."

Axel opened his mouth to say something, but the heavy church doors swung open with a bang. An assault of sunlight made Gretchen and Axel squint.

A very big woman stepped into the doorway and blocked the light. Gretchen knew better than to stare into an eclipse, but she couldn't help it. The woman weighed three hundred pounds after a four-day fast. Crammed into a cleavage-heavy, lime-green dress that would have been loud at a retro 1970s disco party, this woman wasn't afraid of being seen. Gretchen would have guessed that she was in her mid-sixties, but her copper wig made it hard to gauge. The woman took the cigar out of her mouth, spit in her hand, and put it out on her palm.

"Now that's an entrance," Gretchen said.

The woman walked to Gretchen with the left-to-right hobble of a woman her size. Every step seemed painful. Her ankles looked like hams jammed into too-small flats. Her knees shook with each step.

"Gretchen," the woman said. A statement, not a question.

"Thank you for coming," Gretchen said. She wondered if she was staring at the woman's chest. There was a lot of it to stare at. It made up sixty percent of Gretchen's sight line.

The woman leaned in, her eyes darting over Gretchen's features. Their noses almost touched at one point. Her breath smelled like a Havana ashtray.

"Were you friends with my mom?" Gretchen asked, taking a step back.

"You got the devil in your eyes, girl," the big woman said. "Hellfire, spit, and fight."

"I don't want to be rude," Gretchen said. "This being a funeral. But you're creeping me out, lady."

The woman let out a roar of a laugh. Like an explosion. Heads turned from inside the church. She gave Axel a hard slap on the shoulder that made him wince.

"I'm going to watch out for you. You're fourteen kinds of wicked," the woman said, walking into the church.

Gretchen watched her waddle to the back pew, then turned to Axel. "What in the hell just happened?"

With Pepe and Louder accompanying him, Kurt played an acoustic version of some song that he must have written in the last few days. When Kurt's voice cracked, Gretchen felt her throat go dry.

> *When I played cards with Mom, she knew I was bluffing.*
> *Thought I could trick her, but I knew next to nothing.*
> *She wasn't always kind, sometimes downright mean.*
> *But she always had time for a scared, confused teen.*
>
> *I'll miss my mom. I can't believe she's gone.*
> *I'll miss my mom. Now who will I lean on?*
> *Not close to perfect, that I know for certain.*
> *I'll miss my mom, as we close this final curtain.*

Gretchen glanced back at the woman in the green dress. Seated in the last pew, the woman gave her a wink and a smile.

Gretchen leaned toward Axel and whispered, "You've never seen her before?"

"Shh. Kurt's singing. He's really good."

"He's always been great. You weren't around to notice. Seriously, that lady is trouble. She weirds me out. She sure as shit ain't church folk. And she ain't no friend of our mother's. Friends don't smile at their friend's funeral. Friends don't wear that dress, tits spilling out like a boob waterfall."

"In a different context, I might appreciate a boob waterfall."

Gretchen punched his arm.

Kurt finished the song on a long, quavering note. Walking to his spot in the front pew, he placed a hand on the casket. He sat down next to Gretchen, who put her arm around him and gave him a tissue.

Pastor Lucas took the pulpit. He lacked the showmanship of the televangelists that Bertha loved. Tepid lemon water to their Red Bull and vodka shots, sermon-wise. After some boilerplate funeral scripture, he moved on to Bertha Ucker's life. It read like an impersonal dossier: place of birth, education, late husband. He avoided any mention of the scandal that surrounded their father. Pastor Lucas claimed that Bertha loved tennis, which was news to Gretchen. Even though he padded his speech with made-up pastimes, it only took him a few minutes to cover her life.

Following his remembrance, Pastor Lucas led them in a soulless rendition of the hymn, "I Am Waiting for the Dawning." The bulk of the crowd sucked the life out of the already-bummer tune, but Gretchen could hear the lime-green-dress woman wailing with genuine spirit over the drone. It made her like the big lady a little bit, but not enough to get past the creepiness.

When the hymn ended, Axel walked to the dais, took out some notes, and cleared his throat. "Thank you all for coming to say goodbye to Bertha Ucker. Weird saying her full name. To me and Gretchen and Kurt, she was Mom. She—our relationship—I'm going to—"

Axel stopped himself, folded up the notes, and put them in his pocket.

"I'm going to cut the shit. Sorry, Pastor Lucas. I hadn't seen my mother in two years, and when I finally did, she was dead. We had a complex relationship. She gave us a lot of independence growing up—some would say emotional abandonment. Even neglect. You say 'tomato.' But that's neither here nor there.

"Everyone knows our story. When our father was murdered and the thief stuff came out, it destroyed Mom. She retreated into her own world, on her own. The town had a choice. You people could have had her back, but she got no help or sympathy from Warm Springs or this church that she had been a part of most her life. Instead, she got distrust and disdain. Who knew people still shunned?

"She attended this church, but I didn't see any one of you speak to her after that day. You sure as hell didn't want your kids hanging out with us. None of you—no one—ever gave us the benefit of the doubt. You left her to watch Brother Tobin Floom on the TV. He—a stranger—was better to her than you people ever were. I used to think that was sad, but looking out at the lot of you, I'm realizing that she was better off with that money-grubbing Holy Roller than with a bunch of two-faced hypocrites. She should have moved from this fucking place. Sorry again, Pastor Lucas."

Kurt leaned over to Gretchen. "Should I do something?"

"You do and I'll never forgive you. I want to see how he wraps this up."

Axel laughed. "You were probably hoping I'd put the 'fun' back in 'funeral.' That you'd socialize and eat and have a good time, because college football ain't started yet. I couldn't do it. I find all of you contemptible. I find this town deplorable. I hope the whole damn place burns to the ground and the desert sand swallows up the ashes so there's no evidence Warm Springs ever existed."

Axel took a step away from the microphone, snapped his fingers, and returned to the dais. "Refreshments will be served in the Bible study room after the service."

For a moment the church was as silent as—well, a church. Until the green-dress lady burst out laughing. She blew a two-finger whistle and applauded. "You tell 'em, kiddo!" she screamed.

Axel walked off the dais and sat back down between Gretchen and Kurt.

"Mom would have hated that," Kurt said, "but that doesn't make what you said any less true."

"I have never loved you more than I do right now, big brother," Gretchen said. "I didn't think you could beat your job-quitting speech, but this was historic. Please tell me that someone took video."

"No better place than a church to perform an exorcism," Axel said.

Gretchen was surprised to find the Bible study room full of people. Apparently, people were cool with public chastisement if free food was involved. Even a measly spread like the one in front of them: a marked-down, dried-out veggie tray, a variety of two different cheeses, a tube of Pringles, a paper plate of cookies, and a maybe-it's-a-casserole. Two-liter bottles of store brand soda and a coffee urn were the beverage choices. There had been some Ritz crackers and dry salami, but Pepe had made quick work of them before the first parishioner got to the table.

Gretchen and her brothers huddled in the corner. Louder joined the group, giving Gretchen and Axel each a hug. She put a hand on Kurt's arm. "You okay?"

"Someone has to say something," Kurt said. "I don't want to ruin the funeral—although Axel might get that prize—but you can't just claim a cookie is fresh-baked if it isn't. That's fraud."

"Nobody cares, Kurty," Gretchen said.

"Yeah," Louder said. "I don't think it matters."

"I care," Kurt said. "Those over there, those are Chips Ahoy, plain and simple. You could blind-taste-test me all day. I know my store-boughts. Mrs. Conley claimed she baked them. I'm going to find her."

Kurt walked into the crowd and looked around the room. Louder followed, turning and giving Gretchen a shrug.

"Poor guy," Gretchen said. "And poor Mrs. Conley if he finds her."

"Is that's Kurt's girlfriend?" Axel asked.

"That's Amanda Lauden," Gretchen said. "Louder. They've been best friends since like third grade. How do you not know her?"

"Because I suck."

"Do you see that gigantic lady?" Gretchen asked.

"She doesn't seem like she would be a very good hider."

"Who is she?"

"I'm your aunt," the big woman said, making both of them jump. She stood directly behind them like a three-hundred-pound ninja.

"Shit!" Gretchen yelled.

From across the room, Pastor Lucas gave her a headshake.

"Come on, Pastor Lucas," Gretchen said, raising her voice so that the pastor could hear her. "Axel said a lot worse."

"Did you just say you were our aunt?" Axel said.

"I'm your father's sister. Everyone calls me Mother Ucker."

"Oh, I bet they do," Gretchen said.

"It's good to finally meet you kids," Mother said.

"People pull scams at funerals all the time," Gretchen said. "Long-Lost Relative is a classic. If that's your scheme, I'll save you time. My mother didn't have any money. Neither do we. There ain't a nickel to gain."

"I do love the fight in you," Mother said, "and your instinct for distrust. Nobody's going to get nothing past you. Full of raw potential."

"And you're full of shit," Gretchen said, saying "shit" softly and glancing toward Pastor Lucas.

"Do you have some kind of proof that we're related?" Axel asked.

"The whole story is long," Mother said. "One you'll want to hear. Short version is that your mother hated her in-laws. She didn't want anything to do with any of the other Uckers."

"She told me that much," Gretchen said. "What kind of bad are you?"

Mother laughed. "The good kind."

"How much more family do we have out there?" Axel asked.

"Aunts, uncles, and a truckload of cousins. You'll meet them. If you want. It's up to you."

"Still haven't seen any proof," Gretchen said. "In fact, you dodged the question."

"I don't want anything from you kids. I want to help you. I want to bring you back into the family. Uckers look out for one another." She took a black-and-white photograph out of her bra and handed it to Gretchen. It was warm to the touch.

"Let's meet," Mother said. "Next Saturday, a week from today. Let's say noon. Bring Kurt, too. I'll give you all the proof you need. We'll talk about your future."

Gretchen looked at the photo, Axel leaning over her shoulder. Six children, two girls and four boys. The oldest girl was unmistakably Mother Ucker, not quite as big, but definitely on her way. The other girl could have been Gretchen's sister. But the face that Gretchen stared at was the oldest boy. The one who looked like Axel. Gretchen silently pointed at him.

"That's your father," Mother Ucker said.

"What do you mean you'll talk about our future?" Axel asked.

"I have plans for the three of you."

"Could that have sounded more like a threat?" Gretchen said.

"Why would your aunt threaten you?" Mother asked. She scanned the room. Her eyes landed on the man with the bad hairpiece and pasted-on eyebrows. "I'll contact you about Saturday," she said, and walked to the door.

"How?" Gretchen said. "You don't have our information."

"Of course I do," Mother said. She glanced at the bald man, who turned and made eye contact with her. And then Mother was gone. The bald man followed a few seconds behind her.

"What do we do with that?" Gretchen said.

Kurt walked back to the two of them. "I took care of it."

"What?" Axel asked, still in a daze.

"Mrs. Conley apologized for her cookie fraud. I made her cry a little. I cried, too, but I think we worked it out. Everything's cool now." Kurt nodded toward the photograph. "What's that? Why are you making those faces at me?"

CHAPTER 9

Kurt missed his mom. He wanted to make her lunch. Instead, he parked himself on the couch in the living room and played guitar.

At Bertha's desk, Axel pored through the stacks of papers that constituted their mother's financial records. The envelopes, files, receipts, paper scraps, and checkbooks filled an old US Army four-drawer metal filing cabinet.

"Did Mom have a system?" Axel asked. "There are bills from two months ago mixed in with twenty-year-old receipts. I found a full book of S&H Green Stamps from 1985 inside a Green Stamps Ideabook. A ukulele was circled inside. If I find fourteen more books, maybe we can still get it. It's a sweet-looking uke."

"I don't know anything about the finances," Kurt said.

"How did you and Mom pay the bills and stuff?" Axel asked. "Where did the money come from?"

"She got checks," Kurt said. "I gave her whatever I made. It worked out."

"Things don't work out without a plan," Axel said.

"Sometimes they do," Kurt said. "Sometimes they don't."

The doorbell rang. Kurt and Axel stared at each other until Kurt blinked. He stood up and went to the door, then soon returned with Joe Velasquez.

Joe Vee—as he preferred—was the only lawyer in Warm Springs. He mostly handled drunk driving and workers' comp cases, but he was the go-to guy for local legal needs, unless you wanted to drive for forty-five minutes. He had cornered the legal market in Warm Springs. Not everyone liked Joe Vee, but everyone knew him.

"What can we do for you, Mr. Velasquez?" Axel said.

"Joe Vee. Everyone calls me Joe Vee. Sorry about Bertha. It's a terrible loss. Nice lady."

"I didn't see you at the funeral," Axel said.

"I was fishing in San Felipe. Sorry. Heard you gave the crowd a bit of what for. Can't say they don't deserve it."

"You got your briefcase," Gretchen said, walking into the room. "Is this business?"

Joe Vee nodded. "I wanted to pay my respects, but yeah, unofficial official business, if you know what I mean."

"I don't," Axel said. "None of us do."

"It's about your mother's will."

"Oh good," Axel said, pointing to the stack of paper. "I've been looking for some sense of where her finances were."

Joe Vee rubbed his five o'clock shadow and set his briefcase on the coffee table. "Do you want to sit down? You should probably sit down. Why don't the three of you sit down?"

"That doesn't sound good," Gretchen said. She didn't budge, crossing her arms over her chest.

Kurt sat on the couch, picking up a pillow and hugging it.

"I wrote a will for your mother about a year ago," Joe Vee said. "This isn't Lawyer Joe talking. This is plain old Joe Vee down the road. I shouldn't be talking to you about any of this until it's all squared, but there's things you should know."

"Things?" Kurt asked.

Joe Vee popped open his briefcase. "I could read all the legalese, but to be honest, I cribbed most of it from a book. A law book, but I'm going to cut to the chase—give you the CliffsNotes. Love those things. Wished they'd had them for law school."

"Focus, Joe," Axel said.

"Here it is," Joe Vee said. "You kids aren't in the will."

"What?" Kurt said.

"Who else would be in the will?" Axel said. "A long-lost relative, a secret lover, her favorite squirrel? She didn't know other people."

"I shouldn't be doing this. Not exactly 'ethical.'" The fact that Joe Vee put the word "ethical" in air quotes was a clue to his ethicalness.

"Yeah, you keep saying that," Gretchen said. "We get it. Huge favor. Thanks."

"I tried to talk her out of it, but your mother left everything—the house, money, some small investments—to Brother Tobin Floom."

"Are you kidding me?" Axel said.

"She loved his show," Kurt said.

"The televangelist?" Gretchen shouted. "The guy on TV that wears all the gold and asks people for money?"

"That's the one," Joe Vee said.

"Can we contest it?" Axel asked. "What do we do?"

"Come to my office this week. I'll give you the rundown of your options. I'm going to have to crack the books and learn about this stuff. The law is complicated. Whatever you do, I have to file the will in probate court this week. That starts the ball rolling."

"Brother Floom was her favorite," Kurt said. "She watched him every day. He was always there for her."

"I can hold off on the filing," Joe Vee said. "End of the week. Say I was out of town. That'll give you time to get whatever stuff you want from the house without a hassle."

"The house, too?" Kurt asked. "Where do I live now?"

"Sorry, kid. Even if you contest, you're going to have to move out until it's sorted."

Joe Vee set a manila envelope on the coffee table. "Here's a copy. Don't show it to no one, because you're not supposed to have it yet. Wish I had better news."

"Not your fault," Axel said. "Thanks for the heads-up, Mr. Velasquez."

"Joe Vee." He handed Axel a business card and walked to the front door. "Let's set up something this week."

The lawyer left. Axel picked up the envelope. Gretchen sat down next to Kurt. She put her arm around him and hugged him.

"Brother Floom," Axel said. "Brother Tobin freaking Floom."

"It's not like I wanted anything," Gretchen said, "but that's messed up."

"Our house isn't going to be our house anymore," Kurt said. "I've never lived anywhere else."

"You can stay with me," Axel said. "I have plenty of room. At least until I'm foreclosed on."

Kurt hadn't been in his mother's room since the day she died. Out of habit, he knocked softly before opening the door. He stepped inside, feeling the stillness and quiet.

A gold Brother Floom prayer cloth sat draped over the top of the dresser, with ceramic figures of Jesus, Mary, and a cross on top of it. He didn't want the prayer cloth, but he'd decide on the ceramics later. They had sat on the dresser since he could remember. Moving them felt wrong. He would wait until the last minute.

Kurt opened the closet. It smelled like his mother—cigarette smoke and rose perfume. He closed his eyes. It was like she was standing next to him.

"Do you need some help?" Gretchen asked.

Kurt opened his eyes, wiped his face, and turned to his sister. She stood in the doorway, looking as if she didn't want to enter too far into the room.

"Maybe," Kurt said. "I don't know."

"I can take care of Mom's stuff if you want."

"You'll just give it all away."

"That's obviously what Mom wanted. She wouldn't have given it to the preacher otherwise. But that doesn't mean you shouldn't take the things that mean something to you."

Kurt shut the closet door. He looked around the room and walked to the nightstand. "I'm going to keep her Bible. Unless you want it."

"It's all yours, Kurty. The only thing I'm taking is the picture in the hall. It's how I want to remember all of us."

"I don't remember us ever being a family," Kurt said. "I mean, you're my sister. I love you. But do we know each other?"

"Sometimes it takes a tragedy to bring people together. Even Axel is trying. That's close to a miracle."

"There must be more than that photo that you want."

"Not really," Gretchen said. "The past has messed me up enough. I'm not going to consciously bring more of it along with me. Okay, I might take the microwave, but that's only because mine shit the bed last week when I left a spoon in a bowl. It went full Zuul."

Kurt carried the last of his stuff into the upstairs bedroom in Axel's McMansion. Twenty long boxes of comics. Carefully packed action figures and figurines. Six insanely heavy boxes of records. Three computers and assorted hardware. Boxes of games and gaming stuff. His guitar. One duffel bag full of clothes made up Kurt's entire wardrobe.

All the other stuff that they had kept went into Axel's garage. The random collection of items could best be categorized under the informal heading of "I don't know—maybe one of us will want this thing—let's just throw it in the truck and decide later."

By the end of the day, Axel and Kurt stood red-faced and sweaty, staring into the packed-to-the-rafters garage that held their entire childhood, their whole past. Kurt drank his Gatorade so fast, most of it ran down his cheeks.

"Mom's gone," Kurt said. "She's really gone."

Axel put a hand on Kurt's shoulder. "I'm starved. Let's get changed. Tacos sound good?"

"I have never said the phrase 'No, I don't want tacos' in my life. Tacos always sound good."

Kurt and Axel headed into the house. They stopped before entering their respective rooms.

"Thanks for letting me stay here," Kurt said. "I'll try not to cramp your style."

"I don't have any style to cramp. You're family."

"Speaking of," Kurt said. "When do you think our new aunt will call to meet up?"

"I'm not one hundred percent convinced she's really our aunt," Axel said.

"My friend Rasputin authenticated that photo, said it was legit."

"Well, if a guy named after the Mad Monk confirmed it, I'm sure it's okay."

"Raz is the preeminent forger of Magic: The Gathering cards in North America, so."

"I barely know what any of that means," Axel said, "and you shouldn't be associating with forgers."

"That means he can spot a forgery. If he says the photo was unaltered, that's fact."

"Let's say she is our aunt," Axel said. "Mother Ucker—yeesh—did not look like the kind of aunt that knits afghans and puts five dollar bills in birthday cards. We can't trust her."

"You're giving me advice about trusting people?" Kurt said. "You got hoodwinked by your girlfriend."

"Exactly my point. You can't trust anyone."

"I can trust you. I can trust Gretchen. I trust my family."

"Not all family," Axel said. "We couldn't trust Dad. Or Mom. She gave everything away."

"It was hers to give."

"You don't have to take her side anymore. You don't have to do what she says. You know that right?"

Kurt was starting to get angry, which was not an emotion he was comfortable with. Luckily the doorbell rang and Axel went to answer.

When Axel didn't come back after a minute, Kurt got curious and walked downstairs. The front door was open. "Hey, Axel. You can't set up my taco expectations and then not deliver. That's a Geneva-convention-level rule."

He walked out the front door. Someone threw a sack over his head. Before he could react, his hands were tied behind his back, and he was moved expertly across the lawn and—from the sound of the sliding door—into a van.

He definitely wasn't getting tacos now.

CHAPTER 10

The van accelerated and braked suddenly. It felt as if every turn was taken on two wheels. Axel wouldn't have been surprised to find a twitchy cartoon mustelid behind the wheel.

Kurt remained silent while Axel shouted a volley of muffled questions as they slid around the back of the van.

"Where are you taking us?"

"What's your plan?"

"You must have a plan."

"If this a long trip, is there any way I can get some lumbar support?"

"Nobody abducts someone without a plan."

The radio turned on full blast. Mexican pop music drowned out his remaining queries.

A half hour later, the van came to an abrupt stop, slamming Axel into the back of the front seats. The driver turned off the engine.

"This has to have something to do with Gretchen," Axel said. "She probably stole from the wrong person."

"What are you talking about?" Kurt said. "Gretchen isn't a thief."

"How do you think she makes her living?"

"She buys and sells comic books."

"Yeah, that sounds like Gretchen."

"Wait," Kurt said. "Am I her fence?"

The door opened, and the sacks on their heads were removed. A man in his sixties stood at the open door of the van. He had a bushy red beard and a mop of red hair and wore a Hawaiian shirt, which on closer view was made up of small *Playboy* covers.

"Who are you?" Axel said. "What's going on?"

"Don't do anything stupid," Hawaiian Shirt said.

Axel had a good view out the front windshield. The van sat in the empty parking lot of Hofbräuhaus, a German restaurant. The big sign featured the comical illustration of a fat Bavarian man in lederhosen holding two big steins of beer. Under the restaurant's name, it said, "Family Style. Oktoberfest Nightly." Weeds grew a foot high in the cracks of the asphalt.

Axel had driven past the abandoned restaurant in Lemon Grove a dozen times on his way to the Spring Valley Swap Meet. It was one of those businesses that had always been closed, the building empty for decades.

Hawaiian Shirt helped Axel and Kurt out of the van. "No funny business."

If Axel hesitated for too long, the situation would only get worse. He and Kurt had to make their escape. They couldn't wait a second longer.

"Now!" Axel shouted and ran toward the line of hedges that hid the lot from the street. The massive parking lot stretched for fifty yards. He made about twenty of the fifty before something hit the back of his head, causing him to fall forward. His chin hit the asphalt. He bit his tongue and tasted blood. Rolling onto his back, he saw what hit him: a five-pound bag of birdseed busted at one seam. Hands grabbed his ankles and dragged him back to the van.

"What am I going to put in my feeder?" Hawaiian Shirt said, lifting Axel to his feet.

"'Now'?" Kurt asked, standing exactly where Axel had left him. "Was I supposed to know what 'Now' meant? No wink? No head nod? No signal?"

Axel wiped his mouth, smearing blood across his face.

Hawaiian Shirt handed Axel a handkerchief and dug a finger into Axel's mouth. "I've seen worse. I told you not to do anything stupid." He wiped his finger on Axel's shirt and walked toward the front door of the German beer hall. The sign in front said "Closed," but Hawaiian Shirt never lost stride, pushing the door open.

Axel and Kurt followed.

The massive beer hall looked like a church. Leaded glass windows depicting German maidens and griffins gave just enough light for Axel to make out the surroundings. Oversize steins, coats of arms, and alpenhorns decorated the opposite wall. Axel half-expected to be greeted by the lederhosen-clad cartoon character from the sign.

"It's like being in an abandoned German amusement park," Kurt said.

Something exploded. Axel screamed and dove for cover under one of the big wooden tables.

Confetti and balloons rained from the ceiling. Men, women, and children jumped out from every conceivable hiding place yelling, "Surprise!"

A big hand-painted banner unfurled. It read, "Welcome to the Family."

"I knew it," Kurt said.

Gretchen walked out from a side door, her hands in her pockets. She wasn't restrained but didn't look happy.

"I bith off the tip of my tongue for thith," Axel said.

Fifteen minutes later, Axel—untied and pissed off—sat across a big wooden table from a smiling Mother Ucker. Gretchen sat next to him, equally perturbed.

"I see where you get your name," Gretchen said.

Two stout German women in traditional garb filled the table with food: all manners of sausage, sauerkraut, spaetzle, potatoes, and white asparagus. Their cleavage spilled out as they leaned over to set each plate down. Big, frothy steins of beer sat untouched in front of them.

"Dig in," Mother said, picking up a sausage with her bare hand and taking a bite. It made a loud snap and spattered fat onto the table.

"You're like a female version of Henry the Eighth," Gretchen said. "Only bigger."

Mother laughed. "I could rock a turkey leg."

"I would eat," Axel said, "but my tongue is so swollen, I'm afraid I'd choke."

"Is he always such a baby?" Mother asked.

Gretchen nodded.

Axel looked around the room to check on Kurt.

Kurt stood in the middle of the hall, surrounded by a dozen relatives. He shook hands and introduced himself to each of them, including the children. Kurt looked as happy as Axel had seen him. A little girl held Kurt's thumb in one hand, his pinky in the other. Kurt curled his arm and lifted her in the air. She squeaked and laughed and asked him to do it again. One of the older men said something. Kurt laughed like it was the funniest thing he had ever heard.

"Where's the guy who drove us here?" Axel said. "I'd love a brief word with him."

"Fritzy had to pass on the party," Mother said. "Some bad blood. He didn't want to overshadow your arrival. He's a little nutty."

"No shit," Axel said.

"All families have a lunatic or three. The kidnapping was Fritzy's idea, and once he gets an idea in his head, it's best to give in. What was the harm really?"

Axel pointed at his mouth, incredulous. "This was the harm."

"Everyone here, all these people," Gretchen said, "these are all Uckers?"

"A good chunk of the Southern Cal contingent, at least. There are Uckers all over. It's something that we got this crew together today. We might be family, but there's some animosity in the room. A couple blood feuds had to be truced out. Fritzy and a few others stayed clear."

As if on cue, a commotion started at the other end of the hall. Axel turned to see two men wrestling on the ground.

"It's about time," Mother said. "They can finally work it out."

One of the men grabbed a fondue fork and stabbed the other one in the leg. The stabbing complete, the stabber stood up, dusted himself off, and reached out a hand to help the stabbee up. The stabbed man pulled the fork out of his leg and accepted the hand.

Show over, everyone in the room went back to what they were doing. It didn't appear to be their first fork stabbing. Even the children didn't seem to care.

"What kind of family is this?" Axel asked.

"Michael will be the first to admit he had that coming," Mother said. "He pulled some shit. Bertha never told you about us?"

"Nothing at all," Axel said.

"She did what she thought was best for you," Mother said. She picked up another sausage, thought about it, and tossed it back on the plate.

"Why are we only meeting you—everyone else—now?" Axel asked.

"Your mother and father cut us off," Mother said. "We're a bad influence. After she died, that coupon expired. You're all grown up. It's time you know who you are."

"Can we get to the part where you tell us what you want?" Gretchen said. "My mom warned me never to trust an Ucker. That's where you're starting with me."

Mother lifted her stein, held it up in an unspoken toast, and drank its entire contents in one tilt. She wiped her mouth with her forearm, let out a big "ah," and motioned to one of the hausfraus to have it refilled.

When she got her fresh beer, she took a sip and said, "Your Holy Roller mother knew Henry was a thief when they married. He promised to reform. The only way for him to stick to that vow was to break from the family."

"Is this like a family of criminals?" Axel asked. "Are the Uckers travelers or something?"

"The Uckers are thieves," Mother said. "Have been for centuries. We dabble in other arenas, but that's the nature of being a crook. We're professionals. Like a guild."

"A guild of thieves?" Axel said. "A little *Game of Thrones*-y, don't you think?"

"You're saying our father never stopped stealing?" Gretchen asked.

"He stopped," Mother said. "For a while."

"Did our mom know that he had started again?" Gretchen asked.

"At the end, yes, maybe," Mother said. "I don't know. When she found out, I'm sure it was the lie that hurt the most."

Axel remembered that day. The world turning upside down. Everything going to hell.

He watched Kurt play cards with some of the Ucker kids. They had a three-card-monte game going. Kurt lost and laughed about it when they showed him how they manipulated the cards.

"Everyone here is a thief?" Gretchen asked.

Mother shrugged. "It ain't like the movies. Where everyone has a single skill and that's all they do. Being a criminal is about two things: opportunity and willingness. When you read a real thief's rap sheet, it's a recipe of leftovers: a few cups of B and E, a helping of mail fraud, a pinch of theft, and a healthy dollop of confidence scams. We got our hands in everyone's pockets. There's a place for the three of you. If you're interested."

"You want us to join your criminal organization?" Axel asked. "And do what? Steal?"

"That job at the bank wasn't any better than what we do," Mother said.

"How do you know about—I quit that job."

"Your sister is a thief."

"I don't know what you're talking about," Gretchen said.

"Of course you don't, sweetie."

"It's nice to meet you, Aunt Mother, but we aren't joining a cabal of thieves," Axel said, standing.

"Let's hear her out," Gretchen said, a hand on Axel's arm.

"You aren't serious?" Axel said. "Oh yeah. Of course you are."

"You're living under the ridiculous notion that stealing is wrong." Mother smiled.

"How silly of me," Axel said, but he sat back down. "You're going to convince me that thievery is good? This I want to hear. Just to see the inner workings of a delusional mind."

"Is it wrong to steal something back that was stolen from you?" Mother asked.

"Trick question," Axel said. "That's not stealing. It's still your property, even if it's in someone else's possession."

"Touché," Mother said. "What if you couldn't retrieve the specific item but took something of equal value?"

"I don't know," Axel said. "Gray, but still about justice. It depends, I guess. You're pretending that the police don't exist and there isn't a system to deal with this kind of thing."

"Have you seen the clearance rates for property theft?" Mother said. "Let's talk about your taste in women."

"Oh yeah," Gretchen said, clapping her hands theatrically. "Let's talk about that."

"Definitely not," Axel said.

"Did you go to the police when Stephanie Holm conned you?" Mother asked.

"Who?"

"That's right. You know her by the name Priscilla Hamilton. A.k.a. Missy Macklin, a.k.a. Felicity Monroe, and about fifteen other aliases. Her real name is Stephanie Holm. She makes a living by making smart people do stupid things."

Gretchen nudged Axel with her elbow. "She called you smart."

"I—" Axel said, but Mother raised her hand, quickly shutting him down.

"What if I told you that I could get your money back?"

"I—" Axel said. Again the raised hand.

"She made you look like an asshole. The money is small potatoes, but she made you fall in love. That was mean."

Axel opened his mouth to protest but then nodded.

"Is it morally wrong to get your money back? Would it be ethically inappropriate?"

Axel thought about Priscilla. He thought about how she had made him feel. He thought about the note she had left. All the hope she had taken away. Axel thought about those horrible gluten-free muffins. "It's not like she doesn't deserve a little retribution, I suppose. It would be justice. Just not courtroom justice."

"And it took all of a minute for me to convince you. Wait until we spend more time together. You're going to see that there are enough people that need to be ripped off to keep a good thief busy. Your ex-girlfriend is a warm-up, a test run, a dress rehearsal. The beginning."

"You want to go after Priscilla for real?" Axel said. "I thought we were hypotheticalling."

"There are no hypothetical plans," Mother said. "Only good plans and bad ones."

"But after Priscilla," Gretchen said, filling her plate with food. "You have something bigger planned, don't you? What's the score? The crown jewels? The Hope Diamond? I don't care. Count me in. This is what I've been looking for."

"What happened to 'We can't trust anyone' and all that stuff?" Axel said.

"Come on," Gretchen said. "You're curious."

"Priscilla is an easy sell," Axel said. "Who else are you going to convince me to steal from?"

Mother leaned in, dropping her voice. "We're going to rob your grandfather."

"We have a grandfather?" Axel said.

"Oh, you most certainly do," Mother said, "and he stole from you."

"How could someone we've never met steal from us?" Axel asked.

"Because Dolphus Ucker no longer goes by that name," Mother said. "For the last dozen years, he's called himself Brother Tobin Floom."

"Shut the front door," Gretchen said.

"And he didn't just steal your money and your house," Mother said. "Fifteen years ago, he got your father killed."

PART TWO

CHAPTER 11

Stephanie Holm foresaw a disappointing weekend. The pickings were thin, mostly professional women who looked like they leaned toward penis. She was on the prowl for a fortyish middle manager type with self-confidence issues.

Mark Land Symposiums never yielded the same caliber of marks that a Tony Rogers event drew, but she had fished those waters to depletion and needed to let that ecosystem regenerate.

There was time. It was only Saturday morning.

Stephanie reached the front of the coffee line. "Large black coffee. One hundred and twenty degrees. I'll know. Are these muffins gluten-free?"

Before the barista could answer, she heard a name shouted behind her.

"Priscilla? Is that you?"

Stephanie turned. Axel Ucker stood at the café entrance. She pinched the bridge of her nose and softly said, "Overlap. I didn't account for overlap."

She turned and smiled, eyes sympathetic. "Axel? How are you? How have you been?"

"Lady, there's a line," the barista said, setting her coffee on the counter.

Stephanie held up a finger for Axel to wait and turned to the barista. "I'm saying hello to an ex. It's a delicate moment. Nobody here is late to deliver a baby or anything important."

"I care why?" the barista said. "Do you want a muffin or not?"

She put on a big smile. "Yes. Can you heat it up, put butter on it? Lots of butter. Really lubricate it. Butter the living shit out of it. Have you seen *Last Tango in Paris*?"

"Of course, I'm aware of Bertolucci's seminal film."

"So you know where I'm headed with that buttered muffin?"

"The coffee is three fifty," he said. "Can you give me the money and get out of my life? I don't get paid enough to put up with entitled assholes."

"Good for you, coffee monkey. Don't take any shit." She dropped a ten on the counter. "Keep the change."

"Fucking philosophy degree," the barista said.

Stephanie walked to Axel. Before he could speak, she gave him a bear hug. She turned his body slightly to the right in order to get a better angle on the only exit and avoid getting boxed in.

"How long has it been?" Stephanie asked.

"Three months, twelve days," Axel said.

"I'm so sorry about the note. I hurt you. I can see that now. I was in a vulnerable place." She tried to cry, but her face froze in a strange grimace. She needed motivation, a trigger. She thought about the time she lost her phone—it had been a real bitch reentering her contacts.

Axel grabbed Stephanie's shoulders firmly and held her at arm's length. "Cut it out, Priscilla—if that's even your name. I know you conned me."

"What are you talking about?"

"Give me some credit," Axel said, his voice loud enough to turn some heads. "I'm not particularly stable. After you left, I lost the house, my job. A perfectly good recycling bin got a kicking it didn't deserve. My mother died. I got kidnapped by insane relatives. They tried to recruit me into a criminal gang. I'm running on fumes."

"Whoa there, Hoss," Stephanie said. "You can blame me for a lot of things, but I didn't kill your mother. Also, I didn't do any of those other things."

"You ruined my life," Axel said. "I have proof. You're going to jail. I've got evidence. I'm making a citizen's arrest."

"Is that a real thing?" Stephanie asked.

He grabbed her arm. Out of the corner of her eye, Stephanie saw someone pull out their cell phone. She did not need her face going viral on YouTube.

"You need help, Axel. I don't know what to say, other than—" Stephanie kicked off her heels, dropping two inches in height, and shouted, "I can't believe you fucked my sister!" She threw the coffee at his chest, kicked him in the nuts, and ran out the door.

The café in the convention center was on the third floor. Elevators were traps. Already bummed about the shoes she had been forced to abandon, she ran down the concourse. Looking over her shoulder, she caught sight of Axel about forty yards behind her. He lurched forward, one hand on his crotch, and ran for her like an angry prospector.

She hit the stairs and took two at a time. Axel's shouts of "Priscilla!" followed her. After reaching the first floor, she darted through the massive lobby toward the front door. Ten seconds from safety. She looked over her shoulder. When she turned back, a young woman carrying eight cups of coffee in two paper trays stood directly in her path. They collided, coffee flying everywhere. Both Stephanie and the woman hit the ground—then the coffee hit them.

It took Stephanie a moment to get her bearings.

The coffee woman sat up, dazed and soaked, and looked at her with huge eyes. "Are you okay? Are you hurt?"

Stephanie turned to the stairs. Axel hopped off the last step and headed with purpose toward her. He had his whole hand down his pants, adjusting his junk.

Stephanie, fear in her eyes, turned to the woman. "That man."

"Is that guy chasing you?" the coffee woman asked. "What's he doing with his balls?"

"He thinks I'm someone named Priscilla. He exposed himself to me upstairs. He said he wants to beat me to death. With his cock."

The coffee woman dug in her messenger bag, tossing a three-ring binder and papers to the side. "Like hell he will."

Axel reached Stephanie and stood over her. "Get up, Priscilla. You're going to get what's coming to you."

"Nobody's getting a dick-beating today, pervo," the coffee woman said, pepper-spraying Axel's eyes from three feet away.

Axel screamed, grabbed his face, and stumbled backward. He slipped on the spilled coffee and landed in a sitting position.

The coffee woman gave Axel a couple of good kicks in the stomach. He went fetal. She turned to Stephanie. "Grab my stuff. We have to get you out of here."

Stephanie nodded and grabbed the binder, papers, and messenger bag and cradled them in her arms.

The coffee woman kept the defenseless Axel at bay by hitting him with another stream of pepper spray. He screamed.

Stephanie pulled her away, pointing toward a huge security guard stomping over. "We should go."

"What's going on here?" the guard asked.

"That man attacked her," the coffee woman said. "With his dong."

"Not on my watch." The guard picked up Axel with one hand. "You're coming with me, buster."

The coffee woman walked toward the women's bathroom. Stephanie glanced to the front door and considered leaving, then looked down at the bag and papers in her arms. She caught up to the woman in the bathroom.

"Your stuff is right here," Stephanie said, setting it on the sink counter.

"Thanks," the coffee woman said.

"I should be thanking you. I had no interest in getting hit with a dick. Even if it probably wouldn't have hurt, now that I think about it."

The coffee woman looked at herself in the mirror. "I'm covered in coffee." She took off her shirt and put it under the water in the sink. Stephanie found herself staring at the woman's nude torso. She was young, pretty, and in shape. She was also covered in ink. A dragon, some quotes that were too far away to read, a dollar sign, a dozen more.

When the woman turned and smiled, Stephanie looked down at the cover of the binder on the counter. The title read, "San Diego–Poway Highway Proposal, Routes, Maps, Proposed Land Buys."

The woman wrung out her shirt, put it on, and looked in the mirror. "Great. A wet T-shirt contest."

Stephanie took off her jacket. "Try this. It should work until you can get something else."

"Thanks." The woman smiled, took the jacket, and put it on. "Are you doing the symposium, too?"

"I am."

"Perfect. That puts us on the same schedule. I have gym clothes in my car. I can return your jacket." She buttoned the front of the jacket and reached for the binder and her stuff. "Thanks for grabbing my stuff. I'd be in hot water if I lost it. Top secret." She smiled and winked.

Stephanie handed the woman the notebook that she definitely wanted to read. There had been talk about that highway expansion for years. That kind of inside information was potentially the $1 million find that could get her out of her current $300,000 racket.

"I'm Patricia," Stephanie said. "It's really nice to meet you."

"Gretchen. Nice to meet you, too."

CHAPTER 12

Did Gretch have to spray my face twice?" Axel shouted, pouring milk into his eyes to stop the burning.

"You're getting milk all over the back of the van," Kurt said.

"Isn't there something they use in the movies instead of real pepper spray?"

"Authenticity," Kurt said, stripping out of the security guard uniform in the cramped space. "The more truth in the lie, the less lie there is to defend."

"Did you get that pearl of wisdom from Mother?" Axel asked. "You're spending a lot of time with her."

"She's full of wisdoms," Kurt said. "You could learn lots. She's a good teacher."

Kurt hopped in the driver's seat and started the van. He peeled out of the parking lot, fishtailing onto the street.

Axel slid around the back of the van, the milk flying from his hand and splashing against the wall. "What the hell, Kurt? Inconspicuous. We made a scene in there. There's a monster on the side of the van. Slow down."

"Bloodface is not a monster," Kurt said. "He's a fallen seraph."

"I don't care."

"Uncle Fritzy taught me some driving stuff. Uncle Fritzy says that driving slow is for old women and Latinos."

Axel blinked, his vision returning. "Did he use the word 'Latinos'?"

"He used a racister word," Kurt said. "I corrected him, but old people have a hard time with new nomenclature. They like the old words they know for things. Like possessions they don't need but still aren't willing to part with."

"Like comic books and action figures."

"No, not like those. Collectibles are for collecting. It's in the name." Kurt took the next turn quickly, sending Axel flying from one end of the van to the other. "Sorry about that." Kurt did not sound sorry.

Axel looked out the back of the van in the direction of the convention center. A black Town Car slid through traffic and got right behind them. His vision wasn't one hundred percent, but he was pretty sure he recognized the man in the driver's seat—or rather his poor choices in fake hair. Driving the Town Car was the bald man that had been at their mother's funeral. It's hard to forget someone with crooked eyebrows.

Axel moved closer to get a better look. "Do you know anyone with alopecia?"

"Which one's that? Is that when a person has a third nipple?"

"No body hair."

"Nope. Why?"

"We're being followed by one."

Kurt looked in the side mirror. "The Lincoln?"

"It swerved like it was in a hurry, then settled in behind us."

"Only one way to find out," Kurt said. "Hold on."

"To what?" Axel yelled, pushing his hands against the roof of the van for support.

The streetlight in front of them turned from yellow to red. Cars on the cross street moved into the intersection. Kurt floored it toward the thinning gap between the cars.

Axel's vision had cleared enough for him to see his imminent death through the front windshield. "Cars. Bus. Crash. Splode."

"I've been practicing." Kurt smiled, calm.

When he reached the intersection, Kurt pulled the parking brake. The van slid sideways, took a sharp right turn, and miraculously entered the flow of traffic without hitting another vehicle.

"Half Drift!" Kurt yelled.

Axel flew against the side of the van for the billionth time. He stayed down, wondering why he had kept trying to stand.

"It's better to let your body go slack than to tense up," Kurt said. "I read that somewhere. Calm, blue ocean, Ax."

"Calm, blue up yours."

"Is the Lincoln still back there?" Kurt said. "I got some evasive maneuvers I'd love to try out."

Axel looked out the back. The Town Car made the turn and accelerated in their direction. "You pulled ahead. He's not pretending like he's not following anymore. What do you think happens if he catches up?"

"We aren't going to find out." Kurt hit the gas.

Axel lost his balance and slammed against the back door of the old van. It opened. He grasped the interior handle as he fell out, just missing hitting the asphalt. Half in the van, Axel watched the road fly inches from his face, small pieces of gravel peppering his cheek.

The van threaded the traffic, changing lanes erratically. Axel got his other hand on the handle and hooked his ankle on the edge of the back door. All he needed to do was one sit-up. He prayed that the muscle memory from that one Pilates class he took with Priscilla was still in there.

With a loud "haawwgruffla," he pulled himself into the van and slammed the door shut.

Kurt turned. "Be careful. The lock on the back door is broken." He flipped a U-turn and headed in the direction of the Town Car, then took a sharp right down an alley. Kurt found a side street and pulled the van into an apartment parking lot.

Axel made his way to the front seat. His heart raced like an out-of-shape baby bird's heart after said baby bird had just run a marathon for baby birds. They sat in silence. Kurt smiled from ear to ear.

"We lost him," Axel said.

Kurt picked up the milk carton. "Was that my milk you poured in your eyes?"

"It was in the ice chest."

"It's empty. Where's the rest of it?"

"All over the back of the van."

"What am I supposed to drink with my Oreos?"

"You got a real thing about cookies," Axel said. "There's bottled water."

"Stop. Just stop." Kurt held up a hand. "You can't be suggesting I dip cookies in water. That's insanity. And how do you dip something into a bottle? Sometimes you're so oblivious."

"A bald guy with crooked eyebrows?" Mother Ucker said. "Yeah, that's no big deal. He's FBI."

"Say again?" Axel said.

Axel and Kurt sat across the table from Mother Ucker in the abandoned beer hall, which acted as the unofficial Ucker HQ. Axel had only met a handful of times with Mother since their initial meeting. Kurt, on the other hand, spent time with Mother and Fritzy at least once a week.

"The Federal Bureau of Incompetence," Mother said. "They've been trying to get something on me for years. They couldn't find an ass at an orgy."

"I totally ditched a Fed," Kurt said, holding up a hand for Axel to high-five.

Axel left him hanging.

"Can we all get back to the part where the FBI was chasing us?" Axel asked.

Fritzy walked into the hall from the back. He had a small safe on a hand truck.

"Hey, Uncle Fritzy!" Kurt yelled. "You won't believe it. I ditched a Fed. You should've seen me. At one point, I threw a Dipsy Doodle and then put some French Pastry on it. Like you showed me."

"Get out of town!" Fritzy yelled back.

"Ran a reverse Wile E. Coyote on his butt."

"Impressive," Fritzy said, leaving the hand truck and joining them. "You're ready for my advanced class. Meet me here tomorrow morning. I'll find you a helmet."

Axel stood up, sat back down, and stood up again. He thought steam might come out of his ears. "That means we—me and Kurt—are now on the Feds' radar, too. Which I don't consider to be great."

"Was it Harry?" Fritzy asked Mother.

"Who else?" Mother said. "He's a determined bastard."

"A bald man named Harry?" Axel asked.

"I never thought of that," Mother laughed.

"Harry Cronin," Fritzy said. "He's had a bug up his ass for us for a while."

"We're going to end up going to jail forever," Axel said.

"You won't go to jail forever," Mother said. "Jail is where you're held before trial. It's temporary holding. Prison, on the other hand, I can't make any promises about. Most Uckers do some time."

"If Mother and Uncle Fritzy aren't worried," Kurt said, "I don't see why we should be. They're more experienced."

"We set a confidence game in motion, and there's a Fed on our ass," Axel said.

"I won't let anything happen to either of you," Mother said.

"See," Kurt said. "It's fine."

While Kurt got getaway driver lessons from Uncle Fritzy, Axel had started the process of creating an official dossier for Brother Tobin Floom and his ministry. Background information, historical biography, business associates, anything he could dig up on the faux padre.

Axel loved a good mystery—falling into an internet wormhole and seeing where it led, digging deeper and deeper into the web and sifting through the facts and fictions. The biggest problem was that ninety-nine percent of internet content was opinion. Not raw data, but some non-expert's interpretation that may or may not be based on any truth. The only way to wade through the clutter and find actual data was to start with the boring. Dates and locations and numbers and names. Public records, newspaper announcements, statements of fact.

Along with the internet mining, he was reading Brother Tobin Floom's autobiography, *God's Humble Servant: My Great and Humble Journey*. Fifty pages into the book, Axel was positive that Brother Floom (and/or his ghostwriter) didn't know what the word *humble* meant.

From the introduction: "I asked myself a question. While the Lord can choose to speak to anyone—He is the Lord, after all—why does He speak directly to so few people? Why does He speak to me? I prayed on this. And you know what the Lord said? He told me that, like in the Bible, He speaks only to prophets. Does that make me a prophet? Am I enlightened? Chosen? Special in some way? It's not for me to say, but would the Lord speak to me if I wasn't? Not my words. His words. God's word."

Brother Floom's other books were not what Axel would describe as theological texts. No dense monographs on the moral implications of Abraham's decision to sacrifice his son. While the book *God Is Not Poor* cited scripture, it was eighty percent *The Power of Positive Thinking*—not coincidentally also written by a Protestant minister—with a new set of vocabulary words, a healthy amount of illustrations and graphs, and a personal spin on the relationship between faith and prosperity.

Those were the only two Floom books available as e-books. Axel had ordered used copies of Floom's two out-of-print books. By their titles—*The H.E.A.V.E.N. Method to Eternal Prosperity* and the cumbersomely titled *You Can Have It All: Money Isn't the Root of All Evil, the Lack of Money Is the Root of All Evil*—he guessed that they would be more of the same.

The official Brother Tobin Floom Ministry website provided names and staff profiles for the six different physical locations that made up its operational core, including the headquarters in San Diego.

In a recent investigative piece about televangelists, *Fortune* magazine listed Brother Tobin Floom as number twelve in personal wealth. But that number only represented a fraction of his portfolio. The bulk of his investments would not be in his name, but on the ministry's books. Structurally similar to any corporation, but in the case of a church, one hundred percent tax-free income. The ministry had substantial equity, including Floom's $4 million home in Orange County.

According to Brother Floom's autobiography, he grew up in rural Oklahoma. The son of a preacher himself, he was schooled in the Bible and traveled from town to town spreading the Word with his father. He began preaching at the age of eight. He took over his father's ministry at twenty-two, fifty years earlier, and built it into the empire that it had become. He made the switch from church preaching to the television thirteen years earlier.

Axel, of course, knew this was all bullshit. The man's name was Dolphus Ucker. He was Axel's grandfather. And he was a conman.

CHAPTER 13

Kurt maneuvered the van through a series of orange traffic cones that Fritzy had laid out in the parking lot. After a few successful turns, Kurt clipped one of them. Overadjusting, he hit a few more cones on the other side of the lane. He stopped and looked at the damage in the rearview.

"I'm sorry, Fritzy," Kurt said. "I knocked a bunch of them down."

"I set them up closer and closer as you went," Fritzy said. "Until there wasn't room. A kind of test. The trick is not letting it affect you. Bump another car or miss a turn, you got to stay in control."

"Did I pass?" Kurt asked.

"You did okay. Let's call it a C-plus."

"Should I run it again?"

"I ain't got the energy to set all them cones back up."

"Thanks a lot for teaching me this stuff."

"My boy never had no interest. I tried to teach him. It feels good to pass some knowledge down."

"Did I meet your son at the party?"

"Naw, he wasn't there. He's—" Fritzy stopped talking abruptly. "I got an idea. You want some more real world experience. I know a speed trap you could run. Try to ditch a cop. You can't tell Mother, though."

"Better not," Kurt said. "I already got a little too crazy the other day. Let's stick to the parking lot."

"Okay, but we're going to do something dangerous, or what's the point?"

"That a fair compromise."

"I want you to drive right at that light pole. Fast. When you get about thirty yards away, simultaneously crank the wheel and pull the E brake. It's going to feel like you're going to flip, but I don't think you will."

"You don't think I will?"

"Probably not," Fritzy said. "We'll find out."

"This van doesn't have airbags."

"You want to learn or what?"

Kurt hit the gas, the speedometer climbing steadily if not quickly. The light pole fast approached.

Fritzy pushed a hand against the ceiling and yelled, "Now!"

Kurt hit the parking brake and turned the wheel. The van shook as it slid to the side. They just missed the pole but continued to skid out of control. Kurt cranked the wheel the other way, the back end fishtailing. He felt the tilt of the van. The steering wheel vibrated. Then everything stopped, and the van landed back onto four wheels.

"A-plus, kid," Fritzy said. "That's a B for the day."

"That was awesome. Horrifyingly awesome."

"If I can get my hands on a ramp, I'll teach you how to car ski, but we'll need a different ride." Fritzy opened a can of beer and handed it to Kurt. The foam ran over his hand. He opened one for himself.

"It kind of feels like this is what it's like to have a dad," Kurt said.

Fritzy gave him a weak smile. "I wouldn't know."

Kurt and Mother waited by the junkyard office while Michael Ucker hitched the trailer to the back of the rental truck. The single-wide mobile office that sat on top looked a little banged up, but it would serve its purpose.

"Don't tell Michael anything about what we're doing," Mother said. "He'll angle his way in. The office is a set rate, not a percentage of the take. He doesn't got to know nothing."

"I wasn't going to tell anyone anything," Kurt said. "We're committing crimes. That's not small talk."

"You can't always trust family," Mother said.

"I can trust you, though, right?"

"Definitely not." Mother winked.

"Speaking of family," Kurt said. "There's something that's been bugging me. I get that Dad was a thief and all that, but why do you think he went back to thieving if he stopped?"

"From what I pieced together—I didn't have a lot of contact—he lost his job at the gypsum factory around the time you got sick."

"I don't know anything about that. I was too little."

"Sepsis, if I remember right. Medical bills piled up."

"He went back to crime because of me?"

"Not because of you. Because of bad luck and bad timing. He did what any good father would do. And Dolphus did what any bad father would do. He swooped in. They partnered on some jobs."

"Until the last one."

Michael wiped his hands on a rag as he walked to them. "How long you going to need it? Hildy thought she might have something going in October and has it reserved for then."

"Not more than two weeks," Mother said. "Probably less."

"It's a standard office setup inside. Desk, chairs, corkboard, filing cabinets. You're going to have to dress it for whatever scheme you got, though. What exactly are you doing?"

"Like I would tell you." Mother laughed.

"I need to have a word with Kurt here," Michael said.

"He ain't going to tell you nothing neither."

"He's a grown-ass man." Michael put an arm around Kurt and walked him away from Mother. Mother started to follow, but Kurt waved her off. They strolled down a row of old rusted cars. Dogs barked somewhere close. They sounded ferocious.

"How's your leg?" Kurt asked. "Never seen no one fork-stabbed before."

"No big deal," Michael said. "Only two tines. Not the first time. Probably not the last. I was surprised he didn't go steak knife."

"You guys know that you're not like other families, right?" Kurt asked.

"All families are messed up," Michael said. "Has Matty got you mixed up in something sinister? She's my cousin, but she's shifty, even for an Ucker."

"She's helping me and my brother and sister get some money back," Kurt said.

"Be careful is all. She's not a Good Samaritan. She don't do nothing without getting the lion's share of a thing."

"We ain't got nothing to take that ain't already been took," Kurt said.

"You need anything, you let me know," Michael said. "DJ told me to thank you for the card you sent him. You got real friends in this family."

"I figured a funny card was just the thing for someone in prison. Everyone likes *The Far Side*."

"He appreciated it. If you want to tell me about what the score is, you can. You can trust me."

"I appreciate that," Kurt said. "Mother really is helping us. You got nothing to worry about there."

"I doubt that," he said. "You know, I don't even know where she lives. She keeps it a secret, in case she needs to hide after screwing one of the family. She always needs to have the upper hand."

"I'll keep that in mind."

"And then I told Mother that I wouldn't tell anyone about anything," Kurt said. "And then Michael was all 'Don't trust no one,' and then I was like, 'Okay.'"

"But you're telling me right now," Louder said.

"You're my best friend. I'm obviously going to tell you everything."

"Your new family is a trip, that's for sure."

Louder's face looked big and distorted through the fisheye lens. It got even more rounded at the edges as she drew it closer. The screen went black when she shoved the lipstick camera up her nose.

"Gross," Kurt said. "I'm going to have to baby wipe that now."

"Boogers are sterile," Louder said. "That's science fact."

Kurt checked the video surveillance equipment one piece at a time. It had taken him a half hour to untangle the cables. He wanted to be thorough. If something was going to go wrong, it wouldn't be because of him.

"Are you like a real-life criminal now?" Louder asked.

"I haven't committed a crime yet. Other than reckless driving and maybe fraud, and I witnessed a stabbing. Is impersonating a security guard a thing?"

"More like cosplay."

"Crime is my family's trade. I'm honoring family tradition."

"My family's only tradition is microwave Peep wars every Easter. That and binge drinking. Which isn't nearly as cool as it sounds."

CHAPTER 14

Gretchen knew a Sunday sermon when she saw one. A secular sales pitch with all the fervor and passion of any preacher's plea for salvation. Fire and brimstone and merchandising.

On Sunday, the final day of the Mark Land Symposium, the speakers threw out all the stops. An emotional and spiritual fire sale. The main message from the pulpit seemed to be that if Gretchen and the others wanted to progress more in life, love, and business, they needed to keep coming back. Nothing was an overnight fix. Change wasn't easy. One weekend was a good start, but the work was for a lifetime. That was the Mark Land way, the Mark Land vision, and the Mark Land promise. Not coincidentally, all checks should be made out to Mark Land Symposiums Worldwide LLC.

The speaker enthusiastically presented the seven-step method for achieving a true metamorphic breakthrough. The PowerPoint looked like someone had Photoshopped a food pyramid and replaced it with Mark Land products. Where grains would have been, Mark Land's Six-Month Goal Achiever Super Planner and Scheduler was inserted. Products and events—growth opportunities, as pitched—were available for purchase and booking after the presentation. All major credit cards accepted, including Diners Club, which Gretchen hadn't known was still a thing.

Sitting next to Gretchen, Stephanie Holm took feverish notes. Gretchen suddenly felt self-conscious that she wasn't taking notes. Would Mark-Land-True-Believer Gretchen take notes, even if Mark-Land-Is-Full-of-Shit Gretchen wouldn't? That was the question. She wanted her first deep cover assignment to be successful. As adept as she was at burglary, she was out of her comfort zone.

She was overthinking it. She needed to use as much of the truth as she could. Any good liar knew that. Fake Gretchen and Real Gretchen should be identical twins. And Fake Gretchen wasn't taking any notes.

"Ha," she said in triumph.

"What's so funny?" Stephanie whispered.

"Nothing," Gretchen said, digging for a save. "I watched a video of a farting hippo earlier. The image jumped in my head."

"That's a good one," Stephanie said. "Sounds like a buzz saw."

"And it just keeps going."

The two of them laughed, covering their mouths. They got a few stares, two bad kids in the back row passing notes.

Stephanie and Gretchen had spent the better part of the weekend together. Gretchen could never be sure which parts of Stephanie's personality were her and which were Patricia—her current alias—but Gretchen had laughed more in that weekend than she had in ages.

The speaker paced the stage, talking about finding meaning and direction in one's life. Gretchen didn't need to shell out eight hundred bucks to have someone show her the way. She knew where she was headed. If she could just figure out her relationships, she would have life in the bag.

That was the way things were. There was always something that didn't work. You fix one thing, and another falls apart.

"Life has no inherent meaning. We are not born with meaning, and it's not going to fall in our lap. You can search and search, but it's not out there either. It's in here. And in here." The man pointed to his head and his heart. "You have to create meaning for yourselves. You are not entitled to anything. You don't deserve anything. Life is neither fair nor unfair. It is a blank slate. Tabula rasa."

Tell Gretchen something she didn't know. You had to be middle or upper class to see that as any kind of insight. Poor people didn't dwell on fairness. They made the best with what they had. For the Venti-half-caf-latte crowd, this might be revelatory, but regular folk had no truck with the idea of a meritocracy. The American Dream was a nice idea, but if you took it too seriously, you ended up spending your life chasing something out of your grasp. The American Dream was what made Americans so pissed off. Everyone's told that they could accomplish anything. When they don't, they blame themselves, hate themselves, and then blame immigrants to feel better.

"What do you want? That's your homework. When the symposium ends, the real learning begins. I want you to ask yourself a simple question. I want you to ask yourself what your goals are. What do you truly need in your life? This is in addition to everything that we've worked on this weekend. Finish constructing your dream boards and charting your progressional life moments, but I want focused writing on your goals. Find a partner to act as a challenge collaborator."

Stephanie turned to Gretchen. "You want to be study buddies?"

"Are you sure?" Gretchen said. "You could ask someone more experienced. I'd understand. I'm not sure how good a challenge collaborator I am. Mostly because I don't know what a challenge collaborator is. I mean, I'm in. It would be great to learn from someone with your experience, but I want you to get something out of it."

"I'll get something out of it," Stephanie said.

"If we can do it without cracking each other up."

"Where's the fun in that?" Stephanie said. "How about we meet up later tonight? Say seven thirty? I can pick you up, and we can grab dinner."

Gretchen hadn't expected it to be that easy. She didn't know if Axel would have everything ready, but she couldn't pass on the opportunity.

"I have to run by my office," Gretchen said, "but after that I'll be free. It's not that far from here."

"They make you work on Sunday?"

"I'll make that one of my goals. To work less."

"I'll pick you up when you're done," Stephanie said.

"If it's not too much trouble."

"No trouble. I want to know more about you. Your work is part of that."

"It's not that interesting. Roads and plans, lines on maps."

Stephanie placed a hand on Gretchen's knee. "I have a lot to teach you. If you'll let me."

Gretchen was pretty sure that she was going to let her.

"Are you sure this place is going to be ready by seven thirty?" Gretchen asked, giving the temporary office the once-over.

Axel pinned standard government posters and charts on a corkboard. He jabbed extra holes in each of the corners with a pushpin. It would have been better to rent a building, but time hadn't allowed it. A temporary mobile building on a construction site seemed plausible enough as a fake land office.

"I didn't know you would be so quick," Axel said. "It's only got to hold up to a cursory inspection. She's going to be here ten minutes and focused on the paperwork you leave out. If you want to help, put some coffee stains on that desk blotter. Everything is too orderly and new."

Gretchen walked to the coffee machine, poured a cup of coffee, let a little spill over the edge, and made some rings on the desk.

"Priscilla is—" Axel said.

"Stephanie," Gretchen interrupted.

"Right," he said.

"Although for the time being, call her Patricia so I don't get confused."

"I'm going to talk about her as little as possible," Axel said.

"I can see the attraction. She's cool as shit. Way funnier than I thought she would be. I expected an ice queen."

"She's not cool. She's evil. She's whatever she thinks you want her to be. She's a manipulative bitch that's going to get her comeuppance."

"Wow," Gretchen said. "I never pegged you as vengeful. I have mixed feelings."

"She shat on my heart," Axel said. "The karmic scale is getting balanced. That's enough coffee stains. Don't overdo it. There's some lint in that plastic bag by the door. Can you throw it in some corners?"

"You have a bag of lint?"

"It's actually lint mixed with dust and hair."

"Hair?"

"It binds the dust."

"Eww. I'm going to let you handle the room linting." Gretchen plopped down in the desk chair, took a drink of coffee, and made a disgusted face. "This coffee is awful."

"It should be. I added brown watercolor paint." Axel stood back from the corkboard with his hands on his hips. He dog-eared a couple more corners.

Gretchen grabbed the trash can and spit into it. "Full disclosure, Stephanie kinda sorta hit on me, definitely hinted at possible amorousness."

Axel turned to Gretchen. "Why would she hit on you? You're a woman. She likes men. I'm a man. She liked me. A man."

"We've had this conversation before," Gretchen said. "Some people like men. Some people like women. And some people—believe it or not—like both. I'm sure you've heard of them. Or watched pornographies that depict it. Why do I have to explain bisexuality to you every couple of years? It's not a complex concept."

"I know, but she doesn't seem like—"

"Doesn't seem like what?"

"Nothing. Never mind."

"Good call," Gretchen said. "Besides, we don't know if she liked you at all. You were her mark. It could have been an act."

"You're her mark now. She's hitting on you for the same reason."

"I know," Gretchen said. "I'm just messing with you."

"Not funny," Axel said. "I don't want to think about you two together. You're my sister. That would be like incest. Incest adjacent, at least."

"I didn't think the two of you ever did it."

"But I wanted to. I thought about it so many times that I count it as actually happening. She still pops into my erotic thoughts, and I don't want you anywhere near that cesspool."

"Don't worry. It's only our first date. I won't let her get too handsy. Maybe brush a tit or get up on some inner thigh. Nothing where my bathing suit covers."

"For that, you're linting the room."

"Nice place," Stephanie said, walking into the temporary office a few hours later. "It's—uh—quaint."

"It's filthy," Gretchen said. "They don't supply a maid."

"Or a broom," Stephanie said, kicking at some lint.

"This was supposed to be a temporary office, but I've been working here for two years." Gretchen laughed. "Leave it to City Planning to have one of their offices condemned and then never finish fixing the issue. That's the government for you."

Stephanie casually flipped through papers on the edge of the desk. Her expression showed complete disinterest. "What kind of things do you do? Do you plan cities?"

"It's boring," Gretchen said. "Mostly transportation development and land-use analysis, coordination with state and federal—blah, blah, blah. Don't get me started, unless you need to go to sleep. There's no way you would find any of it interesting."

"I might surprise you," Stephanie said.

"Oh dang," Gretchen said. "I have to grab something from my car. Do you mind waiting here for a few minutes?"

"I hope I didn't scare you off." Stephanie grinned.

Gretchen looked away shyly and shook her head. "Help yourself to some coffee. It's not fresh, but it's—actually, steer clear of the coffee. It's disgusting."

Stephanie laughed and plopped down in the desk chair. "I'll entertain myself. Get your stuff done. Don't mind me."

Gretchen walked down the steps of the trailer, across the open yard, and into the parking lot across the street. She got in the back of the van, where Uncle Fritzy and Kurt monitored the screens from the cameras in the trailer.

"You're doing great, sis," Kurt said.

"Did she take the bait?" Gretchen asked.

"Took it, ate it, shit it out, and went back for more," Fritzy said.

"You're one gross dude, Uncle Fritzy," Gretchen said. "Does it come natural, or are you trying?"

"All natural." Fritzy turned and gave her a wink. "She tried a couple of filing cabinets but then went to the desk. She's reading exactly what she's supposed to."

Gretchen watched Stephanie take photos of the paperwork that they had left in plain sight for her to find.

"You did a good job playing coy when she hit on you," Fritzy said.

"Thanks," Gretchen said. "You think she was hitting on me?"

"Definitely. She wants to put her vagina in your vagina."

"Is that even how—?" Kurt looked confused.

"Ignore your uncle," Gretchen interrupted. "How long should I give her?"

"One more minute," Fritzy said. "No more. You don't want her too deep in that material. Your brother did a good job, but he's no engineer. The more bullshit you throw at her, the more likely she is to smell it."

CHAPTER 15

According to the ministry's website, Brother Tobin Floom was currently touring sub-Saharan Africa, bringing Christianity and fellowship where it was most needed. The prosperity gospel and numerous televangelists had found a receptive audience on the African continent, where Pentecostal fervor gibed with old traditions.

In recent years, Brother Tobin Floom performed fewer live sermons and instead devoted most of his time to his television appearances and arena-size events. The last few episodes of *Health, Wealth, and Salvation* had obviously been edited together with footage of Brother Floom on a soundstage and with stock footage of an audience. It hadn't gone unnoticed either. Questions arose on the message board on Floom's website, most of them showing concern for Brother Floom's health. There was no official response from either Floom or the ministry.

The Living Word Chapel in Mission Viejo acted as Brother Floom's ministry headquarters. Brother Floom made surprise appearances, but most often the congregation got the acting pastor Mervyn Whitlock. Five feet tall with the energy of someone who was five feet one, he looked like a younger, smaller version of Brother Floom, down to the white suit and gold handkerchief. Axel, ninety-six percent sure that Whitlock was coked out of his gourd, loved watching the little barrel of energy preach. Axel had met a few people who were naturally enthusiastic, but Whitlock was restless leg syndrome in human form.

Axel parked in the lower parking lot and got on the shuttle bus to the church entrance. The church grounds were massive. The place felt like a college campus, with outbuildings and a gymnasium. On the hill above the church, a giant cross looked down on the place of worship.

The three other parking lots had been full. Sunday evening services drew big crowds, especially when the church booked local favorites the Young Lions to perform. Having appeared on Brother Floom's show multiple times, they were on the brink of national notoriety. With a new song getting some airplay on Air1, they brought in sweater-clad teens; middle-aged women who told themselves it was about worshipping God, not the tightly pantsed young men; and a number of smiling men with odd postures and hair-sprayed coifs stiffer than a Ken doll's.

A toothy, big-eyed young woman greeted Axel at the entrance to the church. He had seen her before. She never blinked. Ever. She handed him a program. "Welcome back. Good to see you again."

"Thank you," Axel said. His efforts to establish himself as a regular in the congregation were starting to yield results. "A perfect day for fellowship."

"Amen to that." She smiled and turned to the couple that entered behind him. "Welcome back. Good to see you again."

Axel turned away, disappointed. He thought he had developed a rapport with Allteeth Noblinky over the last two weeks, but her dismissive rebuke told him that had been in his head.

Was he really so lonely that he had monitored the degree of affection he had received from the church greeter? He missed his relationship with Priscilla. Even if it was based entirely on a lie. Even if it was fraud. At least he had someone.

Upbeat music—the new tune from the Young Lions—played over the sound system as Axel walked down the aisle to the front. An usher handed out a stapled brochure that listed the workshops being held that week. Over thirty different groups and classes, including a selection of online courses. Most were free but usually required some literature or a workbook. Axel wasn't cynical enough to see everything that the church did as a money grab. It was a business, but that didn't mean they weren't making an effort: kids' programs, marriage counseling, after-school teen opportunities, to name a few.

The Second Christian Reformed Church in Warm Springs hadn't prepared him for the unsubtle assault of a megachurch. The Living Word sermons were high-energy events that felt like a mash-up between a rock concert, a self-help seminar, and a time-share pitch. Light on content, but full of passion, enthusiasm, and hope, they were an appealing form of entertainment and an effective form of salesmanship. There were worse ways to spend an evening. Elmer Gantry would have been proud. Sinclair Lewis would have been horrified.

As everyone else found their seat, Axel shifted his attention backstage and to the line of doors that led to the administrative area of the building. Like any concert or theatrical production, there was a clear divide between the front of the house and backstage.

A dozen men in identical suits paced the outer aisles, occasionally speaking into walkie-talkies. Not quite security, but also not quite not security, they acted as the front lines, the pawns on the board. They all had the posture of that one guy in the bar who wants to fight. Axel referred to these men as the 300, naming them after Gideon's army in the Bible. Not to be confused with the movie *300*, which was a completely different story about 300 different soldiers fighting against different impossible odds. Apparently 300 was the sweet spot for defeating massive armies and 301 was overkill—299 and you're screwed.

Axel spotted Reverend Whitlock at the side of the stage talking to Thrace McCormick, the director of operations for Tobin Floom Ministries. He was one of the few people that reported to Brother Floom directly. If Axel was going to infiltrate the organization, McCormick would be the gateway. Tall, thin, and humorless, the sixty-something

Thrace McCormick was camera-ready to be cast as the undertaker in a spaghetti Western.

When Whitlock left to check something on the stage, a woman approached McCormick. He had charted the personnel and their roles in the organization, but she was someone new. New and beautiful and in charge. Axel started to sweat, even in the frigid air-conditioning of the church.

The woman took McCormick to task about something. She didn't yell and kept a smile on her face—obviously not wanting anyone to notice—but the look on McCormick's face communicated everything. McCormick looked like he had been served a shit sandwich with extra shit and a side of french-fried shit. Rather than complain, he ate the shit buffet.

All Axel knew was that she was about his age and blond and had blue eyes and that she was beautiful and he wanted to meet her and talk to her about interesting things and maybe take her to Barcelona and eat tapas, but he was nervous about meeting her and maybe this was love and maybe she felt the same way even though they hadn't met but there was such a thing as fate and destiny, but that was all stupid but yeah, he was definitely in love. Because look at her.

When their conversation concluded, McCormick walked away. The woman scanned the crowd before walking through one of the doors to the administrative area. Her eyes met Axel's for a second. One second, tops. No more. But enough. They had a moment. Axel felt it. He knew she did, too.

Without planning or forethought, Axel stood and distractedly read his program as he strolled the perimeter near the front of the stage. Nobody noticed him, a member of the flock killing time before the service. The 300 weren't out in full force, as the crowd was still thin. He wasn't sure what he thought he'd accomplish other than getting kicked out, but he found himself walking to the side door that the blond woman had disappeared through. The door with the sign that read "Authorized Personnel Only."

He ended up in a long hallway with doors every thirty feet. He tried knobs. All of them locked.

Two of the 300 turned a corner. They walked toward him but hadn't spotted him, both looking down at one of their cell phones.

"Wait for it," one of them said. "Wait for it." And then they both busted up laughing. "Knocked that brother out."

Axel's whole body said "Run," even if he knew he wasn't in danger. This wasn't Nazi headquarters. It was a church. All he had to do was act confused and ask where the bathrooms were.

He chose a different tack. If you weren't where you belonged, the best thing to do was act like you did. He learned that sneaking into movie theaters. He was wearing a cardigan, for Christ's sake. He pulled out his cell phone and fake-pressed a button as if receiving a call.

"Jerry Junior. Sorry I couldn't take your call. I was on conference with Creflo. He's fine. Says hello. Anyhoo, those dates you sent me don't work. I can do Memphis in November, but Knoxville is out. No, no conflict. I just hate Knoxville."

The 300 gave him a look as they passed in the hall but didn't lose stride. He gave them a nod that attempted to convey both "Keep up the good work" and "I'm more important than you, so don't speak to me." His nods were more expressive than most people's nods. It was all about using every neck muscle.

Axel kept up the one-man show. "Creflo mentioned maybe some events in England with Kenneth or Joel, but if we're going to do something internationally, it's not going to be in that novelty-tooth factory they call a country. Let's go tropical. Costa Rica or Belize. I'll email you an action plan."

Axel gave the 300 a glance right before he turned the corner at the end of the hall. He watched them walk out into the stage area without giving him a second thought. He took a deep breath and put his phone in his pocket.

When he looked up, he almost ran right into the blond woman he had seen moments earlier. She was more beautiful up close. He might have made a squeaking sound.

"Are you okay?" the woman said. "You made a squeaking sound."

"I don't think so."

"I didn't know a human over two years old could hit that register. Like a dog toy."

Axel opened his mouth to reiterate his unsqueakiness, but when his eyes met hers, he got lost in them. Blue pools that he wanted to swim laps inside. Azure skies devoid of clouds. Some other blue thing that was really, really blue.

"You're staring at me in a way that makes me wish I had Mace or pepper spray or a Taser. I don't usually say the word 'testicles' in church. But if you don't blink soon, yours will be kicked into your abdomen."

Axel shook his head, snapping out of his stupor. "No, don't. I'm sorry. I'm lost. You startled me. My name is—" He needed a name. "My name is Christian. Fletcher Christian." Axel winced at his new name. That's why you plan and don't do things impulsively. "I don't work here. I was. This is going to sound—I was in the parking lot at my job downtown. The Lord spoke to me. He told me to come here. To offer my help. I'm not sure how or why or what, but when you get the call to action, you act, right?"

"Right," she said, backing up another step, quite possibly to get into proper nut-punting range for full leg extension.

"I sound crazy. Do I sound crazy? I do. It's not like God has ever told me to do anything before. This was a first for me."

"He told you to come here and do what?"

"I don't know. Help. I was in the crowd out there. Looking for a sign. Felt as out of place as a fat guy named Ichabod. Figured someone back here might show me some direction."

"Come with me," she said. "I can help you."

"Thank you. Thank you so much. You're an angel."

He walked down the hall with her, trying to think of something to say. Everything that came into his head sounded stupid, so, in a rare first, he kept his mouth shut. He could ask her to marry him later.

"Here we are," she said, opening a door.

Axel followed her into a big room. Ten young men and women sat around a table covered with envelopes and slips of paper. A laptop open in front of each of them. The men and women alternated between reading slips of papers, typing into the computers, and closing their eyes and briefly praying.

"This is the prayer request room. It's where all volunteers start. Whether God told them to come here or not." She winked. "They get so many prayer requests that the crew has to work around the clock."

"Is that kosher?" Axel said. "Don't people think that Brother Floom or Reverend Whitlock is reading them? That's what I thought."

"Too many," she said. "It's more of a gesture anyway. God hears all prayers regardless. He's God." She waved over an eighteen-year-old with bad acne. "Tobias will show you what to do. Brother Floom thanks you for your service."

"But," Axel said.

"Tobias, this is Fletcher. A new volunteer." And she was gone, leaving Axel standing in a room of teenage and twentysomething Christians who looked happier than sober people should.

He took the only empty chair. Tobias set a stack of envelopes and a laptop in front of him. He smiled, revealing braces. "It's easy. Open the envelope, and separate any cash or checks. Then read the letter, enter the name and address in the form on the screen, and pray for whatever the request is for. If it isn't clear, a general wellness prayer will do."

Axel got to work. Most of the requests were what you would expect. Mother's hip surgery. Struggle with alcoholism. The bank is foreclosing. Fletcher Christian prayed over those letters, doing his level best to take the job seriously. Axel figured that even if he had lost some of his religion, his character was a true believer. God would understand. He wouldn't punish the innocent for Axel's deception.

"I have a question." Axel waved Tobias over. "I put these to the side. I got one here that's requesting I pray for the eradication of all Muslims on the planet. Rather violently. And another one about turning a gay son straight. What do I do with those?"

"Give me the Muslim one," Tobias said. "The gay son you can pray on. God will help."

Axel didn't argue, but if God wanted to do something about the gay kid, he could figure it out on his own.

CHAPTER 16

Kurt watched Louder walk in a circle around his sparsely furnished room. He lay on his air mattress lazily strumming his guitar.

"So the way I see it," Louder said, "I can either find a place in Warm Springs—Pepe offered me the other half of the garage he sleeps in, which was sweet but horrifying—or I can go to a community college that'll take me and focus on the ethnomusicology degree I've been talking about since junior year."

"You should totally do that," Kurt said. "You're the smartest person I know."

"Are you going to stay here?" Louder asked. "Not here here, but in San Diego?"

"I don't know," Kurt said, setting down the guitar. "I got stuff I got to do, but after that I don't know. You and Pepe are all that's left for me in Warm Springs."

"There's Dairy Queens up here. Grossmont College will take anyone. If you ain't coming back, I ain't either. We'd have to work on Pepe so we can continue to Skinrip, yeah?"

"Absolutely," Kurt said.

Louder shoved Kurt to the side. "Move over."

Kurt shifted to the edge of the bed, and Louder lay down next to him. They stared at the ceiling.

"How you doing?" Louder asked. "You know, with all the other stuff. With your mom. With the rest of your family. With everything."

"I can still hear Mom's voice sometimes. Usually scolding me in some way. Telling me what to do. I used to be able to finish Mom's sentences. I miss the old house. This place is big, but weird-shaped. It's like it's built to look at, not live in."

"Yeah," Louder said. "All the houses on this street are freaky. Like the location for a movie that Gwyneth Paltrow would recommend on her website."

"It sounds weird, but I miss sneaking around to play music. It felt dangerous."

"Seems like it's dangerouser now. Learning how to drive a getaway car. You're going to have to show me some of your moves." Louder looked at her watch. "I got to go, K. Let's do band practice this week. Pepe's good for Wednesday or Thursday."

"Cool," Kurt said.

"Cool." Louder rolled off the air mattress and hopped to her feet. She grabbed her backpack and with a smile and a wave left the room. He heard her stomping down the stairs and out the front door.

Kurt wasn't sure how much of a bad boy he was, but he couldn't deny the fact that he was an Ucker. It was God's decision to make him who he was. He wouldn't have been born into this family if it hadn't been his fate.

Since moving to San Diego, Kurt filled his day with distractions. When he was alone and had time to think, he got sad and confused and fearful of the future. Time might heal his wounds, but it didn't mean they didn't hurt when he was still bleeding. Until a scab formed over the wound, movies and comic books and movies would have to do. He hadn't just lost his mother. He'd lost their routine.

"Exercise," Kurt said, standing up and heading out of the room. He had started walking every day, exploring the neighborhood, clearing his head, and trying to come up with a plan for the next thirty years. The idea of a push-up or getting on Axel's exercise equipment held no appeal, but a walk was meditative. He grabbed a sweatshirt, tied it around his waist, and opened the front door.

"Monkey flunker," he said, almost running into the man standing on the front step and poised to knock.

"Hello, Kurt." The man's voice was surprisingly high for his size. A mezzo-soprano in a baritone body. It took a second, but Kurt recognized him.

"I know you," Kurt said. He hadn't gotten a good look at the man in the Lincoln that had followed them, but how many people were completely bald and wore fake eyebrows? One eyebrow was cocked in a way that made the man look like a semicolon-face emoticon.

Confirming Kurt's suspicions, the man flashed a badge in Kurt's face. "Special Agent Harold Cronin. Federal Bureau of Investigation. We need to talk."

"Am I under arrest? What did I do? Am I in trouble? Do you have a warrant? I want a lawyer. I didn't do anything. I have rights." Kurt tried to control the quaver in his voice, but law enforcement had always made him nervous. Maybe it was his Ucker blood.

"Have you done something that would warrant getting arrested?" Cronin asked. "Or any of those other actions? Are you confessing to a crime?"

Kurt felt sweat pour from the back of his head down to the small of his back. He steeled himself as best he could, trying to remember how horribly law enforcement had treated his mother. He would never forgive them, including this jerk. He wouldn't give the G-man an inch. If you can't be brave, pretend to be brave. If that doesn't work, be a smart aleck.

"Yes, I want to confess to a crime," Kurt said. "In my youth, I wasn't kind. I didn't rewind. Is that in your purview, or more of an FCC-jurisdiction kind of thing?"

"Jokes won't make the situation that you're in any less serious."

"That's literally what jokes do," Kurt said. "That's their sole function. Do you not understand jokes?"

"You've recently been seen associating with Mathilda and Frederick Ucker."

"Mathilda?"

"A.k.a. Mother."

"Is it a crime to spend time with my aunt and uncle?"

"Yes, when your aunt and uncle are known to be dangerous psychopaths," Cronin said. "You might not believe me, but I want to help you."

"If I'm not under arrest, frick off. I'm going on my walk." Kurt locked the front door. He took a step down the walk, but the man grabbed his arm.

"You're going to help me," Cronin said, his face close to Kurt's. "Your aunt and uncle have hurt a lot of people. It's time they went down."

"There's nothing you can do that's going to make me help you harass my family."

"I'm not going to harass them. God, no. I'm going to arrest them."

"If you could, you would have already." Kurt pulled his arm away from Cronin and walked to the sidewalk. "If you're not off the property in the next two minutes, I'm going to call the police. Show them my arm bruises. Good day."

"That's too bad," Cronin said. "I wanted to leave your sister out of this."

Kurt stopped and felt his hands become fists.

Cronin took his phone out of his pocket and nodded for Kurt to come over. After a moment he did. Cronin hit play on the screen. Footage appeared of Gretchen breaking into the back door of a property. Cronin turned it off and put his phone back in his pocket.

"I've got video footage of your sister breaking into three different houses. If I wanted to arrest an Ucker, I could do it tomorrow."

"What do you want?" Kurt said.

"I have no interest in arresting Gretchen," Cronin said. "I'm a federal agent, for crying out loud. I don't care about some stupid B and E. She can steal all the comic books she wants."

"She was stealing comic books?"

"I assumed that you knew. Figured you were in on it."

"I don't know what you're talking about."

"I've been after the Uckers for over a decade," Cronin said. "They use people. If they haven't already roped you into some scheme, they will. Don't be fooled. Eventually, you'll end up on the side of the road with nothing and the police bearing down on you. That's how they operate. It doesn't matter that you're blood."

Kurt gave Cronin his best steely glare, although probably more of a pewtery glare.

"Think about it," Cronin said. "Take your time. It's a big decision. I understand loyalty. It's the reason I'm talking to you and not your brother. You're a man of your word."

"Don't play good cop with me."

Cronin pulled out a business card from his breast pocket and handed it to Kurt. "All I'm asking for is eyes and ears into their operation. You can trust me. Information when I need it."

"And me, Gretchen, and Axel stay out of jail?"

"Exactly," Cronin said. "I have no interest in the three of you. I want Mother Ucker."

"I lost my father, my mother, my house, my hometown, and most of my possessions. I got no plan of losing anything else, particularly my new family." Kurt tore the business card in half and dropped it on the ground between them.

"However this plays out, you'll still have family," Cronin said. "You'll just see them during visiting hours." He walked away, shouting over his shoulder: "And if I get a hint that you've told Mother or Fritz or your brother and sister about this conversation, everyone is going straight to jail."

"Yeah," Kurt said, "that's what he said. Everyone is going straight to jail."

"You did the right thing coming to me," Mother said.

"He showed up at the house. Threatened Gretchen. Is after you. I don't know what to do, because he has evidence and she could go to jail and I'm out of my league and I made jokes and tried to act tough, but I'm not tough."

Kurt and Mother sat in Pete's Pit, the location for what had become Barbecuesday, their weekly Tuesday barbecue lunch. Just aunt and nephew.

"Let me turn this forty-five down to thirty-three," Mother said. "Slow it down. One thing at a time. Cronin came to see you?"

"Yeah." Kurt took a big breath. "He's got evidence on Gretchen."

"Tell me word for word what he said, as best as you can remember. It's going to be fine. He's been trying to arrest my butt forever. And my butt is huge. You can't miss it, but he has."

Kurt laughed. Butts made him laugh every time. Because they were butts. He laid it out for Mother as best as he could, explaining how Gretchen had roped him into her crimes without telling him.

"Have you talked to Gretchen about this yet?" Mother asked.

"Not yet."

"Don't. Not yet. Not now."

"Why?"

"She needs to focus on Stephanie Holm right now and her role in that scheme. A distraction could get her in trouble, potentially put her in danger."

"That doesn't matter anymore," Kurt said. We have to cancel the Stephanie Holm job. Cronin is onto us. A federal agent is watching us."

"Don't be ridiculous. We're not stopping anything. Leave it to me. I'll handle Cronin, but don't worry the others."

"What do I do if he comes back?"

"Tell him you'll cooperate. We'll feed him bullshit. Keep him on the hook but only leave him with half a worm."

He felt better telling Mother, but still nervous. Even the thought of barbecue didn't remove the stone in the pit of his stomach. He had never faced a problem that barbecue couldn't fix, so he knew things were serious. He was putting his faith in Mother to keep him and his siblings safe. He had to trust her. You either trusted someone, or you didn't. There was no middle ground.

CHAPTER 17

I figured it would be easier to concentrate here," Stephanie said. "We can get room service and discuss our dream trajectories. How versed are you in the seminar jargon?"

"Not very," Gretchen said, accepting the flute of champagne Stephanie handed her. She took a sip. She didn't know the difference between good champagne and bad champagne, but Stephanie didn't look like someone who bought a three-dollar bottle of white wine and cut it with club soda. It didn't burn Gretchen's throat or make her want to puke, so good enough.

Gretchen had walked into the nicest hotel room she had ever been inside. And she had once been comped at the Imperial Palace in Vegas by a pit boss who was trying to get into her pants. He had even thrown in two front row tickets to *Legends in Concert*, employing easily one of the top three Dusty Springfield impersonators in Sin City. She knew what a classy hotel room looked like.

"Not too shabby," Gretchen said. "I'm more of a Super 8 girl. Although sometimes I splurge, pay the extra twenty, and Best Western it."

"Maybe that's a goal we can discuss," Stephanie said, walking to the window to admire the view of downtown San Diego and the bay. "How others perceive us comes directly from how we treat ourselves. I'm sure you see me as one person and I see myself as someone else. Some of it is perception, but we're usually pretending to be someone that we aren't."

The tack of the conversation made Gretchen nervous. She changed the subject. "I never asked you where you're from. Did you fly in for the symposium?"

"I'm local. I live in La Jolla. When I do a symposium, I like to stay close. The conference hotel is a great base of operations. I can focus on myself, on the work. I don't want to drive through traffic after I've done elemental process work or energy embodiment all day. I can come up here. Meditate. Knock out twenty minutes of yoga. When all else fails, crack open a bottle of champagne, sit in the Jacuzzi, and relax."

"There's a Jacuzzi?"

"On the veranda. It holds four people," Stephanie said. "I kicked it on. Just in case."

"We might have to find two other people," Gretchen said.

"Why would we do that," Stephanie said, "when we have it all to ourselves?"

"I don't like to share either," Gretchen said, and gulped the remainder of her champagne. "Although it feels like we're wandering toward late-night Cinemax territory, if we're not careful."

"If we're lucky."

Even though Gretchen knew that Stephanie was a con woman using an assumed name, she found herself losing track of the line between Stephanie and her character. There were too many planes of deception. It felt like Christopher Nolan were directing the weekend.

"This sure beats that office I work in," Gretchen said.

"No kidding," Stephanie said. "Do your coworkers have a sheepdog? There was a lot of hair on the ground. Nasty."

"I barely notice anymore. They give me so much work to do."

"I see that you brought some with you." Stephanie pointed to the plastic portable file box that Gretchen had set by the front door.

"It's been unusually busy," Gretchen said. "A big project is finally about to be approved, and it'll get fast-tracked. Zero to sixty. That's probably why I'm all over the place. One of the reasons I went to Mark Land. To find some balance."

"It looks like the first priority is to get you relaxed." In one quick motion, Stephanie's dress dropped to the ground, leaving her standing completely nude in front of Gretchen. It happened so fast, Gretchen made a yip sound she had never made before in her life.

"Thanks," Stephanie said.

"Full Cinemax," Gretchen said. "What happens now?"

"Strip down, get in the Jacuzzi, and I'll order sushi."

Gretchen grew up skinny dipping in the canals and had always been ready for a dare. She was a confident woman who wasn't weird around the concept of nudity, but Stephanie threw her off-balance.

Gretchen didn't usually have first-date uneasiness. The fact that it was happening on her first undercover assignment was troubling. She had to get her head back in the game, but naked Stephanie was not making it easy.

Stephanie was at least ten years older than she was but stayed fit. Angular lines, almost severe. Her collarbone looked like it could give you a papercut. Her skin was all one color, not tan-sprayed, still very white, but not blotchy. Stephanie definitely used "product."

Gretchen was the hottest girl at the bus station, but Stephanie was opera-house sexy. The fact that they were both criminals only made the idea more attractive. Criminally, Stephanie was everything that Gretchen aspired to be.

If there was anything more civilized than drinking champagne and eating sushi in a Jacuzzi and looking out at the view of the city and the bay from the twenty-sixth floor, Gretchen couldn't think of it. It fit her redneck view of class. She felt like a feral child who had been brought out of the jungle to learn the ways of humankind. The raccoons that raised her had done their best, but their cuteness and tiny hands could only take her so far.

"Relaxed?" Stephanie asked.

"Very."

"What do you think of the uni?"

"Which one is that?"

"The orange, mushy one."

"To be honest, it's nasty."

"It's an acquired taste, like so many great things."

"What is it?"

"Sea urchin gonads."

"Weird. That sounds like it would be delicious. I'm digging the eel, though."

"What do you want from your life?" Stephanie asked.

"I guess the small talk is done. Big talk on the table."

"That's why we're here. Our dreams, our goals, our future."

"Is that why we're here?" Gretchen said.

"You tell me."

"I've never wanted the things other people wanted. A house, a nine-to-five, kids, a husband—I had one of those, bad idea."

"You have a nine-to-five job."

"Exactly," Gretchen said, catching herself. "But it's not me. Can't stand people telling me what to do. I want to do my own thing. I want to take instead of waiting to be given."

"That, I understand." Stephanie smiled. "More champagne?"

Gretchen held out her glass. Stephanie poured it to the top, spilling some into the water. They both laughed.

"Sometimes I feel broken," Gretchen said. "Together, but broken. Like I have all the pieces, but they're not attached and I'm trying to hold them together to maintain the shape. But once I get one piece in place, another falls off. A balancing act that's in a constant state of collapse. And I'm not even convinced that if I keep it together that it would make me happy."

"What helps you to hold it together?"

"Greed."

"Interesting," Stephanie said.

"Nothing focuses me more than wanting more than I have. Doing what I need to get more. Not accepting limitations others tell me exist."

"No limits," Stephanie said. "What about relationships? Are you seeing anyone right now?"

"I'm single."

"That's good news."

"Why is that?"

"Have I been subtle?" Stephanie said. "I got you naked in a hot tub. We're a camera crew and a funk bass riff shy of a porn shoot. If you can't tell that I'm trying to get in the pants that you aren't wearing, then I have failed miserably."

Gretchen laughed. "So this meeting isn't about optimizing my dream board or channeling my inner goddess."

"Not unless those are euphemisms," Stephanie said. "Because I can definitely see myself wanting to channel your goddess."

"We're going to need more champagne."

CHAPTER 18

Axel needed to get himself out of the Living Word Chapel's version of the mail room. The entry-level position of "Prayer Request Room Facilitator" had all the majesty of a job at the DMV. Open envelope, register money, enter contact information, sort, categorize, pray, repeat.

Axel did his best to believe as much as he could in the moments he prayed, trying to have respect for the devout writing to the ministry. So many of the stories were tragic and heartfelt. He hoped God heard their pleas. It was hard, though, not to feel a little squeamish about someone struggling with their finances sending a big check to the church. They were planting the seed of faith to reap the tree of wealth, or whatever metaphor was being offered at the moment.

Scuttlebutt around Prayer Central was that Brother Floom was planning a tour of small towns in America. With more competition on the airwaves and among the megachurches, ratings and attendance were on the decline. With the noticeable reduction of personal appearances, word was that Brother Floom needed to reestablish his relationship with his base.

That was the opportunity Axel and the gang needed to get Floom. A tour was chaos and pulled everyone out of their routine. If they were going to steal their money back, it would happen on the tour.

He had been getting closer to Virginia. Ever since the day he ran into her on the third level of the underground parking garage—okay, he had followed her down there—and caught her smoking a joint, they had bonded. She didn't ask what brought him down there, just handed him the joint. He took a rip off it, and they had been pot buddies ever since. It was their secret. It felt intimate.

When Virginia walked into the prayer request room, she approached Axel with a goofy smile on her face. "Mr. Christian, I have a few things to discuss with you concerning a joint venture with Mary Jane Hyer at four twenty. Do you have twenty minutes?"

"Tobias?" Axel said to his supervisor.

"I need to borrow Fletcher," Virginia said, the two of them already walking to the door.

Once in the hallway, they both laughed. Axel said, "Subtle. Very nuanced."

"Most of those kids aren't even allowed to watch TV. The odds they know any drug slang are very low."

"Hey, I've been hearing rumors," Axel said. "Is it true there's going to be some big tour coming up?"

"Yeah, it's going to be announced soon," Virginia said, her voice flat, almost angry.

Axel had prepared his pitch. "I know it's outside my current role as prayer lackey, but in my former life, I was a creativity liaison and live-performance-optimization specialist."

"You used a lot of words but said nothing."

"That's what my business cards said." Axel laughed. "In English, I was a concert promoter and talent scout."

"Yeah, I wouldn't tell people that either," Virginia said. "Not exactly professions that elicit trust. You don't hear the phrase, 'a concert promoter for God' often."

"That's why I'm here," Axel said. "Redemption. I saw myself for who I was. And myself was a scumbag. Pardon my language."

"Is 'scumbag' a swear word?"

"Everything is a swear word in church."

"You're talking to the wrong girl. Ezekiel 23:20 used to make me giggle as a kid. Still does."

"'Whose flesh is as flesh of the asses,'" Axel said. "Yeah, I pretty much know all the times 'ass' is used in the Bible, as well."

Virginia laughed loud. Making her laugh gave Axel warm cockles. He could die happy. His cockles had been cold for some time. When she stopped laughing, she said, "You want to help on the tour?"

"I thought maybe my experience could be better used. Playing to my strengths. Maybe even why I was sent here."

"You want out of the prayer dungeon."

"Desperately."

"You'd have to convince Thrace or one of his orcs—I mean, assistants. He's a tough nut to crack."

"Oh, okay. Do I just—how do I?"

"Follow me," she said.

He started to protest but, distracted by her loveliness and her perfume, followed her. She smelled great. He wasn't even sure if it was perfume. It smelled more soapy than perfumey. Less Gladey and more fresh-cut-grassy. Like she just got out of the shower and rolled in flowers and cinnamon.

"Do you mind me asking?" Axel said. "What's your job here? I see you around, but I haven't quite figured it out. I don't see you working. I looked you up on the website, but you're not on it."

"That's a little creepy," she said. "I don't have a job per se. I do this and that."

"At my old job, we called that being a pilot."

"A pilot?"

"You take a pile of papers and pilot over there."

Virginia laughed. Seriously, when you find a woman that gets your jokes—especially the bad ones—you keep her close. That's gold right there. Her laugh was the only evidence he needed to know in his heart that they were meant to be together.

"I've been with the church my whole life," she said. "Never had an official title. Except Brother Tobin Floom's daughter."

Axel tripped over his own foot and face-planted on the ground. He bit his tongue and tasted blood. He had to stop doing that. Or invest in a mouth guard.

"Are you okay?" Virginia said, reaching to help him up. "Oh God. You're bleeding."

"I'm okay." Axel lifted the bottom of his shirt and dabbed at the blood. "Tripped. Bit my tongue. Not too bad."

"Don't use your shirt." She reached into her handbag and handed him a paper tissue.

Axel looked down at the blood on his shirt and tucked it in. "You're Brother Floom's daughter?"

"Yep, that's me," Virginia said. "The preacher's daughter."

"Like a stepdaughter or adopted or maybe one of those things where—"

"Here we are," she said, ignoring Axel. They had stopped in front of a double door. "I would stop thinking about me and think about what you're going to say."

"Say to whom?"

Virginia threw open both doors and walked into a large conference room. Axel followed slowly. Inside, a dozen men sat around a long table, blue folders in front of them. It had all the telltale signs of a meeting. That didn't stop Virginia from interrupting. Axel froze, all eyes on the two of them. Including Brother Tobin Floom himself, who sat at the head of the table.

"Hey, Daddy. Everyone," Virginia said. "This is Fletcher Christian. I think he would be a big help in coordinating the tour. And he's willing to work for free. Come on in and introduce yourself, Fletcher. Give them a good look at you."

"Is that blood on your shirt?" one of the men asked.

Thrace McCormick's stare burned a hole in Axel's forehead. He wasn't a cuddly man to begin with, but he looked genuinely pissed off. For someone who worked in a religious setting, he seemed strangely capable of violence.

"Hello," Axel said.

"Go on," Virginia said. "Tell them about your creative liaisoning. It's impressive stuff."

If he wasn't so nervous, he would have found it funny. He was being encouraged by his aunt to pitch ideas to his grandfather, the man who stole from his mother and might have been responsible for his father's death, events that would lead to him—Axel—facilitating a con with his partners, who were his aunt, uncle, brother, and sister. Axel really kept it all in the family.

If anything, it was appropriately biblical in its incestuous complexity. Everyone was related. Everyone was lying to each other. And everyone was going to eventually get smited . . . smoten . . . smittered. Hurt.

"What did you say?" Mother asked. "What happened?"

Axel, Mother, and Fritzy walked through a giant warehouse full of costumes, using flashlights for illumination. According to Fritzy, the building was storage for one of the big movie studios in LA. He just happened to know the security code, because of "this thing I did this one time."

"Are you sure this is safe?" Axel asked. "I can't afford to get caught now."

"No one can afford to get caught ever. We wouldn't have brought you if we thought there'd be any trouble."

"We're not in the right section," Fritzy said. "All these clothes look like they were used in some lace-and-doily chick flick called *The Amorous Adventures of Darcy Cumberbutt*." He walked ahead, his flashlight scanning the racks and racks of costumes and props.

"What happened with Dolphus?" Mother asked. "How did you react when you saw him? How did he react? What did you say?"

"At first, I stared like an idiot," Axel said. "Seeing the man himself in person at that moment. I wanted to confront him right then and there."

"You didn't, though," Mother said. "Tell me you didn't."

"Of course not," Axel said. "I'd much rather steal his money than hit him with harsh words. It was Grandpa himself that snapped me out of my stupor. He motioned me in with one hand and said, 'Have we met before? You remind me of someone.'"

"He probably saw your father in your face," Mother said. "You are the spitting image."

"Once I lifted my jaw off the floor, I gave my pitch, a bunch of management doublespeak about productivity, morale, metrics, optics, and other words I only have a minimal grasp on. The kind of thing some marketing hack would think was genius. 'MBA' doesn't stand for 'major bullshit artist' for nothing."

"Did it work? Are you in?"

"They didn't say no," Axel said. "The problem is Thrace McCormick. He didn't hear a word. He looked at me like I ran over a litter of kittens, then backed over them because I missed the runt. He sees me as ambitious, the young buck with new ideas trying to eventually angle for his job. I don't think it helped that I was there because of Floom's daughter. The two of them do not like each other."

"The daughter is a good ally to have."

Fritzy approached. "I found the section. Up ahead. It's marked *God's Little Acre*."

"Why didn't you tell me that Virginia was his daughter?" Axel asked. "Your half sister."

"I didn't put two and two together," Mother said. "Stupid of me."

"You're going to want to get close to that girl," Fritzy said, waggling his eyebrows. "Real close."

"To my aunt?"

"I didn't say bang her, kid. Get close."

"The eyebrow thing implied banging," Axel said. "When I was all done, Dolphus nodded and said, 'Satisfactory. Very satisfactory.' That's it. Like he answered a question no one asked."

"You're in," Fritzy said. "If the old man likes you, that's gold. It's his show."

"Don't put the champagne on ice yet. Thrace informed the room that while 'this ambitious volunteer' had some good ideas, he had to assess the personnel needs for the tour and couldn't guarantee any volunteer positions at that time."

"Which means that you're going to have to kneecap someone if they take your spot," Mother said. "In a manner of speaking."

"If you need me to plant some coke in someone's locker," Fritzy said, "I can score some yeyo. I know a guy."

"I have a plan," Axel said. "One that does not require yeyo."

"No offense, but I'm not so sure about your plans," Mother said. "Good ideas, but the execution? I took a look at some of the notebooks you gave me."

"You know how many hours I put into each one of those plans?"

"Great research, but no hands-on feel for the moment. It's like stage dialogue that's never been read aloud. Good on the page, but it won't play on the stage."

"Which plans?" Axel said. "Which ones, for example? Specifically. You're wrong. They're great."

"The nail salon jobs," Mother said. "A huge flaw in that one."

"You don't know what you're talking about," Axel said.

"She does," Fritzy said.

Axel gave him a look. "The nail salons is a solid plan. What's wrong with it? A cash business. Low security."

"You don't want to touch a nail salon in Southern California," Fritzy said. "Not unless you want to get killed. And not in a good way."

Mother pulled some clothes from the nearest rack. "Nail salons in Southern California are all money-laundering fronts. The last thing you want to do is steal from the—what nationality was the nail salon? Russian? Korean? Ukrainian?"

"Korean," Axel said.

"The last thing you want to do is steal from the Jopok. They don't play. No guns in Korea, so you're going to be looking at axes and swords or a piece of wood with broken glass embedded in it. Koreans can turn anything into a weapon. Nobody wants to get stabbed by a sharpened carrot. The marijuana dispensary—that was a stronger plan. Man-bun vegan yoga hippies. It matters who you rob, not just how."

"I didn't know that," Axel said. "Maybe I have some things to learn about nail salons, but I planned this Priscilla thing to perfection. I found the land. Gretchen will reel her in. It's going to play out just how I said it would. You wait."

"You're the boss," Mother said. "We're just here to play the parts as written. Now pick out my costume."

CHAPTER 19

"You can't be serious," Gretchen said. She stared at Mother, who walked out of the back looking like an inflated adult Strawberry Shortcake. "I didn't say anything when you came out here in the gingham dress, but the pigtails are too much. You're just shy of penciling freckles on your cheeks."

"I'm following Axel's plan," Mother said. "The only way for him to see that his plans are ludicrously overcomplicated is to see them play out. He's too overconfident for his lack of experience."

"Do you want to rent a potbelly pig and just kind of hold it for the whole meet? It would be adorable."

"I don't know what growing up in that town did to you kids, but he has this belief about how city folk see country folk. The more country, the more gullible."

"Axel is only happy when he's the underdog," Gretchen said. "If he's not, he'll make himself one."

"His score. His plan. Come what may."

Gretchen kind of hoped it would blow up. Stephanie would eventually figure out that Gretchen was a part of it either way, but maybe if she didn't lose any money on the scam, it wouldn't be a deal breaker.

Money aside, the last thing Gretchen wanted was for Mother to embarrass her. She had too much respect for Stephanie as a thief. She could get over losing her, but she hated the idea of looking like an amateur. Gretchen wanted to impress Stephanie before the woman hated her.

"What's the harm in toning it down?" Gretchen asked.

"Axel's notes say 'country bumpkins.' The word 'bumpkin' is underlined. He drew pictures. Picked out this dress himself. It's the right idea. You got to be the character that they want you to be. Not what they expect. That's the commodity we trade in, what the world runs on. Once you know what someone wants, you can control them."

"And Axel thinks Stephanie wants bumpkins?"

"She wants an easy mark."

"Axel might have dated her, but he doesn't know her. Easy holds no interest. She wants a challenge."

"You've known her for a couple of weeks."

"That's all I needed," Gretchen said. "You going to walk in carrying a jug of moonshine with three big *x*'s on the side, too?"

"No, but I can get one for Fritzy." Mother laughed. "Everyone likes soft targets. She's a lioness looking for the gimpy gazelle. We're going to be them folks the local news interviews after the tornado trashes the trailer park."

"You think Axel was a soft target?"

"That boy's got more issues than a magazine stand," Mother said. "He trusted her quick, hitched his wagon to a shark. My guess is that this isn't the first time he got worked by some broad."

"His heart gets broken every couple of years," Gretchen said. "He believes in love at first sight."

"Yeesh. A romantic. The softest target of all." Mother put on lipstick in the mirror. "This woman has probably never met a farmer but sure as shooting has a picture of a farmer in her head. I'm going to walk into the meet straight from her imagination. Grab Fritzy's 'Make America Great Again' cap, and let's make some money."

Gretchen's role in the scheme was officially over. Her character existed to put the fabricated documents concerning the new freeway expansion in front of Stephanie's eyes. Mission accomplished. Everything that followed was handled by Mother.

The meet that night was to sign the seven-day escrow and deliver the upfront cash. Nothing too fancy. A meal, a signature, money. Put a lie in someone's head, play to a person's greed or emotions, and let them give you their money willingly. Stephanie wouldn't know that the expansion was a scam until at least a few years later, when she would notice that no expansion ever happened.

With a large black coffee on the table in front of her, Gretchen sat at the Starbucks across the street and prepared to watch the show on her phone. Mother's broach gave a clear view of the Garlic Garden. Fritzy sat to her right, looking like he was at a casting call for a *Green Acres* reboot.

Gretchen put in her earbuds. The loud hum of the restaurant filled her head and forced her to lower the volume. The Garlic Garden had that vibe of a place that country folk would consider fancy. A bottom-less-bread-basket kind of place. Mother was not even close to the largest person there.

Stephanie walked to the table and sat across from Mother and Fritzy—or, as they were unfortunately calling themselves in this scenario, Adelaide and Jedidiah Chickensworth.

"You're a godsend, sweetie dear. An absolute godsend," Mother said in an accent that sounded like a southerner making fun of a non-southerner attempting to do a southern accent. The Irene Ryan School of Hillbilly Vernacular.

"We're right gratitudinal for your hospitableness, young missy," Fritzy said through the toothpick in the corner of his mouth, making Mother's accent plausible in comparison.

Stephanie didn't blink, but Gretchen was pretty sure she was trying to keep a straight face. "A pleasure to meet you both in person. I appreciate you taking time out of what must be a busy schedule. I assure you this is an opportunity where everyone benefits. What we call a win-win situation in the business."

"Win-win situation. Ain't that clever." Mother pronounced the word *situation* like she'd never heard it before. Like it was four words: *sit, Jew, way, shun.* "You hear that, Jedidiah? I told you she was a smart cookie. We wasn't busy, sugar. Unless you count Jed scratching his balls."

"I told you that was a duckweed rash."

Stephanie believed that a highway expansion was about to get approval to go through the Chickensworth ranch, at which time it would shift from agricultural to commercial property. The current assessed value of the land was listed as $3,000 an acre, but that had been recorded when the land was arable. The real value of the land was zero dollars an acre, give or take a dollar. Adjacent to the former site of a crop duster's airstrip, it had recently been designated unusable due to the amount of pesticide residue in the soil and groundwater. That information had yet to be reflected in the assessed value of the land. Unless you were planning on starting a DDT farm (which wasn't a thing), it was worthless. Stephanie had offered $5,000 an acre for the sixty acres. Of that $300,000, a third would be in cash.

"We done been growing beans on that there land for nigh on four decades, don't ya know," Mother said.

Gretchen face-palmed, wondering how Wisconsin made its way into her southern accent.

"It's always been my dream to own a bean farm," Stephanie said.

"Has it now?" It sounded like it was Mother's turn to try not to laugh.

"My grandfather was a bean farmer."

"It's good, honest work," Fritzy said. "It most surely is."

"Truly so, but it's high time we retired. These old bones are creaking more than a staircase in a haunted house. Jedidiah's knees are shot."

"I got the arthritis, I do. Ache like the dickens when it rains. And even when it don't. On top of my nut rash, it's hellish."

Stephanie turned toward the front door and then back. "I was going to ask, Do you find the process of deficit irrigation affects the efficiency of the fertilizer on the bean propagation?"

"Oh shit," Gretchen said out loud.

Mother didn't miss a beat. "We done did it the way we always done. The furrow irrigation we use allows us to control some of the saturation. Luckily the loam is rich, so we don't rely as heavily on fertilizer. Ain't that right, Jedidiah?"

"Prefer horse to cow, manure-wise," Fritzy said. "All shit ain't the same. Don't cotton to bullshit."

"That's a beautiful broach," Stephanie said, staring directly into the camera.

Gretchen held her breath. Stephanie stared right at her, like she could see her through the phone. Stephanie winked. "Shit, shit, shit."

The guy at the table next to Gretchen gave her a wave. She ignored him. He waved again, smiling. She popped out the earbuds. "Yeah? What?"

"What're you watching? From your reaction, I'm guessing *Game of Thrones*."

"Are you kidding?" Gretchen said. "I'm busy."

She moved to put the earbuds back in, but the guy scooted closer on the cushioned bench. "I'm Tom."

"Seriously?" Gretchen said.

"I'm a writer. I'm writing a novel about a novelist and his complicated relationships with the female sex, but it's really about the role of the modern man in a postfeminist society. At the same time, it's a humorous take on modern dating. There's also time travel."

"You don't understand hints or social cues, do you?" Gretchen asked.

"I was nominated for a Pushcart Prize."

"Listen, you cartoon character, I would usually enjoy messing with a guy like you, but I am in the middle of something important. If I change my mind—I won't—I assume you'll be here tapping on your laptop and harassing whatever woman is sitting next to you."

"Why all defensive? I'm a nice guy."

"The saddest thing is you believe that."

Tom began to say something.

"If you're about to tell me that I would be a lot more attractive if I smiled or something equally stupid, consider this a warning not to." Gretchen put the earbuds back in her ears. Tom stared at her for a moment and slid back to continue his musings.

Looking back at her phone, Gretchen realized she had missed something big happening. A short, bald man was now sitting at the table. She recognized him from the Mark Land Symposium but didn't know his name.

"I know it's not what we agreed to, but due to the cash arrangement and time frame, I had to bring someone else in. I hope that doesn't change anything. The money is the same. You will just be doing business with Morris, not me."

Mother's voice went flat. "I thought you were going to grow beans. That was your dream. I'd hate to see the land being used for some other purpose. You dance with the one you brought, sweetie."

"I brought Morris," Stephanie said. "Morris plans on growing beans. Isn't that right?"

"Fava, garbanzo, pinto, black. We're going to do it all." Morris smiled. He rested a hand on Stephanie's thigh.

Gretchen felt immediately jealous.

"You said you needed the money quickly," Stephanie said. "This is the only way I could accomplish that. If you want to back out, I understand."

Gretchen had no idea what she had told Morris, but could see him envisioning himself and Stephanie settling down on the bean farm together. Poor Morris was getting piggybacked onto their con.

Stephanie had smelled something hinky. And it wasn't Mother and Fritzy's getup. She had known for long enough to bring in Morris. It must have been Gretchen who had given it away.

"Money is money," Mother finally said.

Morris slid the all-you-can-eat breadstick basket to the side, placed a briefcase on the table, and opened it facing Mother and Uncle Fritzy. It held five $10,000 bundles of hundos.

"This is fifty thousand," Mother said. "We said one hundred."

"We couldn't swing that," Stephanie said. "I shifted the money into the contract. When escrow closes, you'll still get the same amount."

"That wasn't what we agreed on," Mother said.

"It's the only one we can do."

A long silence followed.

"Okay," Mother finally said, "but dinner is on you."

Stephanie nodded and laughed, staring directly at the camera.

"I'm going to need my briefcase back," Morris said. "It's monogrammed."

"Were we supposed to bring a bag or something?" Fritzy asked.

Mother took out the money and put it into her purse. Morris took the briefcase back.

"What are your plans for retirement?" Stephanie asked. "You and Jedidiah?"

"Get a little place outside of Branson," Mother said. "You a Kenny Rogers fan?"

"Who isn't?" Stephanie said. "I know when to hold 'em, and I know when to fold 'em."

"I bet you do, honey," Mother said, her accent dropping away completely.

"She knew." Mother fumed, taking her hair out of the pigtails as she stomped around the German restaurant. Her footsteps shook the floorboards and echoed through the large hall. "The bitch knew. Did you get sweet on her and talk out of school?"

"Go to hell, Mother Ucker," Gretchen said. "I did my part. I didn't say shit."

Mother stared her down. "I believe you. We probably rushed it."

"Why didn't she walk away?" Gretchen said. "Why go to the meeting? Why go through with the deal with someone else?"

"Put it on layaway. Hedge her bets. Morris owns the land now—or at least thinks he does—and I'm sure she figures she can get it from him when she wants. No risk, same reward. Maybe got a finder's fee. She didn't fold. She checked."

"We got the money."

"Half the money. And it wasn't hers. We lost. Tied, at best."

"Axel doesn't need to know, right?" Gretchen said. "Let's give him the win, let him believe he got his revenge. She gutted him."

"You mean lie to your brother?" Mother said.

"I've been doing it for years. It's super easy. This time, it would be a nice gesture. A kind of your-ass-doesn't-look-fat-in-those-jeans lie."

"Fritzy?" Mother shouted across the room.

"Girl's got a point," Fritzy said. "Don't matter much. Doesn't sound like it was on him that it all went tits up. Give the boy a victory lap."

"The confidence boost might help him going into the Floom thing," Gretchen said.

"He ain't ever going to learn if he thinks a bad plan worked," Mother said.

"It was my fault," Gretchen said. "I must have blown it somehow. Stephanie's a pro. I was out of my league."

"She's an amateur compared to Dolphus," Mother said. "We'll have to make sure Axel's next plan works better. Give it more oversight."

Back at her apartment, Gretchen watched *Dawn of the Dead* to get her mind off Stephanie. She drank a beer and ate some microwave pork rinds, liberally pouring sriracha on them. When her phone beeped, she paused the movie but didn't look right away. She knew who it was.

Stephanie texted her an address. Somewhere downtown.

When she walked into the dive bar, she saw Stephanie in a pool of light at a back booth. The sound of the pool table and some David Allan Coe on the jukebox told her it was her kind of place.

She sat down across from Stephanie, but kept her eyes down.

"What were your plans after you ripped me off?" Stephanie asked.

"I don't know what you're talking about."

"Can we not do that?" Stephanie said. "I thought I was the only one that trawled self-help seminars. Tell me if I'm right. I figure you spotted that guy chasing me and saw the chance to play hero. That was a great in. Quick thinking."

Gretchen hadn't thought about it, but there was no reason for Stephanie to associate her with Axel, which was good. That would only complicate things.

"You don't seem mad," Gretchen said. "Why aren't you mad? Or hitting me? Or calling the cops?"

"I am not a fan of the police. We're in the same business. I'm a con woman, too."

Act surprised. Act surprised. Act surprised. "What? Really? You?"

"You have to work on your acting."

"When did you know?" Gretchen asked.

"If something seems too good to be true, it is. You didn't make me work enough. You reeled me in too quickly. The fishing line broke. Impatience hurt you. This is the kind of thing you have to stretch out over a month or two, not a weekend. You practically forced those fake documents on me—which would have fooled me, by the way. Good work there. Also, you over-linted the office. I don't mean to be critical. I feel like I'm giving you notes on your performance. A lot of good ideas, but it had the feel of—not quite an amateur, but someone who has planned a lot on paper but hasn't seen their work on its feet."

"That pretty much nails it."

"If we're going to do this thing, we're going to have to agree on one thing. We can't lie to each other anymore."

"Do what thing?"

"If we're going to become partners, of course."

"I tried to steal money from you. Why would you want to work with me? Or do you mean partners like—I'm confused."

"You tried to steal money from me," Stephanie said. "That's sexy as hell. It's business. You were doing your job. Doesn't mean that we can't get to know each other better."

"What's in it for you?"

"I think you know," Stephanie said. "And I think you feel the same way."

"We've only lied to each other."

"With words, yes. Words are always lies."

"How do I know this isn't another scam? Revenge for what I did?"

"Oh, you can't," Stephanie said, smiling. "People can't trust other people, because people suck. But that doesn't mean this isn't real and we can't try it."

"I hope you don't take offense, but I have to ask you something."

"Shoot."

"Are you insane? I mean like for real."

"Nuttier than a porta potty at a peanut festival."

"At least we have that in common," Gretchen said. She leaned over the table and kissed Stephanie.

CHAPTER 20

Kurt and Louder walked to the open mic at Mugs and Quiches in the Kensington area of San Diego. Due to an unfortunate situation involving the police and six grams of hash, Pepe was on sabbatical.

It had taken Kurt some time to get the itch to play music. When it hit, he didn't want to waste it. Open mics acted as the perfect low pressure environments to play in front of a crowd. No stakes, the audience made up almost exclusively of other performers waiting for their turn to play.

"Hey, everyone. My name's Kurt. This is Louder. Tonight we're Kinrip or Two-Thirds of Skinripper. This is a new one. I hope you like it. Ready, L?"

Louder ran a drumstick down the front of her washboard and nodded. She had constructed a percussion instrument on a pole, with a washboard in the center, a symbol on top, and various pieces of scrap metal below, including some tuning forks, a cowbell, and some triangles.

Kurt followed on the guitar.

Grab all my old comic books, throw them into a box.
Stuff my coin collection in a pair of black socks.

I got a tarnished trombone that's screaming out,
   "Hock me."
Need a coach-class ticket, got to get to Milwaukee.

I can taste the peanuts on the flight over there.
Got a six-hour stopover, I'm stuck in O'Hare.
I can already see us stretched out on the floor.
In front of the TV, watching Death Wish 4.

Got to get to Wisconsin.
Watch some Charles Bronson.
Want to be in Wisconsin.
Checkin' out the Bronson.
With you. With you.

All those classic movies, you'd think he'd won an Oscar.
Don't matter none to me, 'cause the Chuck-man
   rocks her.
Seen 'em all a million times, don't bother me in the least,
When I'm up against the beauty and I'm watching
   the beast.

Louder launched into a badass washboard solo. What she lacked in precision, she made up for in volume and enthusiasm as she moved around the stage and banged her head in time. In a flurry of noise, the song ended. Louder whooped and threw her drumstick into the crowd. It knocked over someone's coffee, bounced in the air, and hit a guy in the face.

"Sorry," Louder said.

The crowd clapped politely, which was better than booing. Kurt would take it. There was a good chance that nobody in the young audience knew who Charles Bronson was. Maybe one of them would google the name and Kurt would have done his community service for the week.

A loud whistle cut through the soft applause, followed by a booming voice. "What? Are you people deaf? Clap or I'll come over there and show you how. Can't stand people that clap their hands but don't make noise. You aren't mimes. It's offensive."

The crowd clapped more enthusiastically. A few people laughed. A dreadlocked waif with a guitar walked onstage as Kurt and Louder left. She said, "I wish my mom was that supportive. She hates my life choices."

Kurt and Louder walked to the back of the room and sat down at Mother's table.

"You haven't met Louder," Kurt said. "Louder, this is Mother."

"Louder is a strange name for a girl," Mother said.

"Your name is Mother Ucker," Louder said. "If a guy named Hogwash Puddledick walked in, he'd have the second dumbest name in the room."

"I like her," Mother said.

"I haven't made a decision about you yet," Louder said.

Kurt looked back and forth between their staring contest. "How did you know I was here? I didn't tell anyone about it."

"I have my ways." Mother winked. "I wanted to see you play again."

"This is just a goof to stay in practice. The songs I'm writing now are all mundane stuff. The other day I wrote a song called 'I Accidentally Poured Guava Juice on my Cinnamon Life but Ate It Anyway, and You Know What? It Wasn't That Bad.'"

"Not all songs have to open a vein," Louder said. "I like that song. It's about taking what's given to you and making the best of it. Even if you don't think something will work out, doesn't mean it won't."

"It's my truth," Kurt said.

The woman on stage started her set. She strummed on her guitar, her voice just above a whisper.

We heal. We live. We are reborn.
Passion is a constant. Nothing is impossible.
Only a seeker of the dreamtime may create this
source of faith.
We exist as superpositions of possibilities.
Power is the driver of curiosity. Nothing is impossible.
The stratosphere is buzzing with supercharged
waveforms.
Wanderer, look within and heal yourself.

"Can we talk?" Mother asked Kurt as she shot a look in Louder's direction.

"You know what?" Louder said. "I'm going to take off. It's a long drive back to Warm Springs."

"You sure?" Kurt asked.

"She didn't come here to see you play," Louder said. "That's cool. I'll see you later, K. If she asks for money, don't give it to her." She stood up, gave Kurt a punch on the arm, and walked toward the door.

"Aren't you going to walk your girlfriend to her car?"

"She's not my girlfriend. Besides, she can take care of herself. Desert rats bite."

"She's got the hots for you. Trust me. I can read people. And she's a billboard. Let's get out of here."

Harry Cronin sat alone at the end of the bar. He drank what looked like a blue Hawaiian with an umbrella and pineapple garnish, a bold choice for the surroundings. Not a tiki bar or themed in any way, the dive looked like the location for a Hank 3 video. Filthy and rough.

Kurt stopped at the door as soon as he saw Cronin. "What's he doing here? Is this a bust? Is he busting us?"

"Why would I take you here if I thought you'd be in trouble?" Mother asked. "Trust me."

Kurt and Mother walked to Cronin. He lifted his drink. "First one's on me. What can I get you?"

"What do you want?" Kurt asked, still bristling.

"Take it easy, kid," Cronin said. "I know we started off bad."

Mother sat next to Cronin and motioned for Kurt to take a seat. "We worked out a deal—Agent Cronin and me."

Kurt looked around the bar. There didn't appear to be anyone else in the place. Not even a bartender.

"You are mortal enemies," Kurt said. "He wants to arrest you. He told me himself. He wanted me to rat everyone out."

"I should be angry at you, kid," Cronin said. "I told you not to talk to anyone, and what do you do? Immediately tell this one."

"You should know by now that Uckers are loyal to each other," Mother said.

"Your aunt is not the only crook on my shit list, son," Cronin said. "As much as I would like to bust her, she offered me a bigger fish. One that I couldn't resist. Dolphus Ucker has been hiding in plain sight, but nobody's been able to touch him."

"You see," Mother said, "Agent Cronin doesn't care if we thieve a thief. So long as we can hand Dolphus over to him."

"After that," Cronin said, "we can go right back to the cat-and-mouse game we've been playing for decades."

"I wouldn't have it any other way," Mother said. "A ceasefire."

"I don't have anything to do with our grandfather," Kurt said. "I don't see how I could help."

"Not yet, but we'll find a way in for you," Mother said. "You're the only one we can trust. Your brother and sister can't know."

"I'm sensing all sorts of bullspit here. Why shouldn't they be in on it?"

"Blame Mother," Cronin said. "I've been double-crossed by her before. If it weren't Dolphus that I was after, I'd bust all of you right now. I've got your sister for the break-ins. Your brother for the land scam. That's right. I know about that, too. If there are too many Uckers in on the Floom thing, you'll find a way to turn it on me. You and Mother, that's it. Nobody else knows. If I get any indication that they know, I haul all of you in."

"Even Fritzy doesn't know," Mother said. "He thinks I'm at spin class."

Cronin laughed at that. Mother shot him a look. He went serious again.

"I want something in writing," Kurt said. "Something that clears me and Axel and Gretchen."

Cronin reached into his jacket pocket and pulled out a rolled-up document. He flattened it out on the table. The heading read, "Confidential Informant Agreement."

"Mathilda has already signed one. This includes all the language that gives you and your siblings immunity from prosecution. So long as I get my evidence. If you steal from Dolphus but give me nothing on him, you'll do time."

"It's the best deal I could make," Mother said.

"What if we just don't do it?" Kurt said. "What if we walk away right now?"

"I wouldn't do that," Cronin said. "You know how when you feel like pizza, but then you don't get pizza. Even if it's tacos, it's not satisfying. In this case, pizza is arrests. I'm arresting someone, one way or the other."

"I can't lie to my brother and sister."

"They lie to you."

"Life isn't an eye for an eye. I make my own moral choices."

"An eye for an eye works for the Bible," Cronin said.

"It's in the Old Testament. Jesus rejects it in the New Testament. Turn the other cheek."

"If you only take Dolphus's money but don't get me some evidence to convict him, you're not turning the other cheek—you're turning a blind eye."

"That's good," Kurt said. "Can I use that as a lyric?"

Kurt and Louder sat on a large boulder, looking down at the Imperial Valley below them. The lights of Mexicali glowed to the south and the much fainter El Centro straight ahead.

"Right now, L," Kurt said. "You're the only one I trust. Everyone's telling me things, but none of the things sound remotely true. It's all angles and cons and bull."

"You can always trust me, K." Louder punched his arm.

"I love you," Kurt said. "You know that, right?"

Louder punched him harder. "You don't have to say stuff like that. It ruins it. I know. I've known it always. You're my best friend, stupid."

"What am I going to do?"

"Right now, nothing. They're all heading off to do the thing with the preacher. They ain't asked you yet."

"They will."

"When they do, I'll be there with you. So will Pepe. If he gets early release."

"My family is going to steal from a televangelist, and an FBI agent knows we're going to do it. It's a recipe for trouble."

"'Recipe for Trouble' sounds like a Skinripper tune," Louder said, slapping a beat on her knees. "Get a bowl made out of rattlesnakes."

"Add two cups of scorpion venom."

"Stir in the blood of a barracuda."

"And a pinch of Levi's denim."

Together they screamed "recipe for trouble" over and over again until they both started laughing.

PART THREE

CHAPTER 21

Axel focused on one of the offering bags. He needed to know the exact path the money took from a parishioner's pocket to the bank for deposit. Like tilling a field, each velvet sack went up one row and down the next. When it finally made it to the end of the aisle, one of the 300 took it. Twelve sacks. Twelve of the 300. At the end of the song, when the men held what looked like cartoon sacks of cash, bulging and round, they joined each other in front of the stage. Standing in formation, they bowed their heads. A quick blessing and prayer. And then they exited backstage.

That was the part of the journey Axel already knew. The part everyone saw. He looked for a flaw he could exploit but found none. He'd have to look elsewhere.

Despite the changing geography of each venue on the tour, the 300 didn't deviate from their protocol. Whether in a fairgrounds in Georgia or a church in Louisiana, the men found the shortest path from the church exit to the Money Bus. (Just like in the movie *Money Train*, but a bus instead of a train.) None of the 300 appeared to be armed, but they didn't look like men who would be threatened easily either. They had the hard glares of war veterans who had stared down the barrel of a gun before.

Axel had tracked all aspects of their protocol and routine but still hadn't found his way in. The biggest blind spot was what happened to the money once it was in the Money Bus. He hadn't seen anything come out of the bus, only go into it. Axel couldn't watch it all the time, so he couldn't get an accurate read on how long the money remained in the bus, when it was picked up to be deposited, and what methods were used to move the cash.

He needed more time to focus on the bus, but his cover job was getting in the way of his real job.

By the second week of Brother Tobin Floom's "God's Country: The Real America" tour, Axel had settled into his new role as "Volunteer Liaison and Coordinator." The problem was that if he wanted to maintain the position, he couldn't half-ass it. He needed to actually do the job.

Brother Floom's tour was similar to a touring rock show. It involved the same personnel from road crew to security to talent. The fleet of buses and trucks seemed constantly in motion. Once one show was over, the next step was all about breaking down and getting to the next town and doing it all over again. There were a few scattered off days, but those were devoted to travel, not R and R.

His big fear was that he would run out of time before he could form a good-enough plan. There had to be a way to steal the cash. He just had to figure out a few small things. Like how to get to the money, how to remove it without being detected, and how to get away without getting caught. Minor details.

The problem was that it was difficult to be creative after a fourteen-hour workday. The four hours of sleep he got every night felt excessive. He would cut it to three. Maybe then he wouldn't spend half the time staring at the ceiling of his bus bunk, listening to the coughing, snoring, and masturbating of the other male staff.

Thrace McCormick made no secret of not liking him. Convinced Axel was there because he had sucked up to Virginia, McCormick looked for any reason to fire him, demote him, or get him to quit. Luckily, it took a lot to get fired from an unpaid position.

What McCormick couldn't have known was that Axel lived for hard work. He hated shortcuts. He threw his whole self at tasks. Which meant that no matter his failures, he could leave knowing there wasn't more he could have done. One hundred and ten percent wasn't a thing, because math, but Axel came as close as any person could.

McCormick could try to wear him down, but he would lose that battle.

The day before, Axel had spent three hours trying to find pink Post-it Notes. McCormick had asked him to do it personally because of the claimed importance of the task. Axel had survived enough bullshit middle management power plays to know the ins and outs of surviving mediocre pettiness.

Pink Post-it Notes should have been a simple task. Not in the rural South. It turned into an epic journey through the maze of backwater Mississippi. Odysseus's journey home by way of James Dickey.

He drove toward Tupelo, but a guy in Nettleton said there was an office supply store in Eggville. There was, but it had closed in 1986. The gas station attendant in Mantachie gave him directions to Guntown, which was a wash. They only had the traditional yellow ones. Axel got the hairy eyeball from the cashier when he specifically asked for pink, but it eventually led him to Amory, where there was a Staples outside town that carried them. It would have been considerably less frustrating if he hadn't started in Amory. He made a mental note to send a scathing letter to Staples regarding their need to update their website.

Working with the volunteers meant he could go virtually anywhere, as volunteers were a part of every level of the operation, from the front of house to backstage to the buses and road crew. Only one area was off-limits. The area he needed to gain access to.

Everyone called it the Pearly Gates. It was the parking lot or hangar or open field where specific buses were parked. Brother Floom's private travel coach, the bus for his personal staff, the band's touring bus, and the Money Bus were separated and cordoned off from the rest of the traveling road show. The buses could only be approached by select personnel. The 300 kept guard, walking the perimeter day and night.

Brother Floom only left his coach to preach. In transit from the bus to the stage, he was unapproachable. The 300 formed a large outer ring to keep everyone at a distance. Only his entourage was within the literal inner circle. All staff and volunteers were specifically instructed not to interact with Brother Floom. Eye contact was discouraged.

When Brother Floom was on stage, Axel found himself staring at his face and trying to see a family resemblance. There might have been a similarity in their eyebrow region, but to Axel they didn't look related. The Floom character was so fully realized that Axel needed to constantly remind himself that this man was his grandfather.

On one of Axel's luxurious ten-minute lunch breaks, he walked through the parking lot of the fairgrounds, eating a peanut-butter-and-honey sandwich and hoping to bump into Virginia. He knew they were related, but that didn't mean they couldn't be friends. That he couldn't get to know his aunt. Half aunt, to be technical.

Who was he kidding? He still had a crush on her. He knew that was messed up, but he wasn't going to do anything. Talking was not a crime. He liked spending time with her. Wasn't that the way it always was? You found the one, but she ended up being the daughter of your current heist victim and related by blood.

As Axel walked the Pearly Gates' perimeter, one of the 300 walked toward him and silently stood in his path.

"How you doing?" Axel said, flashing his lanyard. The 300 didn't appear impressed by his title. "You got everything you need? I coordinate the volunteers and can shoot some your way if you need more personnel. There's juice boxes in the canteen if you're thirsty."

"Mr. McCormick takes care of everything for us," the 300 said.

"Cool, cool, cool," Axel said. "You ever been to Mississippi before? It's beautiful here."

"I spent most of my twenties here. In the Flatlands."

"That sounds nice. Are the Flatlands worth seeing?"

"The Flatlands is what they call the penitentiary in Parchman."

"I did not know that," Axel said, looking for life behind the man's dead eyes.

"Seven years was a long time. Considering the guy lived."

"It does seem excessive," Axel said. "You know, Proverbs says, 'For a just man falleth seven times and riseth up again.' Seven years, seven times. You've obviously riseth."

"If not for Jesus, I'd be dead or other people would be dead."

"Were you saved in prison? Is that where you found the Lord?"

"I found a lot of things. You like questions."

"Sorry. I'm a chatty guy. Interested in the complexity of human existence. I'll leave you alone. Have a blessed day."

"Yeah. God bless you."

Never had "God bless you" sounded more like a threat.

That had been the fourth one of the 300 he had talked to. He had been wrong about ex-military. It seemed that Thrace McCormick—whom they all identified as their boss—preferred ex-cons for his muscle. Loyalty and faith were strongest with those who needed redemption the most. Men who had time to contemplate their fates. Men capable of darkness but willing to use it for light.

Walking back to the volunteer-corral area—little more than a roped-off spot under a big portable canopy—Axel tried to find an angle to get inside the Pearly Gates. In the tent a floor fan moved around the humidity to create a convection-oven environment. He could bake bread in his pants.

He spotted Virginia. She didn't look like she was having a good day. The telltale sign was when she threw her cell phone onto the ground and then kicked it. Axel read the subtlety of her body language. He was perceptive like that.

"Is everything okay?" Axel asked perhaps the stupidest question that had ever been asked.

"I'm fine," Virginia snapped. "I threw my phone on the ground out of happiness."

Axel picked up her phone, which was miraculously in one piece, although with a cracked screen.

"Sorry," Virginia said, taking a breath. "Didn't mean to take it out on you."

"Want to talk about it?"

"Actually, yeah," Virginia said. "I could use a sympathetic ear. I don't have my—uh—chrysanthemums on me, but I have a stash of chrysanthemums in the bus. We can—" Her expression changed for the tenth time in ten seconds.

Axel turned. Thrace McCormick approached with two of the members of the Young Lions, the Christian bubblegum pop band on the tour.

"Later," Virginia said.

"Chrysanthemums," Axel said.

Virginia winked. "The best time is during Dad's sermon. Meet me at T-shirts."

Thrace and the young men reached them. Virginia gave Thrace a bored stare and walked past him, bumping his shoulder.

"Hello, Mr. McCormick," Axel said.

One of the Young Lions stepped forward. "I'm Robby and this is Todd, but you know that."

Axel reached out to shake. Robby put a signed photo of the band in his hand.

"God bless," Robby said, walking past him into the volunteer tent to hand out more photos.

"You busy right now, Fletcher?" McCormick asked. "I don't care. Drop what you're doing. Brother Floom needs five dozen highlighters."

"Right. Let me guess. Pink ones?"

"Don't be ridiculous. They wouldn't show up on the pink Post-its. Green ones. I've already called, and they're all out of them at the Staples here in town."

"Of course they are."

"You might have better luck in Sulligent or Splunge."

"Now you're just making up town names," Axel said as he walked away. Looking back over his shoulder, he watched Robby and Todd standing a little too close to the young female staffers. The Young Lions looked like they were stalking prey. He caught Todd brushing a woman's breast with his elbow and trying to make it look like an accident.

The band had access to the Pearly Gates. They were in the inner circle.

That's when Axel saw the plan in wide-screen and Technicolor. He would have to do some calculations, get some outside information, but in theory he knew how to get to the money. Hallelujah!

CHAPTER 22

The farthest east Gretchen had been was the Grand Canyon and the only foreign country she had set foot inside was Mexico. She had always felt worldly, but sitting in the hotel room outside Durham, she realized how sheltered her life had been. Desert rats never made it far from the desert. She needed to change that.

When this job was done, she would see the world. London, Paris, Barcelona, Cleveland, anywhere new. She could picture her and Stephanie drinking wine under the Eiffel Tower while they watched a mime in a beret eat a baguette. Or maybe Spain. She would have to find out when the running of the bulls happened or that festival where everyone throws tomatoes at each other. Spain seemed like a wacky place.

Gretchen and Stephanie had seen each other almost every day for the last couple of months. The fact that Stephanie could put aside someone's attempt to steal a hundred grand from her definitely suggested a real connection. It would make a better story to tell their grandkids than "I swiped right."

They hadn't reached that stage in their relationship where they brought each other in on their criminal schemes. That was more of a six-month-anniversary kind of deal. Fifth base.

Respect of privacy was an essential component of trust. As much as Gretchen wanted to tell Stephanie everything, she wasn't ready for the awkward moment when she told Stephanie that the guy she had bilked a while back was her brother. Or ready for when Axel found out she was dating the ex-girlfriend who broke his heart and conned him. It would have to happen eventually, but not at that moment. Procrastination solved everything.

With Axel undercover, Gretchen was doing all the advance work. She wished traveling to each of the upcoming tour sites to take pictures and draw up aerial sketches of the area were more exciting. She was a thief, not a location scout. She wanted in on the action. Boredom made her antsy. If things didn't get dangerous soon, she would end up doing something stupid.

She stared at the painting of koi on the motel room wall across from the bed. There was something off about it. The fish had three eyes. Why would the artist do that? Was it an act of subversion? Did the actual fish have three eyes? Did it come from waters near a nuclear power plant? A *Simpsons* reference?

"Losing it," she said as she popped out of bed. She didn't know where she was going to go, but she was going to get out of that room. Maybe go for a run, followed by a drink. She had clearly become a city girl in the last decade, not as secure with the nothingness of nothing to do.

When her phone rang, she dove for it. "Oh, it's you. Hey, Ax. What's up? Don't tell me you need more pictures of the fairgrounds in Hickory, because I ain't driving all the way back out there."

"The pictures were great. I don't need them, but they were great."

"Awesome. It was only a billion degrees with three hundred percent humidity. My clothes felt like they were made of warm slugs. No big deal. Anything else you don't need that you want me to do?"

"I got a plan. It's written and done, and it's awesome. All the pieces."

"Never doubted you, big brother." She had definitely doubted him.

"Stop what you're doing, and head down here to Mississippi."

"I don't know," Gretchen said. "I'm pretty busy."

"Part one, we get the Young Lions, the church band, fired. Part two, we put Kurt and his band in their place."

Gretchen closed her eyes.

"Gretch, you still there?"

"Do all your plans involve costumes and disguises and everyone playing a character? This isn't Halloween."

"The band has access to the restricted area where the money is kept. A key component of my plan."

"Kurt has no experience as a thief."

"Can you sing or play an instrument?"

"I play a wicked tambourine," Gretchen said. "Maracas in a pinch. I shouldn't have to remind you: Kurt and his band play Viking doom metal. Not exactly their demographic."

"He's played weddings. He sang a pretty song at the funeral. He's a musician. How hard can it be?"

"Whatever you say," Gretchen said. "What do you need me to do in Mississippi?"

"Get the Young Lions fired."

"Intriguing."

"It shouldn't be that hard. They're a Christian band. Drinking caffeinated beverages would probably be a scandal."

"I've already got a few ideas," Gretchen said. "Send me the band's schedule."

When Gretchen hung up, she turned to the picture of the crazy three-eyed fish. "I love it when a plan comes together."

Eighteen hours later, Gretchen waited outside the secure area of the Raleigh-Durham airport. A big smile on her face when she spotted Stephanie wheeling her bag. They hugged, crushing each other.

"Be careful," Gretchen said. "This might be illegal in North Carolina."

"Fuck 'em," Stephanie said, giving Gretchen a kiss on the mouth.

A mother covered her daughter's eyes as they walked past.

"We have other ways to convert her!" Stephanie yelled at the fleeing woman.

Gretchen took hold of her bag.

"Thanks for coming so quickly," Gretchen said.

"It's going to sound sappy, and I'm not a sappy person," Stephanie said, "but it was the longest we'd been apart, and it had been getting to me. I wanted to see you."

"You sap," Gretchen said.

"You're the one that had to come up with a ridiculous reason to invite me out. I'm still not one hundred percent sure I heard you right on the phone."

"If it sounded crazy, then you heard right."

"Crazy is my wheelhouse," Stephanie said. "This is the most romantic date anyone has ever asked me on. If I had found out later that you had done this without me, I would have been apoplectic."

"I got no control over the money. Your share is going to have to come out of my end when the score is over."

"Who cares?" Stephanie said. "I should pay you. Gets me out of the self-help rut. It's become too much like a job. I'm going to finish the few things I'm preregistered for and then take a break. No fun in easy pickin's."

"You don't know how sad it makes me to hear that a life of crime can be drudgery."

"Glamour only exists from a distance," Stephanie said. "Up close, everything is work. I know that's true, because I read it on a brochure for a weekend seminar about finding your self-shaman."

Gretchen thought about stealing comics and how it had become routine. No danger. Profitable, but stale. "It's good to shake things up."

"So let's get shaking."

Gretchen threw her bag in the trunk of the rental car. "Have you ever been to Spain?"

"Once. I was there for El Colacho, the baby-jumping festival."

"That's not a real thing."

"Men dress up like devils and jump over babies."

"They get weird in España."

"It's our kind of country."

Gretchen drove down the highway, air-conditioning at maximum. She and Stephanie sang along to the ZZ Top that blasted on the stereo. Gretchen actually felt both bad and nationwide.

"The Young Lions have a gig this weekend," Gretchen said. "Separate from the larger tour. It will be more casual, easier for us to finagle our way backstage, find the band, pop out a tit, and snap some photos."

"Pop out a tit and snap some photos?" Stephanie said, turning off the music. "We're not doing that."

"You don't have to flash them. I'll do it. You can take the picture."

"That's not it," Stephanie said. "I'll get buck naked. But I didn't fly all the way out here to half-ass this thing. If we're going to do something we'll probably only do once—maybe twice—in our lives, let's go bananas."

"I can't see a context where this would happen again."

"You never know," Stephanie said. "We need to put some creativity into this thing. Show some panache. Simple plans are effective but never fun."

"You sound like my—" Gretchen caught herself. "I'm not looking to ruin their careers. We just need to get them to cancel their tour."

"We're not going to release the photos or video or whatever," Stephanie said. "That gives us carte blanche."

"I love when you use French words."

"Oui," Stephanie said. "If you see a skeevy truck stop on the way, pull over. We're going to need a drool ball and a zipper mask."

"And with that statement right there, I'm sure I'm falling in love with you."

Stephanie's smile left her face as she turned to Gretchen. "Joking aside. I'm pretty crazy about you."

Gretchen smiled. "Emphasis on crazy."

"I mean it."

"I already knew that," Gretchen said. "Me, too."

"How did you know?" Stephanie asked.

"You never asked me why I needed to blackmail a Christian pop group. It's the first thing most people would ask."

"I figured you had your reasons," Stephanie said. "And we're definitely going to need a riding crop."

The Young Lions were playing a charity event at the Tylertown American Legion Hall. Not a disease charity or a disaster charity, but one of those vague organizations that sounded good, but did they actually do anything except raise money? Two minutes online told Gretchen that the Christian Advocates for Faith and Family were a Washington, DC–based lobbying group. Nonprofit, but also nonbeneficial, unless you backed their cause. Gretchen did not.

Gretchen and Stephanie chose their best librarian getups. Every boy's perennial fantasy, the pretty-but-she-doesn't-know-it mousy woman with one too many buttons undone on her white blouse, a hint of bra and cleavage. Her horn-rimmed glasses and pinned-up hair did little to hide her desperate horniness. When the last book was checked out, the orgy started. The basis for an entire subgenre of pornographic scenarios.

There was no doorman or velvet rope, just a kid with a cash-box taking ten dollars from each person. Eighty people, give or take, politely waited for the concert to start. Plenty of room to move around. Christian bands usually played for free in churches, so only hardcore fans bought tickets. It shouldn't be hard to get close to the band. The girls who, with that dreamy look in their eyes, clutched pictures of the band to have signed were more likely to want to pray with them.

"I should have brought a flask," Gretchen said.

"When I snuck backstage at the Whitesnake Twenty-Fifth Anniversary Tour," Stephanie said, "I had to get through three levels of security and give a hand job to a roadie. Even then, I only got a glance at the drummer. The drummer."

"If we finish early, we can still check out the strip joint across the street from the hotel."

"It's called the Booby Trap."

"Au contraire. The Booby Trap Colon A Gentleman's Club. So you know it's classy. It's for gentlemen."

The band took the stage. The three members were very young, very white, very fit, and very haircutted. The drum set, guitar, and keyboard on the stage were quickly revealed to be props. Canned music rose from a loudspeaker. The Young Lions' dance choreography was wholesome-ish, a lot of swaying.

> *We're the Young Lions, Robby, Todd, and Kevin.*
> *Spitting the truth to you about the kingdom of heaven.*
> *It ain't about wanting, but doing, believing.*
> *It might look tough, but them looks be deceiving.*
> *We came to rock for God.*
> *We came to roll for Jesus.*
> *Loud enough, he hears us.*
> *Bold enough, he sees us.*

"They set up all that equipment," Gretchen said, "and nobody's going to play it?"

"I can't tell if they're lip-syncing or not," Stephanie said.

"They plugged in the equipment and everything."

"I don't know if I can do this," Stephanie said.

Gretchen turned to Stephanie. "If you're having second thoughts, I can meet you back at the hotel."

Stephanie laughed and leaned in to whisper to Gretchen. "I meant the music. The blackmail, no problem, but I can't listen to another second of this shit."

While the band played, Gretchen and Stephanie walked three blocks to the nearest Piggly Wiggly to buy some beer, only to be informed that they were in a dry county. The cashier had to explain the concept of a dry county to Gretchen three times. She couldn't get her head around grown-up adults not being allowed to buy alcohol. It made no sense to her. They were still in the United States of America.

They walked back to the American Legion parking lot, beerless and disappointed, just as the concert was getting out. A thirty-minute set was apparently all the Young Lions had in them. Stephanie and Gretchen approached the tour bus just as the three sweaty "musicians" jogged inside, high-fiving each other.

"It might take some work to tempt them into sin," Stephanie said, undoing one more button on her blouse. "There's a fifty-fifty chance they're gay."

The glasses they wore didn't just accentuate the librarian look. They would record everything that happened. They turned on the cameras.

Gretchen knocked on the bus door. It opened. Gretchen and Stephanie walked up the steps. It was a nice travel coach, but it was hard to concentrate on its details with the three men standing completely nude inside.

Gretchen tried to figure out how they got their clothes off so fast. Tear-away clothes, maybe?

"Is that all of you?" Robby said.

"Just us," Gretchen said.

"Great job, Todd. You messed it up again."

"It's not my fault," Todd protested. "I said three like ten times. Three. I wasn't going to let what happened in Tallahassee happen again. I only got to watch but still had to pay. Which wasn't fair."

"It's only the two of you?" Robby said. "There ain't another one of you parking the car or something?"

"Nope," Gretchen said. "We're it."

"I'm going to assume Todd screwed up," Robby said. "That doesn't change the fact that we ordered three hookers and we got two. You're old, and neither of you look Asian to me either. This is a problem."

"We can roshambo for sloppies," Todd said.

"Shut up, Todd," Robby said. "Don't make things worse."

"Did you at least bring the molly?" Kevin asked. "If I'm going to have to watch the two of you bone until I can get jiggy, I at least want to be rolling."

Gretchen turned to Stephanie. "I'm sorry. I really thought this would be a challenge."

"Not your fault," Stephanie said. "On paper, it looked like it would be."

"What are you two whores talking about?" Robby said.

"Oh," Stephanie said. "'Whore' is going to cost you."

CHAPTER 23

Kurt hadn't been back to Warm Springs since the move. He hadn't had any plans to come back, but Louder was throwing a party for Pepe's early release from the hoosegow. It would be just the three of them, but that was their kind of party. Skinripper hadn't jammed in a while.

Kurt had expected to get choked up seeing his house again, but he didn't shed a single tear. He also didn't see his house again. The house was gone. It wasn't there. The spot where it used to be had become a giant hole in the ground surrounded by a chain-link fence. He walked to the end of the block and read the street sign. Sure enough, he was on Custer Road in Warm Springs.

Brother Tobin Floom hadn't just taken his family home but had for some inexplicable reason destroyed it, too.

Walking back, he saw Mr. Panowich, their mailman for the last ten years.

"That you, Kurt Ucker?" Mr. Panowich said. "No mail. No mail-box. No house."

"When did this happen?"

"Not soon after your change of address," he said. "Strangest thing. It didn't happen in a day or a week. It got took apart slow. Maybe they were salvaging."

"It was a good house."

"It seemed it. Every day I came by, another piece was gone. You ever read *The Langoliers* by Stephen King?"

"Yeah," Kurt said. "Good reference."

"How's life in Encinitas?"

"How did you—you're the mailman."

"Officially, a postal worker, but I've always preferred 'mailman.' Friendlier."

"You ever feel lost, Mr. Panowich?"

"Naw. The route don't change, and I got GPS."

"Not for real, but in your head? In your life?"

"All the time, son. All the time. Anyone that tells you different is an idiot or a liar."

Kurt's phone rang. Mr. Panowich gave him a hard slap on the back and walked down the road. "Maybe that's someone calling to get you unlost. Good luck and God bless."

Kurt answered his phone. "Hey, Ax, what's up?"

"Finally figured out your part in the plan. It's got to be you."

Kurt stared at the hole that held his childhood and his past. "Ain't nothing here. I'm ready to help."

"I need you and those friends of yours that you play music with. I got you a gig. The three of you need to drive your van to Louisiana. I figure three days if you stop to sleep and drive in shifts. By the time you get here, you need to be a credible Christian rock band ready to perform three or four songs."

"I have reservations, but I don't even know where to start," Kurt said. "From the over-under on the van making it farther than the Arizona border, let alone across the country, to the assumption that my friends can just drop everything and hit the road for the flippant idea that Skinripper can easily transform itself into a Christian band."

"Details," Axel said. "Say you'll do it, and we'll figure it out."

"The bar is low musically. I've heard enough Christian music to know what it sounds like. If I shoot for parody, I might come close."

"See. Piece of cake. What about your pals?"

"Their names are Louder and Pepe. All I can do is ask."

"If I do my part, you'll be paid to play to a thousand people every night on tour with Brother Floom."

"It's like *The Blues Brothers*," Kurt said. "We're getting the band back together. We're on a mission from God."

Six hours later, the van was packed and the band formerly known as Skinripper (new name TBD) were heading west to Louisiana with Kurt behind the wheel. Louder had been immediately on board, like a wish had been granted. Pepe was a tougher nut to crack. No pushover, he took an entire three minutes to decide to violate the terms of his probation and leave the state.

"You should have seen Margo's face when I quit," Louder said. "I climbed on the counter and announced that I was the real Dairy Queen and they were all my Dairy Bitches. Then I threw my uniform in the fryer."

"Epic," Kurt said.

"Sometimes I wish I had a job, just so that I could quit," Pepe said.

"Dream big, Pep," Louder said.

"The band is your job now," Kurt said. "We're going to get paid to play music."

"Does Christian rock really count as music?" Louder asked.

"The way we're going to play it," Kurt said.

"Wait," Pepe said. "What about Christian music? I'm a Buddhist."

Louder smacked her forehead. "How many times do we have to explain it? It's one thing to smoke some pot, but you're living in a cloud."

"Clouds are cool. Clouds are fluffy and shaped like things. Don't hate on clouds."

"Do you even know what Buddhism is?" Louder asked.

"It's the one with karma and tie-dye."

"I stand corrected."

Kurt hadn't kept a secret from Louder since they were eight years old. She knew everything that Kurt knew about the plan and the heist and Brother Floom. They both agreed that the less Pepe knew, the better. He wouldn't have moral reservations, didn't need incentive, and would go along with them on damn near anything, but he would forget. Or he would end up putting what he did remember on his Myspace page, but that wouldn't have been a complete disaster because that was the equivalent of shouting into an empty well.

"It's what they call in the business 'an artistic pivot,'" Kurt said. "If we keep doing the same thing, our fans are going to get bored."

"We have fans?" Pepe asked.

"This represents an exciting change in our creative vision," Louder said. "It was your idea, Pepe, remember?"

Kurt gave Louder a disappointed look. They had agreed to stop Obi-Wanning Pepe. It was too easy. Like blowing pot smoke in a dog's face.

Pepe looked worried for a second, then tentatively said, "Yeah. Totally. Christian rock."

"Great idea," Kurt said.

"What's the weed policy?" Pepe said. "Have we discussed the weed policy? I'm concerned about the weed policy."

"There is no weed policy," Kurt said. "It's a Christian tour supporting an evangelical preacher and his sermons."

"So everyone brings their own. Every-man-for-himself style. Got it."

Kurt opened his mouth to say something, but Louder shook her head. "He'll just ask again in ten minutes."

"Ask what?" Pepe said. "Oh yeah. What's the weed policy?"

Somewhere in Arizona or New Mexico, Kurt lost himself in the vanishing point at the end of the endless highway. He couldn't understand why anyone would need peyote or any other psychotropic drug. All anyone needed to do was drive a few hours until they hypnotized themselves.

Louder crawled from the back into the passenger seat, snapping Kurt out of it.

"Thanks for coming along," Kurt said. "Pepe doesn't know better. For you—well, it's a big deal. You got a life. Had a job."

"Shut up," Louder said. "You been thinking about songs?"

"I considered just taking some Slayer songs and replacing any mention of Satan with Jesus, but probably too loud and aggressive."

"What about changing the lyrics to our songs," Louder said. "We know how to play those."

"Okay. 'Berserker vs. Berserker.'" Kurt mouthed the lyrics to the first few stanzas to himself. "What if we change 'barbarian warrior' to 'Jesus, our Savior'?"

Louder closed her eyes and bobbed her head. "Kind of grim. 'Jesus, our Savior. Death close at hand. Jesus, our Savior. Blood on the land.'"

"Let me finish," Kurt said. "'Jesus, our Savior. More than a man. Jesus, our Savior. Blood of the lamb.'"

"You're going to have to do somersaults for the next verse," Louder said. "'Vorpal sword of crucible steel. Gutting goblins and orcs with murderous zeal.'"

"Yeah, I'll work on that," Kurt said. "How many songs do we have in the Skinripper music vault?"

"Eight originals and four covers."

"I might have something in the songs I've written over the last few months."

"Those are all about watching movies and reading comic books."

"But poignant," Kurt said. "'Requiem for *Requiem for a Dream*' has depth. The chorus was 'Hey, Mr. Selby? Why didn't you tell me? That you wrote misery porn. Before I bought my frickin' popcorn. I want to kill myself. I want to kill myself. I want to kill myself.'"

"Yeah, they'll love it in the back pews. Uplifting."

"It uses the phrase 'ass to ass' pretty liberally, though," Kurt said. "I'd probably have to change that. Maybe 'Mass to Mass'?"

Kurt, Louder, and Pepe walked into the stifling heat of the tiny Motel 6 room. They chucked their duffel bags on the floor. Louder worked on the air conditioner, pressing its buttons and banging on the side. It made some clicking and whirring sounds before a tiny bit of cool air escaped.

Pepe walked straight to the bathroom and closed and locked the door behind him.

"Did he lock the door?" Louder said. "That's going to be contaminated for hours. I should have brought quarantine tape. Turn the fan on, Pepe."

"It's broke!" Pepe shouted through the door. "It made sparks."

Kurt looked at the two small twin beds. "I'll hit the floor. You two take the beds."

"The floor is filthy," Louder said. "You'd have to add dirt to make it cleaner. Share with me."

"Or I can bunk with Pepe?"

"The bed would collapse. Don't be a dumbass."

Kurt later tried to convince himself that it was Pepe's snoring that had kept him awake all night, but there was something about being in the bed next to Louder that made him feel weird and nervous. He looked at the back of her head for a long time until he felt even weirder.

He'd had a crush on her since they were kids. Their becoming best friends didn't take the crush away. It only became more critical that he didn't say anything. Louder was the most important person in his life.

Kurt smiled and started to drift off, but Pepe's snoring hit a crescendo loud enough to set off a car alarm. Kurt grabbed his notebook and played around with lyrics. He would get some sleep in the van.

CHAPTER 24

The vein on Thrace McCormick's forehead pulsed violently. It looked like an earthworm attempting to wriggle under his hairline.

The prayer room of the church had been converted into a make-shift war room. The closed meeting included the principal leads on the tour—including Axel, a half dozen of the 300, and the Young Lions' manager. Thrace had not informed Virginia about the meeting, but Axel made sure she knew. The look on McCormick's face when she walked into the room was priceless.

The band manager calmly conveyed to the room that the band had made a decision to cancel the remainder of their contribution to the tour, enter rehab for drugs and sex addiction, and get back to their relationship with God.

"Prostitutes and ecstasy," McCormick said. "Which I'm told is a drug, correct?"

"Yes, MDMA or molly," the manager said. "The devil is everywhere."

"Does Brother Floom know anything about this?"

"No," the manager said.

"Small victories," McCormick said. "Make sure he doesn't. No point in upsetting him."

"I agree," Virginia said, obviously not used to being on the same side as McCormick.

"Thank you, Virginia," McCormick said. "Glad you could make it. I would propose that the band delays their rehabilitation and continues the tour under our watchful eye. My men can be present at all times to ensure that they resist all temptations."

The members of the 300 nodded in agreement.

"It seems that there is a video," the manager said. "There is nudity. It is, at present, unsecured. Your ministry would not want to be associated with its content."

"We have a sermon tonight," McCormick said. "Brother Floom relies on the music. For energy and for time. He can no longer preach for three hours."

"Cancel tonight, for sure," Virginia said. Every head turned toward her. "In fact, you should cancel the tour."

Thrace brushed away the idea with his hand. "Not an option. We will return to the classic revival. Old-fashioned hymns. Retro, as they say."

"You could get another band," Axel said. He had created this moment. He had better nail it.

"Bands book months, even years, in advance," McCormick said. "At least, the bands that we're interested in. If I wanted your uninformed opinion, I would have solicited it."

"In my former profession," Axel said, "I used to book bands. I can make a few phone calls. Call in some favors. I might be able to get someone by Bogalusa."

"I still propose that we cancel the tour," Virginia said.

McCormick stared at Axel. "Make your calls. However, nobody performs without my approval. I don't want you trying to give some relative their big break. I want to see a professional looking and sounding band. I want to hear upbeat. I want to see upright. I want to feel uplifting."

"The three ups. Everyone knows those. Got it."

They tried the old hymns that night. The strategy had not proved popular. It made everyone in the church feel like they were at church. The whole point of Brother Floom and the revival was to make it fun and big and entertaining. An extended Sunday sermon was not going to cut it.

The stage was set for the band to join the tour in Bogalusa. Three hours before their audition, Axel met Kurt, Louder, and Pepe on the outskirts of town, in the parking lot of an abandoned gas station.

"It's all set up," Axel said. "Three songs. That's what you're going to get."

"We're ready," Kurt said. "Tired, but ready. I think."

"No, no, no, no, no," Axel said, pointing at the side of the van with the image of Bloodface and the word "Skinripper" written above it. "This can't be here. You have to lose that."

"That's art, man," Pepe said.

"It's hideous and demonic and no damn way," Axel said.

"We'll take care of it," Kurt said. "Sorry, Pepe."

"Aw, man," Pepe said. "I love Bloodface."

"Cover it up," Axel said. "Or paint over it. Get rid of it."

"I don't have enough paint," Pepe said, "but I can maybe modify it."

"Get paint," Axel said. "You have a zombie monster creature on the side of the van."

"How about a Jesus?" Louder asked. "Jesus is like the mascot for Christians, right?"

"Jesus is not a mascot," Kurt said. "He's the Lord and Savior."

"Great," Axel said. "Jesus is great. Just not that demon."

"I could add a crown of thorns," Pepe said, "clean up his face, give him a halo."

"And the name," Axel said. "Skinripper is out. You still need a new name. Maybe the Truthbadours, like troubadours, but with the word 'truth.'"

"Christian bands have horrible names," Kurt said. "It's the only thing that's consistent. Skillet, Flyleaf, Kutless, Pillar, but that's too awful."

"I'm not attached to it," Axel said. "Spitballing."

"That's the worst name I've ever heard ever," Louder said.

"Okay," Axel said. "Take it easy."

Kurt stared at the side of the van. He held up both hands and closed one eye. "I got it. Pep, paint out both sides of the word 'Skinripper,' leave the 'I,' 'N,' 'R,' and 'I' in the middle. That's our new band name. INRI."

"Should I know what that is?" Louder asked.

"It's what Pilate nailed onto the cross," Kurt said.

"Can you get it done in an hour or two?" Axel asked.

"If I hot box some weed," Pepe said, clearly doing calculations in his head, "I can do it in an hour twenty, but I'm going to need you to get me three boxes of Little Debbies. Zebra Cakes definitely and any other two. Plus a gallon of Gatorade and some Twizzlers."

"I'm not getting you any of those things," Axel said. "Just paint the van."

"It was worth a shot," Pepe said.

An hour and a half later, the newly painted van pulled up outside the Bogalusa Freedom Church, a megachurch headed by Pastor Vic Profit.

The paint was still wet on the side of the van. Pepe's new art wasn't Axel's ideal, but it would hopefully be Jesusy enough to pass muster. Axel could see what Pepe was going for, but it looked rushed, less like Christ and more like Zakk Wylde had gotten tuned up in a bar brawl.

Axel grabbed a seat next to Virginia, right behind Thrace McCormick and Vic Profit. He was nervous, but definitely not as nervous as Kurt, who was sweating through his clothes. He looked like he had just been baptized.

The band dressed conservatively, Kurt and Pepe in jeans and button-up shirts. Louder wore a long dress they had bought at a gas station. They had shown Axel some black tunics that had a goth Friar Tuck look to them, but he vetoed them as too Satanic-ritually.

Kurt walked to the microphone. "We are INRI. Thank you for the opportunity to let us perform for you today."

Thrace McCormick loud-whispered to Vic Profit. "I have never seen a man sweat that much. He's a husky one, isn't he?"

Axel considered punching McCormick in the back of the head, but before he could make his decision, Virginia leaned toward Thrace. "The band went out of the way to be here. Show them some respect."

McCormick didn't respond, but Axel could see the back of his neck turning visibly redder.

Kurt walked to the amplifier, turned it up, and returned to the microphone. "This first song is called 'Gestas, the Impenitent Thief.'" Facing the band, he said, "One, two. One, two, three, four."

Loud did not adequately describe the volume that issued from the speakers. In the large auditorium, the sound of the guitar and drums had mass. The sound knocked Axel back in his seat. Heavy bass vibrated in the room. He felt like he was having a seizure.

Kurt growled out the lyrics.

> *Caught as thieves, but didn't want to be famous.*
> *The Gospel of Nicodemus is the one that would*
> *   name us.*
> *For what we did, we didn't deserve to die.*
> *Dismas repented, but I wouldn't cry.*
> *The forgiveness he asked for, I would deny.*
> *The end of my life wouldn't end with a lie.*
>
> *Now I burn in the fires of hell and Dismas in Paradise.*
> *If I did it again, I would think thrice.*

I wouldn't have mocked him, been evil and cold.
I wouldn't have doubted, bought the heaven he sold.
If I'd only known it was for the fate of my soul,
I would have asked forgiveness, but still would have
*   stole.*

"Stop, stop, stop!" McCormick shouted, standing up and waving his arms.

Kurt gestured for Louder and Pepe to stop playing. The church felt twice as quiet after the onslaught of noise.

"Too loud," McCormick said. "Very too loud. While I appreciate that you actually play your instruments, this is not a rock-and-roll concert."

"We were told it was Christian rock," Kurt said. "We put the emphasis on rock. There is a strong tradition from Stryper to Skillet of harder music."

"A miscommunication," McCormick said, glancing back at Axel. "Not your fault. It's hard to find good people. To be clear, that's not what we're looking for."

"Our mistake," Kurt said. "My apologies. If you give me a better idea of what you're looking for, I'm sure we can find the right rhythm—and volume—to fit your taste."

"It has to have pep," McCormick said. "Uplifting with pep. Can you do more than just stand there? The last band had choreographed dancing, which the audience found engaging. And rapping. As much as I abhor the sound of it—borderline blasphemous, if you ask me—the hip and hop speaks to the youths."

"Yes, sir," Kurt said. "The hip and hop."

"They can rap," Axel said. "Can't you?"

Kurt gave Axel a pleading look and turned back to Pepe and Louder.

"Not it," Louder and Pepe said simultaneously.

Kurt turned back to McCormick. "It would be an honor for us to show our versatility. Keep in mind I will be freestyling, so it might be rough."

"Don't apologize before you perform. It lacks confidence." McCormick sat down, looking at his watch. "Let's get on with this."

Axel said a small prayer. McCormick had no idea what good rap was, so it only had to be passable. It felt like that moment in *8 Mile*. One shot, one opportunity. Maybe they would make a TV movie about this moment a decade from now.

Kurt carefully put his guitar in the guitar stand, buying time. He walked back to the center of the stage, pulled the microphone out of the stand, and moved the mike stand to the side. His mouth moved as he mumbled softly to himself.

"Is that one a Mexican of some kind?" McCormick said to Vic Profit in one of those whispers that was louder than his actual speaking voice.

"Give me a beat," Kurt said, more a question than a statement.

Louder and Pepe did what he asked. They gave him a beat. Kurt stomped the stage, rolling his shoulders and gesticulating with his hand in a parody of a rap artist.

Yo. Yo. Yo. Yo.

Axel slunk down low in the pew and dug his hands into the wood seat. He felt like throwing up. His heart raced.

Jesus is Lord, and that's both tight and dope.
My lyrics are cleaner than Ivory soap.
Lord and Savior, he be the King of Kings.
He's more popular than Stranger Things.
On Netflix, yo. With Winona Ryder.
About a weird girl, some kids try to hide her.
It's also got Matthew Modine as a special guest.
He was really good in the movie Vision Quest.

His character wrestles the champ, Brian Shute,
After losing tons of weight in a shiny sweat suit.

Axel coughed loudly. Kurt made eye contact with him. Axel shook his head. Kurt stalked the stage, trying to get back on track.

Jesus, Jesus, Jesus, Jesus.
Lord, Lord, Lord, Lord.
God, God, God, God.
Our Father who art in heaven.
Hallowed be thy name.
Thy kingdom come.
Thy will be done.

Kurt rapped the entire Lord's Prayer. It worked better than Axel would have guessed. When he got to the end, he repeated the word "yo" about twenty times.

"I'm going to stop you there," McCormick said, putting Kurt out of his misery.

The band stopped. Kurt breathed heavily into the mike. "I was almost to the good part."

"I truly doubt that there was ever going to be a good part, son," McCormick said. "That was awful."

"What are you talking about, buddy?" a voice said from the back of the church. Everyone turned. Brother Tobin Floom walked down the aisle toward the stage. A couple of the 300 trailed behind. "The kid's got enthusiasm. Passion. It was zippy."

Virginia rose from her seat, scooted past Axel, and walked to her father. She whispered something to him, but he patted her head and smiled. "I'm fine, Tulip. Just fine."

Reaching the stage, he held out a hand to Kurt. "The power of the Lord ran through you when you spoke in tongues at the end."

Kurt leaned down and shook his grandfather's hand. "Thanks. I improvised."

"You remind me of someone," Brother Floom said. "Have we met? My memory gets hazy."

"No, sir. I am positive that we haven't. I would have remembered."

Brother Floom turned to McCormick. "Hire them. Didn't like the last band. Phonies. A bunch of sissies. These kids got brass. And a Mexican. They're hard workers."

"But, Tobin," McCormick said, "I don't think—"

But Brother Floom was already walking back down the aisle, saying to himself, "Yo, yo, yo, yo, yo." He turned to the 300 that walked alongside him. "It's fun to say."

Axel and Virginia walked out of the church. Virginia shook her head and laughed. "I don't know where you found them, but that was worth it just to see Thrace's head explode. Almost makes me want to sit through the sermon tonight and watch the train wreck."

"The band was caught off guard," Axel said. "They were nervous after a long drive."

"Does it really matter?" Virginia asked. "This tour is a circus. Might as well fill the clown car up to capacity."

"Are you okay?" Axel put a soft hand on her arm. "Is there something going on?"

"If I had my way—which I obviously don't—this tour would be over right now."

"It seems like it's going well. Bringing the Lord to so many people. The crowds have been great."

"And generous. Which is all Thrace cares about. I'm tired of my father getting dragged from city to city. I thought I could take care of him if I came along, but I can't."

"Is he sick or something?"

"Or something," Virginia said.

"It'll work out," Axel said. "Things work out."

"Naive but sweet," Virginia said. "I'm glad you had your parking-lot vision and ended up here. It's nice to have someone to talk to."

"Anytime."

"I still think you're crazy."

"Who isn't?"

"No," Virginia said. "I mean seriously insane. You had a vision. Sorry. You're being nice, and I'm insulting you."

"It's okay. If you need to talk more, we can meet for dinner. We don't hit the road until morning."

"It'll be late. The Waffle House might be our only option."

"Ain't nothing better than late-night hash browns."

"I'm at that hotel a block away. Come to room 207 around ten. We'll figure something out." Virginia gave him a kiss on the cheek and walked away.

Axel put a hand to his face and watched her until she turned the corner around the church. For a moment, he had that first-date feeling. That butterfly nervousness that made his body tingle. Then he remembered she was his aunt. And the butterflies turned to maggots.

"It's not a date, stupid," Axel said, making a mental note to find a good therapist when he got back to California.

CHAPTER 25

Let's get crazy. We're in Louisiana. I'm one espresso shy of robbing a liquor store just to get a rush. I'm bored and I'm in the South. The two of us need to put on some Daisy Dukes, hit the local watering hole, and see if we can stir up some trouble. Make some men fight over us." Stephanie paced the hotel room, opening and closing a butterfly knife.

"Where'd you get the knife?" Gretchen asked.

"A kid was selling them out of his trunk. I bought one for you, too."

"I don't think it's going to get any more exciting."

"I know I'm complaining," Stephanie said. "I understand the drudgery of crime better than most, but that was the most disappointing blackmail frame in the history of extortion. A slam dunk on a five-foot basket."

"I don't want you to go back to SD, but you should consider it."

"Let me help," Stephanie said. "Let me in on the frame. If you leave me here in the hotel room, anything can happen. Maybe I'll head out to the crossroads and make a deal with the devil."

"It's not my place to bring you in. I got partners." Gretchen wanted to push the moment that Stephanie and Axel saw each other to somewhere between later and never.

"I don't want a piece of the action. I just want action. No cut. No share. Something to do. An assignment. I'm dangerous when I'm bored."

"I sympathize. I'm the exact same way, but no can do." Gretchen went through the gear laid out on the bed and put it all into a duffel bag. Flashlight, binoculars, bottled water, dried fruit, beef jerky, cheese balls.

"You're obviously going to be gone awhile. You have snacks." Stephanie picked up the big container of cheese balls. "You eat these? They're gross, unnatural, and leave orange dust everywhere."

"I'm going to be sitting in my car the whole time. I'll orange the rental."

"What's this? You got plants to water or something?"

"That's a urinal for ladies."

"For ladies?" Stephanie said. "Do you hold your pinky out when you pee in it? So what are we staking out?"

"I'm not—"

"Let's not do the back-and-forth," Stephanie said. "We both know that I'm going to wear you down."

Gretchen and Stephanie sat in the rental car in the Walgreens parking lot. The drugstore was open twenty-four hours, so the lights remained on in the lot, but Gretchen managed to find a dark corner with a good view of the church across the street. And most importantly the buses parked in the grass field that abutted the building.

"Ripping off a church is some next-level thievery," Stephanie said. "There's already the whole 'Thou shalt not steal' thing hanging over every thief, but you're really spitting in God's eye and flipping him the bird when you steal directly from him. That's one badass 'Don't tell me what to do' if I ever saw one."

"We're not stealing from God. God doesn't use money. We're stealing from an organization that bilks people out of their money. The preacher is a conman."

"A tree is wood. A pig is pork. Tell me something I don't know."

"We're stealing stolen money."

Stephanie put a hand on Gretchen's face and turned it toward her. "Maybe you are, maybe not, but you sure as shit don't have to justify anything with me. You want to jack a church, you have my blessing. A kid has an ice cream cone that looks delicious, I don't care if you snatch it from him. Other than killing, there ain't no amount of bad that's going to scare me. I understand bad. I understand you." Stephanie gave her a soft kiss. "Now give me the rundown of the caper."

"Caper? Really?" Gretchen smiled. "All the money from tonight's offering will be brought to that bus on the far right, the Money Bus. We know that. What we don't know is if, when, and how often the pickups are for bank transfer. I got to watch that bus to figure out timing and method of transport."

"Simple enough. One last question," Stephanie said, giving it a dramatic pause. "Is that beef jerky just for you, or are we doing sharesies?"

Three hours later, Gretchen fought sleep by naming every kind of sandwich that she could without saying the same sandwich twice. Stephanie slept soundly in the passenger seat. About fifty sandwiches in, Gretchen slowed down.

"Monte Cristo, Philly cheesesteak, French dip, banh mi, Cubano, torta, *bocadillo*, Italian beef, po'boy, croque monsieur, sloppy joe, *choripán*."

A tapping on the window snapped her out of her sandwich hypnosis. For a brief moment, she couldn't figure out where she was.

The tapping continued.

Gretchen took a big breath and centered herself. Probably a security guard rousting them from the lot. Without bothering to wake Stephanie, she rolled down the window.

Axel leaned in. "Had a chance to get away and figured I'd see how it's going. You need anything?"

Gretchen glanced quickly at Stephanie, who faced in the other direction. "Get out of here. We shouldn't be seen together. I'm fine."

"Is there someone in the car with you?"

"Nobody. Someone I met. Don't worry about it."

"You brought a date to a stakeout," Axel practically shouted, then dialed it back. "This isn't a game, Gretch. You can't—"

At that moment, Stephanie woke up, turned on the overhead light, and faced the two of them. "What's up?"

Gretchen felt that thing that was depicted in movies by dollying and zooming at the same time. The person stayed in one place and the background went weird. That's how she felt. It might not have been that long, but it felt like an hour to Gretchen. It was long enough for everyone to recognize everyone else.

Axel vomited on the side of the car, communicating clearly to Gretchen that he was a little upset about Stephanie's presence.

"A little dramatic," Gretchen said.

"What in the hell is she doing here? I can't even understand how she could be here. It doesn't make sense. She should be somewhere that's not here. Not in this car. Or the state of Louisiana. Did you tell her things? What does she know?"

"Calm down," Gretchen said. "Do you want me to answer any of those questions, or do you want to ask like a hundred more before I start answering?"

"She—" Axel started to say.

"I'm right here," Stephanie interrupted, "and not a fan of being spoken about in the third person. I have a few questions myself."

"That's funny, because I'm not a fan of being conned into buying a piece-of-shit monstrosity of a house. Or of falling in love with someone that's a lying-ass liar bitch liar."

"Let's watch the language and the name-calling," Gretchen said. "Steph, I meant to tell you."

"Are you kidding me right now?" Axel said. "I knew her first."

"Again," Stephanie said, "with the 'shes' and the 'hers.' It's annoying. Why don't you climb in the back seat to avoid bringing more attention to us? The church is across the street. We can talk like grown-ups. Or, at least, two grown-ups and a child."

"Am I the child in that?" Axel said.

"She's right, Ax," Gretchen said. "Get in the car. Let's talk."

"What's the point?" Axel said. "This is over. It's all done. We're compromised. There's no way I'm going to trust her—sorry, third person. There's no way I'm going to trust you, you awful liar bitch woman. This is done."

"That's not your decision to make," Gretchen said.

Axel leaned back, looking at the side of the car. "You're going to want to run the car through a car wash. I ate beet salad earlier. This is a white car. If you want to get your deposit back, that is."

"It's under a false identity," Gretchen said. "They'll charge the fake card."

"I'd clean it anyway. It looks like someone got shot up against the door. You don't want to get pulled over with a criminal in the car." Axel walked away.

Gretchen opened the door to get out. Stephanie held her arm, stopping her.

"You talked to him, but we need to talk about this," Stephanie said. "Why didn't you tell me about Axel? Is he your boyfriend or something? Your husband?"

"He's my brother."

174

"Oh." Stephanie let go of her arm. "That's not really a big deal, then. I thought it was a love triangle scenario. A brother is fine."

"It's not fine," Gretchen said. "I brought the woman that he was in love with that ended up conning him to the heist that he planned."

"If he's a pro, how could he take any of it personally?"

"He's semi-pro," Gretchen said. "I got to go. I don't want this thing to fall apart. Keys are in the ignition. Please don't leave. I don't want this to sit until we're back in San Diego. I really don't want you to go."

"Go talk to your brother," Stephanie said. "I'll do what I do. I don't like being lied to."

Gretchen caught up to Axel just before he walked into the church. "Ax, we need to talk about this."

"No, we don't."

Two people walked out of the church. The woman looked perplexed. "It's not my fault. They said the Young Lions would be playing."

Axel pulled Gretchen around the corner of the church. "I will not go to jail or get ripped off again by the same woman. You brought the last person we can trust into something that we need absolute trust to pull off. Best case, she double-crosses us and gets the money. Worst case, she double-crosses us and we end up in prison. Both are not optimal."

"I get you being mad. You should be mad. It shouldn't have happened with Stephanie, but it did."

"She's running an angle on you, Gretch. That's what she does. You don't see it, but she is going to screw you."

"Already has." Gretchen smiled.

"You're joking? You're making jokes?"

"You teed it up for me."

"You only think about yourself. I get it. I do that, too. We pretend like we're a family, but we're not. We've never been a real family. Even on this gig, we're each doing our own thing separate from each other.

175

When Dad died, it could have brought us together. We could have had each other's backs. We didn't. It was every man—and woman—for himself. That's the way we roll."

"I'm not the one jumping ship right before we pull a job. I want to go through with this. We can do this."

"Not with her. Not with you." Axel walked away.

Gretchen watched him go into the church. When he opened the door, she thought she heard Kurt rapping about the movie *Escape from New York*, but it had to be her imagination.

CHAPTER 26

Kurt walked off the stage to the sound of polite clapping. The kind of pity claps that a six-year-old gets after thrashing "Chopsticks" at a piano recital. The sound a participation ribbon would make. Fewer than a dozen people walked out, which he took as a good sign. Rehearsal and preparation hadn't improved his rapping skills. Nor his dance moves. His attempt to do the Worm made one parishioner think he was having a seizure.

Louder high-fived him as he walked past. "INRI rocked the house."

"That was a disaster."

"That was Andy Kaufman–Brother Theodore level brilliance," Louder said.

"They didn't throw a single thing," Pepe said. "They could've. They had Bibles and crosses and other stuff. But they didn't."

"My body is adrenaliney," Kurt said. "Skin quivery."

"That's the biggest crowd we've played for," Louder said.

"Maybe I should do some beatbox next time," Pepe said, demonstrating his beatbox skills, which sounded like explosion noises a child made.

Kurt's voice dropped down to a whisper. "Are you high?"

Pepe winked. "High like a fox."

"We had an hour-long conversation, because you kept forgetting. No smoking pot. We have to be extra chaste."

"Nobody's chasing me," Pepe said. "I didn't smoke any pot. I said I wouldn't, and I didn't."

"Your eyes are redder than a blushing communist cutting onions."

"Edibles, compadre," Pepe said, pulling a Ziploc bag halfway out of his pocket. Gummies shaped like cannabis leaves filled the bag.

"Give me that," Kurt said, grabbing the bag from Pepe and putting it in his pocket. "No more pot."

Pepe pouted but nodded.

"Can we get back to celebrating?" Louder said. "We didn't suck too bad."

The three of them chanted "We didn't suck too bad. We didn't suck too bad. We didn't suck too bad" until Kurt spotted Thrace McCormick out of the corner of his eye. He shushed them.

When McCormick got close, the three of them pretended to pray. Kurt hoped he would go away, but he could feel the man standing next to him.

"Amen," Kurt said. "Oh, hello, Mr. McCormick."

"Abhorrent," McCormick said. "A travesty. Nothing resembling music just happened."

"The audience seemed to enjoy it," Kurt said.

"Quality is not determined by popularity," McCormick said. "Something is either good, or it isn't. You isn't."

Kurt hated that he agreed with his simplistic explanation of popularity versus quality. That was going to bug him for a while. It was like Hitler explaining how great *Raiders of the Lost Ark* was. It would force you to agree with Hitler.

McCormick shook his head and started to walk away, then turned. "Am I mistaken, or did you play the same song twice?"

Kurt thought they had gotten away with that. Their set list was limited, so they played the first song again at the end. "That's our theme. We open and close with it."

"Don't do that. It makes it seem like you only know four songs."

"Yes, sir," Kurt said. "Got it."

"And is there any way to reduce the sweating? Three people asked me if it was raining outside."

"I'll work on it."

McCormick caught sight of something behind Kurt. With his long arm, he pushed Kurt and Louder against the wall. "Make way."

Four of the 300 marched forward, clearing a path. Kurt, Louder, and Pepe remained glued to the wall to avoid getting steamrolled. Once there was a clear path, Brother Tobin Floom in his pristine white suit with gold accessories walked toward the stage.

When he reached Kurt, he stopped and turned to him. "What are you doing here?"

McCormick put a hand on his shoulder and guided Floom away from Kurt. Brother Floom looked back, confused. The crowd's cheer snapped him out of it. His eyes brightened. He clicked into performance mode.

Brother Floom opened his arms to the applauding congregation. A few people whooped and hollered, which kind of hurt Kurt's feelings. They had it in them but chose not to give INRI any of that enthusiasm. Brother Floom stalked the stage a few times and then jumped into his sermon. "What a glorious night for fellowship. Praise Jesus. Thank you for inviting me to your wonderful house of worship."

"Mom would have loved this," Kurt said, leaning down to Louder. "At least, I think she would have. I don't even know what she saw when she saw him. A preacher or her father-in-law. A holy man or a thief."

"We don't got to watch, right?" Pepe said. "I was going to head back to the bus and do anything else but this."

"You two go ahead," Kurt said. "I want to listen for a while."

Kurt found a seat on a stage block. He looked out at the crowd, who were enraptured. All the faces fully engaged with the man on the stage. Except one, who was staring right at him.

FBI agent Harry Cronin had figured out how to straighten his eyebrows, but the goatee he wore was about three shades different. He looked like a Chinese-made knockoff Mr. Potato Head where nothing was quite right. Cronin winked.

Kurt hadn't forgotten the deal they had made, but he had no idea how he would deliver.

An hour later, Brother Floom hadn't lost any steam. There were times when his words got away from him and didn't quite make sense, but his passion never waned.

"We hear the word 'redemption.' We take it to mean that our soul has been saved, which is true. Jesus forgives us, redeems us, gives us second and third chances. We are who we are and not who we were. We are who we are and not who we might become."

Kurt watched from the backstage area, transfixed on a man he had seen almost every day for the last thirteen years. It was strange to see Brother Floom from that angle. The man looked thirty years older in person. The strongest father figure in his life, but like his real father, the persona and the reality were in conflict.

Brother Floom paced, wiping his forehead with his signature gold silk handkerchief. He reached to heaven, one hand filled with a fat Bible that bloomed open. He smiled and joked and yelled and barked. It was like watching an end-of-career farewell tour. A greatest hits album. All his catchphrases and expressions and mannerisms were on display.

It reminded Kurt of his mom. The deep echo of something as simple as sitting on the couch in silence. Since her death, Kurt's relationship to her memory had become more complex, but it didn't make him miss or love her any less.

It must have been how Gretchen and Axel felt when Dad died. He was too young for it to resonate, his father an idea he barely remembered. They had lost someone they had an actual relationship with, someone they had history with, someone they had their quiet moments on the couch with, someone they loved and cared for.

For the rest of the night, Kurt would try to forget that Brother Floom was a character that his grandfather was playing and let himself sink into the show. It was the best way—if for a short time—to be back on that couch with his mom.

"Redemption!" Brother Floom shouted. "Another meaning of the word, the same but different, means to clear a debt. So when we are redeemed, we are paying God back what we owe him. What do we owe? Our souls. Our lives. Our whole selves. Yes, yes, and yes. If we don't give our whole selves over to Jesus, over to the Lord. If we don't have faith in life everlasting, then we still owe him. We are not truly redeemed. Are you on that path? To have redemption, you must change. Are you who you were or who you are or who you might be? I know that I am not who I once was." He glanced back at Kurt, then repeated even slower, "I am not who I once was."

Kurt froze. It felt like a moment of clarity. A communication directly to him.

Brother Floom took a long pause, as if lost in thought. The church went silent. Dead air. An odd feeling. He staggered around the stage looking confused.

After a half minute, Vic Profit took a step toward him. "Brother Floom? Are you okay?"

Kurt looked out to the crowd. He could no longer find Agent Harry Cronin in the audience.

"I am not who I once was," Brother Floom said, snapping the lull and turning back to the crowd. "When I was younger, I did things that, looking back, I wish I hadn't done. Mistakes, regrets, harm. Don't we all have regrets, sins, in our past? I look back and wonder if I am the person who did those things. I am and I am not. I cannot undo my actions, but redemption is possible. I can only be the man I am. And strive to be better. The Lord knows and accepts that. The Lord forgives. People don't."

Brother Floom's voice grew softer as he spoke. At one point, he stared at the lights and spoke with his back to the audience. "Forgive our trespasses as we forgive those that trespass against us. I wish the world heeded that call. Didn't hold on to animosity and pettiness and hate."

Brother Floom turned back to the congregation. He dropped his Bible. The thud echoed to the back. He stared blankly at the faces in the crowd. "Who the hell are you people?"

A gasp rose from the crowd, but also a few laughs.

"Where am I?" Brother Floom said.

Something was very wrong. Brother Floom looked scared and lost. The kind of look Pepe got when he was too high and tried to play a first-person shooter. Without thinking, Kurt stepped onto the stage and walked to Brother Floom.

Behind him, he heard McCormick say, "Do not go out there."

Kurt put a hand on Brother Floom's shoulder once he reached him. "Sir, are you okay?"

Brother Floom turned and grabbed hold of Kurt's face and pulled him toward him. "My son. I knew it was you."

"Why don't we get you some water and a place to sit?" Kurt said, giving a pleading eye to Vic Profit, who took the hint and walked to center stage.

Kurt walked Brother Floom toward the side of the stage. "It's going to be okay, Grandpa."

"What did you call me?" the old man said right before he collapsed. Kurt caught him by one arm and eased him to the floor.

"Someone call a doctor!" Kurt shouted. "Call 9-1-1."

CHAPTER 27

Axel knocked on the hotel room door. He wasn't even sure why he was there. He should be on his way back to San Diego. He didn't have a strong-enough work ethic or sense of loyalty to keep doing a fake job for free. Gretchen bringing that woman was unforgivable and irreparable.

Virginia answered the door. "Come in. Pour yourself a drink. If you don't drink, that's fine, too. I never know, especially with people that had visions in parking lots."

She was already drunk. Not six-whiskey-sours, walking-like-a-boat-on-rough-water drunk, but three-glasses-of-wine, not-able-to-not-smile drunk. The more fun, less chaotic of the two. Virginia welcomed him into the modest hotel room and gestured toward a pile of mini liquor bottles.

"I drink," Axel said, a little too loud, following her into the room. "I mean, not a lot. I'm not an alcoholic or someone who used to be an alcoholic either, which is technically an alcoholic but one that doesn't drink. I find wine to be part of a sophisticated evening."

Virginia laughed. "Are you okay? Your face is really red, and you're sweating. Are you holding your breath?"

"No." Axel exhaled and picked up a mini bottle of vodka. Remembering his last excursion with that particular spirit, he put it back and chose whiskey instead. As if that would have a different result.

"You've got some catching up to do," she said. "Don't think I do this all the time. It's been a long, stupid, frustrating few months, and I'm blowing off steam. You're one of the only people I can stand on this whole dumb, stupid, dumb tour."

Axel took a big swig of the whiskey.

"I always talk about me." Virginia sat on the corner of the bed. "Tell me about you. Do you have any family?"

Axel spit whiskey all over Virginia. It usually took years to perfect the fine misty spray that is the hallmark of a great spit-take. Axel hit perfection on his first try, but his audience had no appreciation for the moment.

"My eyes," Virginia screamed, reaching her hands blindly in front of her.

"Oh crap. I'm so sorry." Axel looked around frantically. He ran into the bathroom, soaked a washcloth under the sink, and hurried back. He placed the dripping washcloth in her outstretched hand.

Virginia wiped her face. "What the hell was that?"

"Whiskey," Axel said. "Went down the wrong way."

"It burns."

"Sorry. I'm so sorry."

"I'm going to not get mad," she said, obviously mad. "What were we talking about? Say something to get my mind off the intense pain."

"Family. We were talking about family. Parents are dead. I have a sister, but we're not talking. I have a brother, too. He's the good one. How about you?"

"Only child."

"Are you sure?"

"That's a seriously weird question," she said. "Why wouldn't I be sure?"

"I don't know."

"I don't want to talk about my dad. Let's try not talking." She took the towel away from her face and blinked her bloodshot eyes open. "Can you turn off the light?"

Axel found the switch and dimmed the lights.

"Why don't you come over here?" Virginia said, tapping the bed.

"Uh" was all Axel said. And then he said it again. "Uh."

"You had to know this was a hookup."

"A hookup?"

"Obviously. It would do us both good to get laid. Don't tell me that you're saving yourself or it's a sin. We're grown-ups. You don't come to someone's hotel room on tour and not know that's what's up."

"I left the water on in the bathroom!" Axel shouted. He sprinted to the bathroom, closed the door, and locked it. He put his back against the door, as if Virginia might attempt to break it down. He counted down from ten, washed his face, and looked in the mirror. "Say good night and walk out of the room. No good will come out of any other choice. She's your aunt. You've done a lot of dumbass things in your life. This is not going to be one of them."

A loud knock on the hotel room door cut off his pep talk, and then he heard voices and the door slam. Ten seconds, tops. When he walked out of the bathroom, he was the only one in the room.

Axel closed Virginia's hotel room door. A couple of doors down, Stephanie closed her door. They turned and saw each other at the same time. Axel heard an Ennio Morricone soundtrack in his head.

"How did you know I was here?" Stephanie squared up to fight, one hand digging in her purse.

Axel put up his hands defensively. "Coincidence. I was seeing a friend."

"Booty call," Stephanie said. "Good to see you've moved on."

"Is your plan to go through my family one person at a time?"

"There's no way I'll be able to convince you, but I'm not running a game on Gretchen. What I got with your sister, it's real."

"Nothing is real about you, Priscilla."

"Call me what you like. Names don't mean anything."

"So if I called you a lying bitch, you wouldn't care."

"Sticks and stones," Stephanie said, her hand still in her purse. "But don't push it too far. I have limits. You're not going to hurt me, but I don't like being annoyed."

"Because I plan on never seeing you again, I've got to ask," Axel said. "Was it handwritten, or computer generated?"

"Was what what? What are you talking about?"

"The breakup note you left me," Axel said.

"Handwritten. I took a calligraphy course once, when I thought I was going to pursue something normal people did. Normal people do that, right?"

"I wouldn't know what normal people do."

"The note had to be cruel. I didn't want you looking for me to try to get back together. I needed you to hate me."

"Congratulations."

Gretchen appeared at the end of the hall. She stopped when she saw Axel and Stephanie. "What are you doing here? Are you okay, Steph?"

"Is *she* okay?" Axel asked. "What about me?"

"You're fine," Gretchen said. "Mother is flying out from SD. She called a meeting. Tomorrow morning. Don't do anything until then."

"What's the point?" Axel said. "We're done here. You ended it by bringing her, not me."

"It might be over regardless of that," Gretchen said. "Kurt called. Floom collapsed onstage tonight. Like mid-preach. They took him to the hospital. I don't know how serious, but collapsing is not the sign of vivacious health."

"Virginia," Axel said, running down the hall away from them.

The first person Axel saw when he arrived at the hospital was Kurt, who chewed his fingernails in the corner of the waiting room. A pool of volunteers and a few of the 300 milled around drinking coffee. Axel sat next to Kurt.

"You okay?" Axel asked.

"I'm fine," Kurt said. "Why wouldn't I be?"

"I don't know. You're sensitive."

"You guys have always called me that." Kurt dropped his voice. "The only reason you think that is because you see me as a kid. I have a normal range of human emotions. I'm not any more sensitive than the next person. You and Gretchen, on the other hand, happen to be narcissists—possibly sociopaths—that only think about yourselves."

"When I walked in, you looked sad. That's all."

"I'm in character," Kurt whispered. "We're playing characters. It was traumatic. He was completely helpless. I caught him on stage as he fell. I thought he died."

"Exhaustion," Thrace McCormick said, giving them both a start. He stood over them, looking even more like an undertaker in the setting. "Brother Floom suffered from exhaustion."

"He's okay?" Kurt asked.

"Resting and recovering. Virginia is with him now. They were laughing and joking a minute ago. I'm on a mission to retrieve some popped corn on his request."

"That's a relief," Axel said. "We were praying for him."

McCormick nodded and walked away.

"Popped corn?" Kurt said. "He said it like he was an alien posing as a human being. Who doesn't know what popcorn is?"

"And another thing, Fletcher," McCormick said, making them jump again.

"How do you do that?" Axel said.

"I need you to coordinate the volunteers. If we're going to make McComb in time for prep and setup tomorrow, we have to be on the road by three thirty."

"In the morning?" Axel asked. "Shouldn't Brother Floom rest some more?"

"The doctor gave him the okay," Thrace said. "The tour continues as planned."

Axel spotted Virginia walking through the double doors from the back of the hospital. He got up without excusing himself and went straight to her.

"Hey," Axel said. "Are you okay?"

She dropped into his arms. Axel held her.

"Keep hugging me," she said. "I want Thrace to think I'm emotional, not thinking. Make it seem like a private moment."

She wasn't going to get an argument from Axel. He would hold her all night if he had to. She felt too good to be his aunt.

"How is he?" Axel asked.

"No worse than before."

"Are you okay?"

"Simultaneously drunk and hungover, but thinking clearly. Sorry about ducking out so quick."

"Why are we acting right now? This is a very long hug."

Virginia gently pulled away and double-checked that McCormick remained out of earshot. "I'm cancelling the tour. Thrace and Dad will fight me, but I'm not going to risk his health for money. That's what all this is about. My lawyers will have everything I need done soon. I'm just hoping Dad makes it to Yazoo City without something like this happening again. That'll be the last event."

"What's wrong with him?"

"Dementia. You must have noticed. The other day he called me 'Tulip.' He called Thrace 'Buddy.'"

"I thought those were terms of affection or like 'Hey, buddy.'"

"Tulip was my mom," Virginia said. "Buddy Matthews was his former right hand. On stage, he's fine—muscle memory kicks in—but otherwise he's forgetting and lost more and more. Thrace keeps him locked away like a performing animal."

"That's messed up."

"I don't like my father that much," Virginia said. "We have a complicated relationship that I don't want to get into, but no one deserves to be exploited."

"You can't stop it before Yazoo City?"

"The legal stuff is complicated. It's better to do it right than do it fast."

"Then, Yazoo City it is," Axel said.

CHAPTER 28

The family meeting was held at a run-down motor court outside McComb. Six people in the cramped room was four people too many. Especially at five in the morning. Mother and Fritzy had gotten into town just before the tour caravan arrived.

Gretchen marveled at how everyone had figured out how to use the space in the room optimally, to be as far away from everyone else as math allowed. It was like they had solved one of those puzzles with a Japanese name. Mother and Fritzy took the only two chairs in the room. Kurt leaned on the TV. Stephanie stayed by the front door, Gretchen on the bed.

Axel leaned against a wood-paneled wall. "The only reason that I'm here is out of respect for the work that has been put in. Don't expect me to change my mind."

"Closing up shop doesn't make sense," Mother said.

"Why is she here?" Axel pointed at Stephanie. "This is a family meeting."

"She's with me," Gretchen said.

"She's the problem!" Axel shouted.

"Grow up," Stephanie said. "Get over whatever happened between us. Move on. You sound like a child that needs to get laid. Okay, that came out wrong."

"Be careful, Kurt," Axel said. "When she's done with Gretch, she'll move on to you. She's working her way through the Ucker family."

"Send her my way," Fritzy said. "I'll put some butter on that dinner roll."

Mother whistled loudly. Everyone in the room winced and raised their hands to their ears. Their neighbor pounded on the wall and told them to shut up.

"I didn't fly out here to listen to a bunch of bitches," Mother said. "No more bullshit. I'm going to talk. You're all going to listen. Do not test me. Fritzy and me, we shouldn't have to be here. I am standing here, because you children couldn't play nice."

Axel blurted out, "Gretchen brought—"

"Hush," Mother said, shutting him up with a raise of a finger. "This might be your plan, but it isn't your call. You aren't in charge. This is a cooperative effort. You cannot shut this down. Everything is in motion. Time and money have been invested. No way you walk away now."

"I can if I want to."

"He's good at that," Kurt said.

Everyone turned to Kurt, who had otherwise been quiet.

Kurt shrugged. "He was always going to leave eventually. That's what he does."

"Remember the morning Mom died?" Gretchen asked.

"No, I forgot about it," Axel said. "Of course I remember that morning."

"Remember what happened?"

"Are you going to blackmail me because of what I was doing in the bedroom?"

"No. I had forgotten that I had caught you jerking off."

Everyone looked at Axel. His face turned dog-dick red.

"When did you . . . ?" Kurt asked.

"Before. Before. Before," Axel blurted out. "Before I knew about Mom. It wasn't weird or perverted. There was a Pamela Anderson poster from when I was fifteen. I had morning wood. What am I doing? I'm not defending myself. I'm not having this conversation."

"So the kid tried to paint the ceiling," Fritzy said. "It's not like none of you haven't dated Miss Michigan. I rubbed one out fifteen minutes before this meeting."

"Miss Michigan?" Kurt asked.

"Michigan is shaped like a mitten," Gretchen said.

"I like Uncle Fritzy," Stephanie said to Gretchen. "It's like he has a degree in filthy uncle."

Fritzy made a strange growl and gave Stephanie a flick of the tongue. "And a minor in carpet cleaning."

"It's like trying to teach a hamster how to read, I swear," Mother said. "Can we get back to it?"

"Are you going to keep your promise, Ax?" Gretchen asked. "Are you going to leave again?"

"It's not about me leaving," Axel said. "It's about Priscilla staying."

"Up yours, Axel," Gretchen said, flipping off her brother.

"He has a point," Mother said. "Your lady friend's presence deserves an explanation."

"I could have left you with nothing in San Diego," Stephanie said. "I went out of my way to find a mark so that you weren't left uncompensated for your work. Why would I do that? Because I didn't want Gretchen to look bad. I saw a future. I had no idea Axel was her brother."

"Why can we trust you?" Mother asked.

"Because I'm in love with Gretchen."

Gretchen turned to her. "I love you, too."

"That's beautiful," Kurt said. "Good for you two."

Gretchen and Stephanie kissed until Mother cleared her throat and Fritzy said, "Someone get a hose. Or a video camera."

"Are you kidding me?" Axel said. "She told me she loved me, too."

"Priscilla did love you," Stephanie said, "but Stephanie—the real me—loves this one."

"Then it's settled," Mother said.

"What the hell are you talking about?" Axel shouted. "What's settled? It's not settled. Nothing is settled. How could it possibly be settled?"

"They love each other," Mother said. "That makes Stephanie family."

"Welcome to the family, Stephanie," Kurt said.

"Have I gone completely insane?" Axel said.

"They're in love," Kurt said. "Look at them. Look how happy Gretch looks. Be happy for her."

Axel turned to Gretchen and Stephanie. "Doesn't matter. It's too risky. I'm out."

"Have it your way," Mother said. "Your role is pretty minor at this point. A few modifications and we can pull it off without you, especially now that we have an extra hand. But don't expect a cut. Which is a shame, as it doesn't change the fact that you were complicit. Walk away if you want all the risk with none of the reward."

Axel's eyes darted around, searching the room for answers. After a half minute, he said, "Damn it, but when she screws us over, you're all going to get the biggest 'I told you so' that you've ever heard. Like an epic one."

"I'll make it easier," Stephanie said. "It's best I go. I crashed your crime. I get it. If you're thinking about me, you're going to screw things up. Amateurs get distracted easily."

"Burn," Gretchen said. "But we're good, right?"

"We're great," Stephanie said. "I'll see you back in San Diego."

They started kissing again. Gretchen wanted to see if they could make out until everyone left the room, but Fritzy held his ground. He wasn't going anywhere.

After a long nap and a shower, Gretchen walked into the church and found a seat in the back. The room looked like the setting for an Asia concert, almost new age in its design and color scheme. Nineteen-seventies modernism transformed over time to modern retro. She spotted Axel talking to Virginia at the edge of the stage.

According to the short article in the local newspaper and on the church website, Brother Tobin Floom had fainted as the result of exhaustion but would be back to bring worship and salvation to McComb that night. The penultimate event before Virginia shut it down in Yazoo City.

Gretchen wanted to maintain her vengefulness for her grandfather, but it was hard to do with someone going through such an ignoble disease. If she finally got the chance to confront him about taking the house or about her father's death, there was no guarantee he would remember. The mystery of that day, when her father died, was moving deeper into the cloud of his senility. She wouldn't feel bad about taking his money, but it rang hollow.

People were still arriving as INRI got ready to play. Walking to the microphone, Kurt looked back at Louder, who gave him a thumbs-up. "Welcome, everyone. We're INRI, and we're going to play some music for you."

The crowd clapped politely.

"We've played a few events, but to be honest, we haven't been very good. We haven't played honest music. That changes tonight. This song is called 'Praise for the Fountain Opened.' A hymn from 1779." Louder counted it out on the drumsticks. When Kurt and Pepe came in with the guitar and bass, they blew off the doors. They sounded like they had in Louder's basement. Pure heavy metal.

Kurt belted the lyrics from deep in his throat.

> *There is a fountain filled with blood*
> *Drawn from Emmanuel's veins;*
> *And sinners plunged beneath that flood,*
> *Lose all their guilty stains.*
> *Lose all their guilty stains.*
>
> *The dying thief rejoiced to see*
> *That fountain in his day;*
> *And there have I, though vile as he,*
> *Washed all my sins away.*
> *Washed all my sins away.*

At the edge of the stage, a tall skeletal man Gretchen pegged as Thrace McCormick screamed at Axel. He did not seem happy with Kurt's music, but Gretchen thought INRI was rocking it. She couldn't stop smiling and banging her head.

"Praise the Lord!" she shouted. A woman a few seats over echoed the sentiment. The room went old-school tent revival, people standing in their seats. One young man became consumed by the power of the Lord and writhed on the floor in the aisle.

Kurt didn't let up, stretching the song into almost twenty minutes of pure rocking. With the last flourish of guitar and drum, the church went silent, except for the kid still squiggling on the floor.

Louder and Pepe exited the stage. Kurt put his guitar in its stand and followed them but stopped when he spotted McCormick with his arms folded in front of him. He walked the length of the stage and exited on the other side just as Brother Floom appeared at the same spot. As Kurt passed, Brother Floom grabbed his arm and guided him to the front of the stage.

The crowd applauded loudly the moment Brother Floom appeared.

"Thank you all for coming," Brother Floom said. "Before I begin tonight's sermon—it's a good one—I want to give my personal thanks to this young man. You've seen his passion and enthusiasm for the Lord as you've listened to his music. Glorious. While the Lord can hear a whisper, sometimes it doesn't hurt to shout. He certainly heard us tonight. What do you folks think?"

The crowd whooped and hollered, wanting to be heard, as well.

"What a wonderful crowd," Brother Floom said. "Beyond being a talented and faith-filled musician—" Brother Floom paused. "I'm sorry. My memory isn't what it used to be. Help me with your name, son."

"Kurt Ucker."

"Fuck," Gretchen said, loud enough for the woman nearest to her to gasp. Kurt just said his name. His real name.

Criminality 101: don't tell people who you are before you steal from them.

Brother Floom stared at him for a moment. "Kurt Ucker. Ucker? That's an unusual last name."

"Yes, sir," Kurt said, "but there are a lot of us. A lot of Uckers."

Brother Floom smiled, put a hand over his radio mike, and said something to Kurt.

Kurt nodded and, with a small wave to the crowd, walked to the side of the stage.

Brother Floom watched him leave. "A hand for Kurt Ucker and his band. God bless." He turned to the audience and then back to the side of the stage where Kurt had exited. He shook his head and laughed to himself before jumping right into his sermon. "You all know the story of the prodigal son. The son that returned. When I was a child, I never liked that story, never understood. It never seemed fair. I always took the side of the older brother. The obedient one. He had done every-thing right but got no reward. He always seemed to get the—" Brother Floom's voice dropped off as he turned once again to where Kurt had exited the stage. "Ucker. Such a strange name."

Gretchen rose from her seat and walked toward the doors.

"My apologies. Senior moment." The crowd laughed. "The older son seemed to get the . . . You all know that Jerry Reed song, 'She Got the Goldmine (I Got the Shaft)'? That's what it felt like."

Gretchen walked through the lobby and out into the parking lot. She called Axel. He picked up immediately.

"Hello. This is Fletcher."

"Did you see Kurt on stage?"

"He wasn't supposed to play that loud and fast."

"Not that. After?"

"No, Thrace was yelling at me. What happened?"

"He introduced himself to Floom with his real name."

"No." There was a pause. "The fairgrounds are supposed to sup-ply that. I'm going to have to find the invoice number for you. Can you hold on?" Axel's voice got more muted. "Excuse me a second, Mr. McCormick."

"What are we going to do?" Gretchen said.

"Okay, I got like one minute," Axel said. "How did Floom react?"

"It threw him. There seemed to be recognition."

"Of course there was. Nothing's going to happen during the ser-mon. Maybe he just thinks it's a relative. It doesn't impact you and me. Meet me in the parking lot right after the sermon."

"Should I get Mother down here?"

"Can't," Axel said. "She's Floom's daughter. He'd recognize her. I'll find Kurt. See what he's thinking. He was quiet at that meeting."

"How long are the sermons?"

"It's a short one tonight. Only two and a half hours."

People tried to exit the church parking lot all at once. Some people lingered, making it easy for Gretchen to get lost in the crowd. She milled around until Axel emerged from the church.

"What did Kurt say?" Gretchen asked. "What's going on with him?"

"I couldn't find him," Axel said. "He's not answering his phone."

"Oh crap. We have company."

Virginia ran out of the front of the church, looked around, and headed straight to Axel.

"Thank you again," Gretchen said with a southern accent. "I will look into the local opportunities to volunteer. God bless you."

"Sorry for interrupting," Virginia said, a frantic tone in her voice. "Fletcher, have you seen my father?"

"No, I've been out here giving information for potential volunteers."

"Nobody knows where he's at. He usually accompanies Thrace's men, but somehow they lost him. He seemed dazed on stage. I'm not sure where he could have gone. I don't know what to do. I'm really worried."

"My heavens," Gretchen said. "Can I help? Brother Floom is a treasure."

"He can't have gone far," Axel said. "He probably got confused and wandered off. I'll get the volunteers to start searching the area. We'll find him."

As if on cue, the screech of tires made them turn. The Money Bus tore around the corner of the church and bounced over a speed bump, scraping the front bumper on the asphalt, shooting up sparks. With the lot full of cars, both parked and trying to get out, the bus rammed through, creating a narrow passage, popping side mirrors off as it went.

Over the bus loudspeaker, the clear voice of Brother Floom resounded. "Set thine house in order. For thou shalt die and not live."

"Oh my God," Virginia said.

Gretchen didn't see the driver, but there was no doubt in her mind who was behind the wheel of the bus. It wasn't a coincidence that Kurt and Brother Floom were both missing. She didn't know why or what had made him do it, but Kurt was going to have a lot of explaining to do.

Gretchen had to give it to Kurt, though. He had the money. Hell, he had the whole damn bus.

CHAPTER 29

Shrapnel flew as the bus sideswiped a Toyota Camry. The screeching made Kurt's brain vibrate, but he didn't let up on the accelerator. He felt the clinging weight of a pickup as the bus dragged it through the parking lot. He wasn't trying to hit anything, but nobody understood how merging worked in Mississippi. Even hopping on the sidewalk wasn't enough to get through the bottleneck.

Daylight arrived after he pushed a sedan out of the way. He pulled out of the driveway and jumped onto the main road.

"I'm going to have to send a lot of apology notes," Kurt said.

He kept the gas pedal to the floor and picked up speed on the straightaway. The church wasn't in the city proper but a few miles out of town on the old highway. That gave him plenty of open road to really put some distance between himself and the church.

Brother Floom continued to preach into the microphone from the back of the bus. Kurt could only hear a muffled echo, the speakers outside.

Kurt flicked switch after switch, trying to turn off the PA. The airplane dashboard in front of him had so many buttons and toggles and switches, he was concerned that he might hit the ejector seat on accident. Instead, he hollered back to Brother Floom. "How you doing back there, sir? Sorry about the turbulence."

Brother Floom stopped his sermon. "You're not the regular driver. What city are we going to now?"

"Yazoo City, here we come."

"And what city were we just in?"

"McComb, Mississippi."

"It doesn't matter, does it?" Brother Floom dropped the microphone and let it dangle from the receiver. He reached into his pocket, found something, and put it in his mouth.

Kurt spotted a side road that looked promising, wide enough for the bus but remote enough that he probably wouldn't see another car. He slowed down and took the turn. Not slow enough. The bus buckled and edged toward tipping. Kurt adjusted and just made it. He had never been behind the wheel of something so big before. He thought it would handle like the van, but the back end felt like it was in another county.

Scrubby woods flew past, decent cover but not quite enough if the police broke out a helicopter. He took another turn—much slower—onto a narrower road that had last been repaired in 1958. Every time the bus hit one of the craterlike chuckholes, Kurt bounced a foot high in his seat. Branches kicked off the roof and side windows.

"I'm tired," Brother Floom said, stretching out on one of the padded seats.

Kurt glanced at the side mirror. Nobody followed. He had taken everyone by surprise. As the bus bounced down the rural Mississippi back road, Kurt simultaneously patted himself on the back and was horrified at the fact that he had stolen a bus. A bus full of money.

Opportunity and willingness. That's what Mother had taught him. The opportunity arose, and in that moment he was willing.

Kurt hadn't planned on stealing anything. While Pepe and Louder went to relax after the performance, Kurt found a quiet spot to sit, think, and eat candy.

The meeting with Mother had been a reminder of how dysfunctional his family was. They had spent most of their adult lives fractured from each other. Why should he expect anything different? He didn't even know if it was possible for them to stay together as a family, let alone as a functioning band of thieves.

It made him wonder what he wanted. When he had been living with Mom, he knew who he was. After her death, he spent his days attempting to be his authentic self, but more often he felt like he was pretending to be someone else. Someone he wasn't.

He had eaten five of Pepe's marijuana edibles before he realized they weren't the package of Haribo Gold-Bears he had snaked from the hospitality tent. Which explained some of the introspection. The last time he had gotten high had been in high school. That had ended with him sitting in his backyard in the rain, crying and eating leftover Frito pie from a Tupperware.

The packaging the edibles came in informed him that each edible contained two servings. Two times five equals ten. He had taken ten servings. It took everything inside him not to immediately have a freak-out. He felt himself slowly go crazy worrying that the drugs would drive him crazy.

At the peak of Kurt's buzz and the height of his paranoia, when he thought he might have everything under control, Brother Floom approached him and asked him to take a walk.

Kurt mumbled a few consonants, but without the vowels to help out, the sounds didn't quite form words. Without the ability to communicate clearly, he shrugged, took Brother Floom's hand, got to his feet, and strolled with him.

Once they walked inside the cordoned-off area where the buses were parked, the men that always surrounded Brother Floom stopped at the perimeter. Kurt concentrated on not appearing high. He started to wonder if he was blinking more than the normal amount of blinking. He stopped blinking, but then his eyes hurt.

"Let's talk in my quarters," Brother Floom said. As they were about to step into Floom's bus, he saw Virginia walk past the men. She hadn't seen them yet, but she headed right in their direction.

"She wants to talk to me," Brother Floom said. "She's angry. I can tell from her stride. It hasn't changed since our wedding day."

Kurt started to correct him, but Brother Floom pulled him in the opposite direction. At the Money Bus, Brother Floom knocked "Shave and a Haircut" on the door. Kurt made a mental note to face-palm later. The security system for the bus they had spent months figuring out how to break into was "Shave and a Haircut." It didn't matter how high Kurt was, he knew that was ridiculous.

The door opened. Brother Floom stepped inside, waving Kurt to follow.

"Wow," Kurt said. Because that's what you say when you see money piled everywhere and scattered on the ground. It looked like the offering bags had been dumped onto a table and someone was in the process of counting and organizing it. Kurt spotted personal checks and bills of all denominations. It was impossible to tell how much. It was easier to figure out mass than value. He figured about three Hefty bags.

That figure didn't include the money in the vault.

The entire back end of the bus was a giant safe. The door was open. Neat stacks of money sat inside. Lots of it.

"'Shave and a Haircut,'" Kurt said softly to himself.

"Give us the room, Jeremiah?" Brother Floom said.

Jeremiah didn't say a word. None of his business. Not his money. The pro that he was, he made one last note in the ledger in front of him, put his pencil behind his ear, and walked off the bus.

Kurt hadn't finished the process of staring at the money. It was that much money. In the presence of piles of money, it was impossible not to fantasize about the things that could be bought with it. No one needed a full-scale replica of Mjöllnir—more commonly referred to as Thor's hammer—but that didn't make Kurt want it any less. It would look good next to his replica Green Lantern Power Battery, even if it crossed universes.

"From the moment I first saw you," Brother Floom said. "Your face, it was familiar. But . . . I forget easily."

"We've never met, but I knew who you were."

"You knew me? How?"

"From the television."

"Of course," Brother Floom said.

"You knew my mother and father," Kurt said.

"Did I?"

"My father's name was Henry. He's dead."

"I'm sorry to hear that."

"He was your son."

"That can't be. I only have a daughter. Virginia."

"Not Brother Floom's child. Dolphus Ucker's child."

"Whose? I'm confused."

"You are Dolphus Ucker," Kurt said. "That's what we came in here to talk about."

"Is it?"

Someone pounded on the door. A female voice yelled from the other side. "Dad? Are you in there?"

"We have to go," Brother Floom said. "I'm frightened."

"What? Where?" Kurt said. "I have so many questions."

"Anywhere. She's going to put me away. In a home. In an asylum. I'm scared of where they'll leave me. Desert me. Don't let them put me somewhere. Help me."

Kurt felt sympathy for his plea. He was also very high. As Virginia continued to pound on the door, he thought about what he could do. He did his best to focus. Then he did the math, pluses and takeaways.

They wouldn't get this opportunity again. He was inside the bus. The bus was full of money. The keys were in the ignition. What was stopping him? And that, children, was how he ended up in a stolen church bus full of money in Swampwater Valley, Mississippi, with a televangelist napping in the back, who he was pretty sure was also high on Pepe's gummies, because they were no longer in his jacket pocket.

As Kurt drove down the back road, his phone vibrated in his pocket. It had been doing that quite a bit. A few people wanted to talk to him.

"Hey, Ax," Kurt said.

Two voices shouted back through the phone, Axel's slightly louder than Gretchen's. A lot of talking and words, overlapping and angry. Kurt held the phone away from his ear. He didn't catch sentences but got the gist. They wanted to know what in the hell he was doing stealing the damn bus, and oh Christ, don't tell me you kidnapped the preacher, too.

"The bus is full of money," Kurt said. "The safe is open. There's more money in it. It's a lot of money. All of it. Nobody followed me, and I'm on a back road somewhere. I got away clean with our money."

Silence followed. And then in a calm, measured tone, Axel said, "Where are you, Kurt?"

"No road signs out this far. I'm in the woods. I took a bunch of turns. Might run out of road. I'm going to find a spot to put the bus. You come to me."

"What about Brother Floom?" Axel said. "He's a witness."

"Not a reliable one. He might have gotten a little high."

Silence for a short while. Then Axel said, "I had a plan. My plan would've worked."

"Head south out of town. I'll send you the GPS when I find a spot."

"You spoiled my plan," Axel said.

"I knew you had some hidden badass in you," Gretchen said.

"Mother's on the other line. I have to take this." Kurt hung up on Axel. "Yello."

Until Kurt saw the cross, he wouldn't have pegged the building for a church. A visible waterline stained the side five feet high, where a decades-old flood had left its mark. One wall had collapsed, but the house of cards remained standing.

Kurt slowly drove the bus into the open end of the church, like it was a garage. It didn't fit all the way, the wheels unable to climb a stack of rafters from the collapsed roof.

While Brother Floom slept, Kurt shoveled the loose bills into every container he could find. The velvet collection pouches, garbage bags, a roller bag that had some clothes inside. He also found a couple of sets of accounting books and other paperwork that might prove useful. By the time he finally got it packed and in stacks outside, Axel, Gretchen, and Louder had shown up in the van.

"Hey, jerko," Louder said. "How could you have a demolition derby without me?"

"You shouldn't be here," Kurt said. "You could get arrested."

"They needed a ride. You know the rules."

"Only Skinrippers drive the Skinrippermobile," Kurt said. "Why didn't you bring the rental, Gretch? This van is not nondescript. It's descript."

"Stephanie took it when she left. Thanks a lot, Axel." Gretchen didn't hide the anger in her voice. "Besides, you said it was a lot of cash."

"It is," Kurt said, pointing at the stack he had made. "Everyone grab a sack or bag or coffee can."

"That's all money?" Louder asked, grabbing two Hefty bags and walking them to the van.

"Getting money has always been easy," Gretchen said. "Not getting caught is the trick."

"It's all rando cash," Axel said. "Small bills. Untraceable. They don't even know how much is here."

"Oh shit," Gretchen said. "Who's this?"

A PT Cruiser barreled down the dirt road, kicking up dust, and slid to a stop, blocking the van in.

"Act natural," Kurt said, holding a roller bag full of money.

"Are you kidding?" Gretchen said.

"What?" Kurt asked.

"Who the hell is that?" Axel asked.

Harry Cronin got out of the car, pointing a pistol in their direction. "Stop what you're doing, and put your hands where I can see them!"

"It's okay," Kurt said. "He's not going to arrest us."

"Hands where I can see them!" Cronin shouted again.

Everyone put their hands in the air, except Kurt. He picked up the stacks of accounting books and paperwork he had found. "Brother Floom is in the bus. I found accounting books. Some other stuff. That has to be what you were looking for."

"Why would I want that?"

"Because it's what you asked me to find. Maybe they are cheating on their taxes. I don't know. I held up my end."

"Churches don't pay taxes, kid," Cronin said. "That paperwork just means that someone is screwing someone else over. Maybe someone skimming and cooking the books to make it look legit. Taking money from the ministry for themselves."

"McCormick," Axel said. "I'd bet on it."

"We had a deal," Kurt said.

"What deal?" Gretchen said. "Who is this guy?"

"He's the FBI," Kurt said.

"Wait a minute," Axel said. "Is that the guy that chased us?"

"Mother knows all about it. We didn't want you to worry."

"Kid," Cronin said. "I hate to be the one to tell you, but I'm driving a PT Cruiser. Do you really think I'm FBI?"

The man's voice dropped two octaves lower and became very familiar. Kurt recognized the voice just as Mother got out of the back seat.

With all the dust, he hadn't seen her in the car. She held a pistol loose at her side.

"Mother?" Kurt said. "Uncle Fritzy?"

"That's Uncle Fritzy?" Gretchen asked.

"It ain't Wendell Willkie," Fritzy said. "The best disguise is a bad one. All you see is the disguise."

"Is this a test?" Kurt asked. "Are you testing us? Testing me?"

"You failed," Mother said. "I warned you that you couldn't trust me. I told you straight out. They're getting helicopters going, so I don't have time for a full villain speech. Fritzy, load the money into the car."

"We're family," Kurt said.

"Don't be stupid, Kurt," Axel said. "She's not really our aunt. She lied from the start."

"Oh no," Mother said. "I am your aunt. Henry was my brother. We're blood. That's true. Those other Uckers you met—they're your kin too. But we're not like a normal family. We're constantly screwing each other over."

"What about Dolphus—Brother Floom?" Kurt asked.

"He's some guy," Mother said. "Not your grandfather at all. I made the grandfather thing up on the fly. Once I figured out what was missing in your lives, what you needed, everything else was easy. It all came together."

"What?" Gretchen asked. "What do you think we need?"

Mother smiled but didn't answer.

"You made it all up!" Axel shouted. "And you accuse me of creating overcomplicated plans?"

"What about the whole pretending-to-be-an-FBI-agent thing?" Kurt said. "I don't get the function."

"Us either," Mother said. "A loose thread. No plan is perfect. We thought it was going to go somewhere, but it never panned out."

"I have so many questions," Axel said. "My brain is exploding."

"But unfortunately, no time for answers," Mother said. "Soon as the car is loaded, we're out of here."

Brother Floom exited the bus. He looked confused, walking directly into what was left of the abandoned church. He found a raised platform at the back, where a beam of light shined on him. "I hope you're ready for an evening of faith and fellowship. Praise the Lord." He launched into his sermon.

Fritzy pushed his back against the Hefty bags in the back. "Money takes up more space when it's all wadded up. It's going to fill the car." He got the hatchback closed and, with rope in one hand and a gas can in the other, walked to the group. "Don't get squirmy or it'll hurt."

"I thought only lazy thieves used guns," Axel said.

"I never said that," Mother said. "I use every tool in the toolbox."

"Are you going to set us on fire?" Gretchen asked.

"Of course not," Fritzy said. "We ain't bad people. Now hold out your arms." He bound her hands and continued the process of tying up all of them.

"Why go through all this trouble?" Kurt asked.

"It started out simple," Mother said. "Got away from itself. It was more improvisational jazz than a finished concerto. I needed you out of the house. That was it initially."

"We left when Mom gave everything away," Axel said. "That means the will is fake, of course."

"Mom didn't give the house to Brother Floom?" Gretchen asked.

"Who would do that?" Mother laughed. "Even if he was her father-in-law, that never made sense. People are so ready to believe things. You mentioned Floom's name at the funeral. I ran with it. A snipe hunt worked for my needs."

"The house is still ours?" Gretchen asked.

"It's not there anymore," Kurt said. "It's gone. She leveled it."

"Can you hurry up with those ropes, Fritzy? I'm going to end up making the whole villain speech."

"It would go faster if you helped," Fritzy said.

"Not with these knees," Mother said. "Look, kids. Your father hid a bunch of loot way back when. That stash is mine. I saw a chance to thoroughly search the house. Piece by piece. Now I know for sure it ain't there."

"You went through all this trouble to search our house?" Axel asked. "Couldn't you have bought us a European vacation or something?"

"I suppose I could have," Mother said, "but I didn't think of it. Admittedly, now that you mention it, that would have been considerably easier."

"What's stopping us from turning you in to the police?" Axel said.

"Turn who in? Someone named Mother Ucker? Your long-lost aunt that convinced you that Brother Tobin Floom was your grandfather who had bilked your mother out of your inheritance so you stole it back by going undercover as a Christian rock band only to be double-crossed? Good luck with that."

"They might believe us," Axel said. "They aren't going to believe we tied ourselves up. The money had to go somewhere." "The cops will think the money burned up with the bus," Mother said, nodding to the gas can. "They'll come up with whatever story makes it easiest for them to close the case. You are functional scapegoats."

"It would be easier to let us go."

"I like you, kids. I do, but you're out of your league. No hard feelings, though. This is business. It's a lot of money."

"You taught us that money was stupid and pointless," Kurt said.

"That's when you should've known I was lying."

CHAPTER 30

While the Money Bus burned, Brother Floom wandered the nearby forest, preaching to the wild mushrooms and woodland creatures. Black, acrid smoke rose through the trees.

Axel, Gretchen, Kurt, and Louder, their hands and legs tied, sat in a circle on the ground. Axel worked his hands back and forth, but it only made the ropes tighter.

"I'll bet you anything that Priscilla was in on this," Axel said. "Mother's inside man."

"Her name is Stephanie," Gretchen said, "and I don't see how her involvement makes sense. We walked right into this situation all on our own. Besides, she had an inside man. Isn't that right, Kurt?"

"I didn't tell you about Cronin," Kurt said, "because I thought I was protecting you."

"You still lied to us," Gretchen said.

"Fuck you!" Louder shouted. "You were using Kurt to sell your stolen comic books. That's right. He told me about that bullshit."

"This is a family matter," Axel said.

"No, it isn't," Louder said. "This is a people-who-are-tied-up matter. I'll say whatever the shit I want."

"She's my family," Kurt said. "More than you two for the last fifteen years."

"You want to go there?" Gretchen said.

"I don't want to go anywhere but home," Kurt said, "but that doesn't exist anymore."

"I told you we couldn't trust Mother," Axel said.

Gretchen laughed. "You're an idiot."

"Holy shit!" Axel yelled. "Wait a minute."

"What?" Gretchen said. "Did you get your hands free?"

"No," Axel said. "If Brother Floom isn't our grandfather and he's just some guy, that means I'm not related to Virginia. She's not my aunt."

"Who cares?" Gretchen asked. "I can't think of something I care less about."

"It changes things," Axel said.

"Did you?" Gretchen asked. "You didn't. Axel, that's incest. I don't believe in a lot of rules, but even that's over the foul line and in the seats for me."

"Who did Axel incest?" Kurt asked.

"It's not incest," Axel said, "because she's not my aunt. And no, we didn't do anything."

"But," Gretchen said, "you wanted to, which is kind of the same."

"That's not the way it was. I thought about it, yeah, but I didn't and I wasn't going to. Thoughts are only thoughts. You can think anything you want. She offered. I could've, but I didn't. And she isn't. And you don't."

"I get it," Gretchen said. "Now that the taboo is gone, it's lost its excitement."

"Shut up," Axel said.

"Hey, Uckers!" Louder shouted. "I'm just a special guest star, but do any of you geniuses have a plan to get us out of this? I, for one, don't want to get arrested or eaten by swamp creatures or whatever else could happen way out here in the sticks. If Axel wants to plow his great-aunt, that's fine with me."

"She's not my great-aunt. We're the same age."

"I. Don't. Care!" Louder yelled.

"I'm working on a strategy," Axel said. "That's why plans exist, instead of people driving buses into the country all willy-nilly."

"Yeah, Kurt," Gretchen said. "What is up with that? You could've given us a heads-up."

Brother Tobin Floom walked out of the forest. His rant had ended, and he stopped to marvel at the burning bus. The interior smoldered. It looked like it had mostly gone out.

"Mr. Brother Floom!" Axel shouted. "We're tied up. We need you to untie us."

Brother Floom walked to them, his eyes wild. "The Lord forgives you," he said, and walked back into the woods.

"Axel, remember how you accused Stephanie of being in bed with Mother Ucker?" Gretchen said.

"A horrific image," Axel said, "but I stand by that accusation."

"Because, as earlier stated, you're an idiot," Gretchen said, nodding toward the road. "Looks like I'm the only one that trusted the right person."

Stephanie took her time walking up the dirt drive. She kicked at a rock, making a game of it. When she reached them, she put her hands on her hips and smiled. "Hey, guys. How's it hangin'?"

"You didn't leave," Gretchen said. "I love you."

"Of course not," Stephanie said. "I forgot to give you your present." In a sweeping flourish, she opened a butterfly knife.

"Let me guess," Stephanie said. "Tons-of-Fun double-crossed you? Axel, you are terrible at this. You should've stuck to being a victim of crime. You were good at that. Play to your strengths."

"We haven't formally met," Louder said. "Pleased to meet you and whatnot, but are you going to untie us? That smoke is going to bring cops."

Stephanie sawed at the rope that held Gretchen. "When you're all free, head straight back to the church. Stay in character. Don't run. Don't panic. Everyone thinks the preacher took off with the bus on his lonesome. Nobody knows any of you are here. Where is the preacher?"

Gretchen got her hands free and pointed toward the forest. Brother Tobin Floom shouted into the air, something about heaven and hell and redemption and the end. It was pretty convincing.

Stephanie handed Gretchen the butterfly knife and pulled out her own. Gretchen worked on Louder's ropes while Stephanie freed Kurt.

"Play your parts," Stephanie said. "You should be fine. Even if he gains clarity, who's going to believe him?"

"We're leaving Brother Floom here?" Kurt said. "Is that ethical?"

"Ethical, shmethical," Gretchen said. "We'll call in an anonymous tip."

"This doesn't make us even," Axel said.

"You're welcome," Stephanie said.

A televangelist stealing a bus and taking it on a joyride garnered attention. Four different law enforcement agencies and a half dozen news outlets blocked the road to the church.

Kurt, Axel, and Louder got out of the van parked a few blocks from the church and walked back as nonchalantly as they could. Gretchen had left with Stephanie. No hugs or goodbyes. No plans to meet up and debrief.

The scene at the church was chaos. Car owners pointed at their damaged vehicles and yelled at police or church personnel. Dozens milled around, talking on their cell phones or taking pictures. Nobody gave the trio a second look. Kurt and Louder went to find Pepe to work on their alibi.

Axel spotted Virginia surrounded by men in suits. A police officer ran to the man talking to her. In a matter of seconds, Virginia was in a police car and a dozen cruisers were speeding away from the church. The news vans got the hint and followed close behind. Someone had eventually communicated the tip they had called in.

An hour later, a meeting was called for all tour personnel. It didn't take a genius to figure out what it was about. Thrace McCormick gave a short statement about Brother Floom and his health. He had been found in the woods, almost incoherent. As of that moment, the remainder of the tour was cancelled. No mention was made of travel arrangements or costs being provided to get home. It looked like Axel would have to catch a ride in Kurt's van.

They never found out what Brother Floom told the police, if anything. However, they weren't brought in for questioning, which was all that mattered. Not that Fletcher Christian could have been found.

They didn't get any money out of the deal, but they didn't get any jail time either. Axel chalked it up to a draw.

While Louder and Pepe bought groceries and gear for the long drive back, Axel and Kurt got their last taste of Waffle House.

"I'm sorry that I lied to you," Kurt said. "We're roommates and everything now. We need to be okay, or it's going to suck."

"We're okay," Axel said. "I don't know if me and Gretch ever will be."

"Give it time."

"We all screwed up in some way. I'm the big brother. I should've done better."

"I spent hours with Mother, and all she was interested in was the house, Dad's money. Fritzy taught me to drive a getaway car. How does that fit into the whole thing?"

"Not everything always makes sense," Axel said.

"Some of the other Uckers warned me about her," Kurt said. "I should have listened."

"There were plenty of red flags. We chose to ignore them."

"Some good came out of all this," Kurt said.

"You're going to silver line this?"

"Someone has to. You met Virginia."

"That's true."

"We also successfully robbed the church, even if the money was immediately robbed from us after."

"You're stretching there."

"The biggie is that Mother went to great lengths for whatever Dad left behind. His stash is a real thing and still out there."

"I hadn't thought of that," Axel said. "We could look for Dad's hidden loot."

"A mystery," Kurt said. "The game is afoot."

"Way to nerd it up."

"That's Sherlock Holmes. That's not nerdy. *Doctor Who* is nerdy. A Dormammu reference, über-nerdy. But Sherlock Holmes, that's a meat-and-potatoes reference."

"Not in Mississippi," Axel said.

"Stereotypes and caricatures don't make you right," Kurt said.

"Excuse me, sir," Axel said over his shoulder to a large man wearing overalls and a baseball cap sitting at the counter.

The man turned. "Yeah?"

"Can you help settle a bet? If I said 'The game is afoot,' what am I referencing?"

The man took off his baseball cap and ran his hand through his hair. "Sorry, chief. You got me."

Axel turned to Kurt and made a smug face. "That's okay. Thanks. We'll figure it out."

The man continued. "Everyone knows it from Sherlock Holmes, but it actually originates from Shakespeare's *Henry the Fourth*. But I surely can't remember if it's *Part One* or *Part Two*. Back to the wall and a gun to my head, I'd go with *Part One*, but I'm guessing on that. I reckon Google will know."

"Thanks," Axel said, turning back to a beaming Kurt. "Shut up, nerd."

Axel and Kurt arrived back at the house on Xanadu Lane. While they had been on the road, the house had been ransacked. They both rolled their eyes at the destruction and left it as it was. They dropped their bags in the anteroom—the word *foyer* was forbidden to say within the walls of the house.

"It's good to be home," Axel said. "Your home, too. You're not a guest. You live here. For as long as you want."

"Thanks, Ax," Kurt said. "I appreciate it." He gave Axel a hug and started walking up the stairs to his room. "Now I'm going to take a twenty-hour nap."

Axel went into the living room and plopped down on the couch. On Fletcher Christian's phone, he called Virginia but only got voice mail.

"Hi, Virginia. It's Fletcher. Calling to see how your father is doing. See how you are. It got pretty crazy, and I didn't want to be in the way. If you want to talk or there is anything I can do, let me know. When things settle, give me a call. I'll try you again in a few days. Bye. It's Fletcher. Bye."

Axel stared at the ceiling. He knew what he wanted. Now all he needed was a plan.

PART FOUR

CHAPTER 31

Mathilda Ucker stretched out on the deck chair and opened her third can of Tecate. Her boyfriend, Fred Kramer, worked the grill, poking at a couple of fat sirloins with a meat fork. He wore a hat and thick sunscreen to protect his hairless body.

Their small condo in Rosarito had been their safe haven for a decade. Nobody knew about it but them. The place needed some work and the waft of the sewage plant down the beach could get rank, but damn if life wasn't the right kind of easy. The sun, the ocean, good food, and cold beer.

"We made money," Fritzy said. "You can drink something better than that Mexican Budweiser."

"Money don't change how things taste. This is what I like. I'm always going to be regular falutin. You can take the girl out of the trailer park, et cetera. How those steaks looking?"

"Another minute. I want to get a good sear."

"Don't overcook them," Mother said. "Anything more than medium rare is a punishable offense. Besides, we didn't make that much money. I swear we took all the ones and burned all the twenties."

"We've earned a break, Matty. I got cruise brochures."

"You knew the score when you hitched your wagon to this ox."

"I'm talking a vacation, not retirement. Ten days. All you can eat and drink. Mexican Riviera."

"I love the work too much to retire," Mother said. "A big-time CEO makes ten million, he keeps working. A thief makes a few grand, and everyone thinks they run off to Mexico and that's it. Like thieves don't have ambition. It's insulting."

Fritzy brought the steaks over to the table, where a tortilla warmer and a bowl of salsa waited for him. He took the lid off a clay pot of beans, sending steam disappearing into the air.

"We did run off to Mexico," Fritzy said, "but I know what you're saying. Some days I miss driving."

"Robbery is better money than stunt driving," Mother said.

"And not nearly as dangerous," Fritzy said.

"You didn't need retirement. You needed a career change."

"Being with you is more than a career change. It's a mission behind enemy lines."

"It's not good to stop working. Especially at our age. Got to keep the mind active. Have a sense of purpose. Retiring is for people that hate their jobs, not passionate people. Imagine hating doing something for so long that all you can think of is the moment you can stop."

"You already got something planned, don't you?" Fritzy said.

"I got some ideas."

"Whatever we do next, I don't want to play your brother. I liked all the disguises. That was fun. But acting like we were brother and sister wasn't my thing. Don't even know why we did that."

"Playing up family was everything. We both had to be Uckers. Part of a loyal family. It's psychology." Mother cut into her steak and pulled the two halves apart. "You overcooked it. Not enough blood. I like blood."

Things hadn't played out as Mathilda Ucker had expected. Not even close. The whole thing had snowballed from a simple distraction to grand larceny very quickly. Not really a snowball—more of an avalanche. Every time she had been convinced that her niece and nephews couldn't make it more convoluted, they managed to weird it up. She liked their spirit, but she had never seen anyone who could take something as simple as stealing money and make it seem like performing brain surgery on bumper cars.

When word had made it to Mother that Bertha was dead, her plan was simple. If Mother could get them out of the house, she could make a thorough search. Henry had to have stashed his share somewhere close. Bertha hadn't spent a dime, as far as she could tell. It had to still be there.

As she was sitting in the back of the church and hearing about Bertha's obsessions with the televangelist Floom, a story built in her head. Three birds, one stone. All she needed was a fake will, and the grandkids would be blinded by revenge and opportunity. It would give them purpose, a focus away from their grief. In a way, she did a compassionate thing in duping them.

A little research and personal observation told her the girl was a thief, the younger boy was a citizen, and the older boy was on the fence. They had potential as a crew.

Revenge is a great motivator. Nothing better than a sense of justice or fairness to balance the scales. Stephanie Holm had wronged Axel. Brother Tobin Floom had supposedly wronged them all. Gretchen, of course, took no convincing. It was fascinating to see Kurt's process. His inner Ucker was deeply embedded, but the goodness that Bertha had shoved into him fought back. Nature versus nurture. Mother was surprised at how much she really liked the kid. Fritzy had definitely taken a shine to him. She held a certain pride that it ended up being Kurt who stole the preacher's money.

Compared to the loot Henry had stashed, the Floom money was a consolation prize. A good score, but a lot of work for the trouble.

Mother had run out of places to look for Henry's stash. She had been convinced that it was in the house. She knew Henry's movements between the last job and his death. Bertha could have hidden it or destroyed it. In which case it was gone forever. The only option left was to get a metal detector and wander the desert one square foot at a time. To her, that's what retirement looked like and why it was so awful.

She knew it was a risk to put revenge in their heads and then double-cross them. Axel never got his revenge on Stephanie. All three kids never got their revenge on Floom. Vengeance now sat dormant in their minds and hearts. That would put Mother in their crosshairs. They would eventually seek her out.

She wished them luck. They could look in all the places they had seen her, but she wouldn't be there. They had limited resources and even more limited skills. She was smarter, more experienced, and meaner.

Mother had lost count of the number of people looking for her: law enforcement, ex-boyfriends, former criminal associates, victims, and a slew of Uckers. So many people wanted revenge, money owed, or justice, but if she didn't want to be found, nobody could find her. In fact, she planned to go right back to work. A rolling stone and moss and all that jazz.

Even if they got lucky and somehow found her, what would they do? What could anyone do? She was Mother Ucker. And she didn't take any shit.

CHAPTER 32

Kurt and Louder were back on stage at Mugs and Quiches. Pepe had violated his probation by going to Mississippi, so he would remain a guest of the state of California for the remainder of the month. Pepe rolled with it. He claimed that the weed was better in jail and he found the yoga classes centering.

Louder worked her homemade washboard percussion. Kurt kept his eyes to the floor as he spoke into the microphone. "I wrote this last night. It doesn't have an ending yet."

Tricked, bamboozled, conned, duped,
Taken for a ride, and played for a fool.
Trust is a shell game with a cheat at the cards.
Hope is a liar that's heartless and cruel.

Maybe I'm a masochist, who knows?
With hope in the future and faith in the Lord.
For all of the bad and wrong in the world,
One act of kindness and I am restored.

Cheat me with lies.
Beat me, I rise.
No matter your guise.
Trick me, I rise.

Axel couldn't stop his foot from bouncing, not from the beat but from nervousness and excitement. Sitting next to Virginia, he watched her watch Kurt sing, then worried that he was watching her too much.

After the dust had settled with her father and the ministry, she had finally called him. It took them a few more weeks to coordinate their schedules—or rather, her schedule, as Axel's was wide open. They eventually arranged this date.

Axel had prepared six versions of what he was going to say, still debating the strengths of the two top contenders. If he was going to make something work between him and Virginia, he had to come clean. Well, not completely clean. He couldn't tell her the truth. Partial honesty would have to do. He had to present a better lie, one that would act as a transitional buffer that might eventually lead to the truth in the future.

Secrets were healthy in a relationship. He had read that somewhere.

Meeting her in front of the coffee shop, Axel went in for a hug. Virginia shifted her body at the last minute. He ended up bouncing against her shoulder. Not an auspicious beginning.

"Thanks for meeting me," Axel said. "How's your dad?"

"He's safe but not really him anymore. I see him as often as I can."

"I saw that Mervyn Whitlock has taken over the bulk of the ministry duties."

She nodded. "He idolized Dad. He'll lead it in the right direction. After the cops found Thrace's second set of accounting books, some housecleaning needed to be done. Mervyn is earnest, at least until he gets corrupted, too."

"I can't say I'm surprised about McCormick," Axel said, "but stealing from a church is so low."

"I was curious if I would see you again," she said.

"There are some things I want to talk to you about."

"Oh wow," Virginia said. "You have that serious voice people get when they have a secret that they've finally got the guts to reveal."

Axel laughed a fake laugh that sounded like a fake laugh. He turned and walked into the café without saying another word.

The rest of the date went well. Despite sitting through two bad poets, a woman singing an eighteen-minute song about menstrual cramps, and a comedian that ran off stage crying halfway through his set because no one was laughing, Virginia was a sport about the place. She appeared to enjoy her Thai chicken wrap.

Virginia nudged Axel. "You're a loyal supporter of these guys, aren't you?"

"Kurt and Louder are family," Axel said. "We've had some trust issues recently, but I still trust the two of them more than anyone on the planet."

"I wish I had that," Virginia said.

"You do," Axel said.

She could trust him. Except for the lies, of course.

What had come to be known as the "Mississippi Cataclysm" (also the name of an upcoming Skinripper tune) had taken a lot out of all of them. Gretchen was hell-bent on finding Mother and getting the money back and then some. Gretchen knew revenge. Axel had the scars from his teen years to prove it. The big, fat form that their defeat had taken gave her a target, but little direction.

When Axel had gotten back to San Diego, exhaustion and pessimism slowed down any enthusiasm for finding Mother and Fritzy. He had been kneecapped, nut-punched, and given an emotional wedgie too many times over the last few months. He had no energy for revenge. Sometimes it's better to stay on the ground than to take more of a beating. Mother had a comeuppance coming, but he would let Gretchen pursue it.

Axel had called it, licked his wounds, cut his losses, stopped throwing good money after bad, quit using cliché phrases, and gotten on with his life. He was resigned to the fact that they weren't ever going to find Mother.

Gretchen called him a week after they got back. It was the first time they had spoken since Mississippi. Her voice was cold and businesslike. "I'm going to brace Joe Vee tomorrow. You want in?"

Axel knew it was a fool's errand, but those were the first words Gretchen had said to him since Mississippi. He couldn't say no.

They didn't say a word to each other on the drive to Warm Springs. When they walked into Joe Vee's office, he looked resigned, having to had known that this day would come.

"I knew this day would come," Joe Vee said, confirming Axel's assumption.

"Who hired you to give us the fake will?" Axel said.

"You know," Joe Vee said. "The big-boned lady. She had the document all prepped. Your mother's signature. Told me to bring it to you, give the spiel, make it sound legit. I got paid. Was promised a bonus, but I'm thinking I ain't ever seeing that dough."

"Every way this was going to play out would eventually lead us back to you," Axel said. "How did you think you were going to get away with it?"

"I live in the moment," Joe Vee said.

"What does that even mean?" Gretchen said.

"Got a problem with the little ponies," Joe Vee said. "I owed money to violent people. I couldn't be worried about today when I was concerned about living through that day. I could deal with you now or them then. You don't look like you cut off fingers."

"Try me," Gretchen said.

"Between me, you, and this desk, I'm not very good at lawyering," Joe Vee said. "I don't advertise it, but I got disbarred three years ago. Nobody checks way out here in Bumfuck."

"Because of you," Axel said, "we don't have a house. She leveled it. You're going to jail."

"You don't want to call the police or nothing," Joe Vee said. "I'm practically family."

"You are not family," Gretchen said. "This asshole is family." She pointed at Axel. "And I resist punching him in the stomach every time I look at him."

"I knew your old man, from back when I was less legit," Joe Vee said.

"How could you possibly be less legit?" Axel said.

"I might or might not have fenced some things or not things for your old man. I liked him."

"Not enough to not screw over his kids," Axel said. "You're going to tell us everything we need to know about our dad, our mom, and the fat lady. And any other damn thing. How do you contact her?"

"I leave a one-star review for the book *Lamentation* by Joe Clifford on Amazon, complaining about the profanity. She calls. We set something up. If I do it now, though, she'll know what's what. She ain't stupid. You want to make contact, you'll have to wait for her to call me."

"You gave us a forged document," Axel said. "You don't have a law license. That's a lot of crimes. You could go to prison."

"I thought I was going to make a bunch of money."

"That's your defense?" Gretchen asked.

"What would be the point of calling the cops? You do that, you're going to have to start calling the police on everyone you know that commits crimes."

"That's what people do," Axel said.

"Where is that going to lead? To anarchy."

229

"You really are an awful lawyer," Gretchen said.

"I provide a service to the less than legally inclined. I could maybe provide that service for you. Let's call it store credit. I can't help you if I'm in prison."

"You can give us any money Mother paid you," Axel said.

"Your brother is talking crazy now," Joe Vee said. "That money is long spent."

Walking out of the lawyer's office in Warm Springs, Axel couldn't decide if Joe Vee was a moron or a savant. But he had been right—there was no upside in calling the police, but potential in him owing them a favor.

"I'm going to find Mother Ucker," Gretchen said on the drive back to San Diego. "I'm going to find her and—well, I don't know what I'm going to do when I do, but I'm going to find her."

"It's time to move on, Gretch," Axel said. "I'd love revenge, but we got nowhere to look. What's the point?"

"I don't care what you do," Gretchen said. "I don't need your help. I don't want it."

"Is this where we're going to leave things between us?" Axel asked.

"It's where it's at," Gretchen said. "It's where you put it."

They drove the remainder of the trip back from Warm Springs in silence. Neither of them even moved to turn on the radio. The silence made more sense.

"How'd you like it?" Kurt asked, joining Axel and Virginia at the table after his set.

"I'm going to grab some drinks," Louder said. "You losers want anything?"

"You sounded great together," Axel said. "I'm good, Louder. Virginia?"

"No, thank you," Virginia said.

Louder walked to the counter.

"A different venue for you," Virginia said. "Different music. I like it."

"Yeah, about that," Axel said. "I wasn't exactly straight with your father or the ministry or you. When I said Kurt is family, I was being literal. Kurt is my brother. He doesn't really play Christian music. He threw INRI together in three days."

"That explains a lot of things," Virginia said. "Ballsy move. What do I care? You tried to get your brother a sweet gig. You ended up pissing off Thrace. Bonus for me."

"Heard he might do time," Axel said.

"I'll believe it when I see it," Virginia said.

"We wrote all the songs on the drive from California to Louisiana," Kurt said. "I think we could have figured it out with more time. Like a full week."

Virginia turned to Axel. "Is that the big secret you wanted to tell me? That you hired your brother? It doesn't seem like a big deal."

"Not exactly," Axel said. "My name isn't Fletcher Christian. And I didn't have a come-to-God moment in a parking lot. I'm barely a Christian."

"Uh-huh," she said, waiting for the kicker.

"You sure you want to do this?" Kurt asked.

"I have to," Axel said. "It's time she knew."

"I meant with me sitting here," Kurt said. "It's making me feel awkward, very third wheelish."

"You're part of it," Axel said. "My name is Axel Ucker, and I'm an undercover reporter doing research for an exposé on televangelists, faith healers, and the evangelical moment, with an emphasis on the prosperity gospel. I pretended to be someone else to get close and see the inner workings of the organization."

"Oh," Kurt said. "That."

"I feel like I'm Jamie Lee Curtis in the movie *Perfect*," Virginia said.

"Excellent reference," Kurt said.

"I'm not going to publish the article," Axel said. "And it's not just because of what happened with your father. It's because—yeah, you were right, Kurt. Can we have a moment?"

"No problem," Kurt said. "I'll check on Louder."

"I'm sorry I lied," Axel said when Kurt left. "When I told you the first lie, I didn't know you. I didn't know I'd have to keep it up. Keep telling lies. I wanted to tell you."

"I appreciate you coming clean," Virginia said, "but I'm not sure why it matters now. What do you want from me?"

"A second chance."

"Did we have a first chance?" Virginia stood up.

"I thought we did."

"We didn't," Virginia said. "I thought we might maybe become friends, but we were mostly just coworkers. I'm done, though. Nothing is going to happen. You told me you lied to me right now. I don't really know you. This isn't a romantic comedy. There's not a lot of depth to our relationship."

"But there could be. We have a connection."

"That's not a thing," Virginia said. "This is going to sound mean—and I'm sorry for that—but just because you want something, because you think you deserve it or it's your destiny, that doesn't mean you get to have it. That stuff's all made up in your brain. Like love at first sight."

"I believe in love at first sight."

"Of course you do," Virginia said. "How many times has that worked out for you? Is there anything more shallow?"

"It's romantic," Axel said.

"It really isn't. It's empty." Virginia set a twenty-dollar bill on the table. "That's for Kurt. I'm going to pick up one of his CDs on the way out."

Axel watched Virginia walk out of the café. When she was out of view, he picked up a newspaper to give him something to do. So he didn't look so alone. So he didn't feel so alone. No matter how alone he was.

Kurt and Louder sat down across from him.

"That did not look like it went according to plan," Louder said. "Bummer, dude. Do you own 'In Your Eyes' on cassette?"

"Too soon." Kurt gave Louder a shove. "Her loss, Ax."

"Thanks, guys," Axel said.

"I just heard a thing," Kurt said. "Did you know that goats pee on their own heads to make themselves attractive to lady goats? The lady goats dig it."

"What?" Axel said, putting down the newspaper. "Why would you tell me that?"

"I don't know. It was interesting. The barista told me, so I'm ninety percent sure it's true. He looked like one of those guys who knows a lot about goats."

"I can't believe she dumped me," Axel said.

"I didn't know you two were dating," Louder said. "Quit shoving me, K."

"I plan everything in my life," Axel said. "In detail. All the stuff that doesn't matter. And the important things, a relationship, family, all that stuff, I just—holy shitballs." Axel snatched the newspaper from the table and reread the front page.

"What is it?" Kurt asked. "Is there a sale at Penney's?"

Axel was too busy reading. Reading about some robberies. The robberies of three nail salons. Robberies he had planned. Robberies pulled off mostly according to those plans. Plans only Mother and Fritzy had seen. And criticized, which was even more insulting now, considering that the robberies had been successful.

CHAPTER 33

Axel might have given up, but Gretchen had no quit in her. She also had a ton of free time, which made not quitting considerably easier. Rather than sit at home and contemplate her next major life choice, she sat in a car for twelve hours a day and contemplated the emptiness of the building in front of her.

Growing up in the middle of nowhere might have sucked. But if boredom and monotony had taught Gretchen anything, it was patience. She could outwait anyone.

The downside of stakeouts was the potential for weight gain. Gretchen had put on six pounds in the last couple of weeks, five of which felt like were in her ankles. She got out of the car and stretched every half hour, but she was hesitant to let her guard down for too long. She chose to remain immobile, with her binoculars trained on the abandoned German restaurant.

It wasn't just the lack of exercise. The taco truck down the block was insanely good. Chorizo and egg in the morning, carnitas at lunch, and *lengua* in the evening were not recommended by four out of five doctors. Maybe if she claimed paleo or Atkins, she could fool her body into thinking it was healthy rather than gout-inducing.

A part of her knew it was pointless, something to keep her distracted until Stephanie got back from her trip to Esalen—some exclusive Tony Rogers retreat. Gretchen had wanted to watch her in action, but the invite list was only for gold-dragon members, whatever that meant. Besides, it cost $5,000. Big fish, expensive pond.

Her phone rang. Axel. Her finger floated over decline, but she chose to accept the call.

"What?" Gretchen asked.

"I got something," Axel said.

"Chlamydia?" Gretchen said. "Never mind. That would mean that you had sex."

"Not likely," Axel said. "It's about Mother."

"I thought you had admitted defeat."

"I know you hate me," Axel said, "but I know where Mother is going to be."

"I don't hate you," Gretchen said. "You were a dick to someone I care about. You never apologized."

"Okay, I'm sorry."

"Not only was that insincere, but I'm not the one you need to apologize to."

"Can we do this later? Where are you at?"

"Later is never, but that's what I've grown to expect," Gretchen said. "I'm staking out the German restaurant."

"Criminals returning to the scene of the crime is a myth," Axel said. "Is it okay if I meet you there?"

"Do you really got a lead on Mother?"

"I do."

"Then I suppose I can call a temporary moratorium on the shunning," Gretchen said. "Bring a salad."

An hour later, Axel climbed into Gretchen's car, brushing the garbage off the passenger seat onto the floor.

"Where's my salad?" Gretchen asked.

"What?"

"I asked you to bring me a salad."

"I thought that was slang or something."

"Slang for what? What could that be slang for?"

"I don't know. That's why I didn't bring anything."

"Slang still means things. Why didn't you ask me what I meant?"

"I didn't want to be unhip," Axel said. "If you're hungry, there's a taco truck down the street."

"You're an idiot."

"Idiot like a fox," Axel said. "Take a look at this."

He handed Gretchen the newspaper he had found in the café.

Gretchen read a few paragraphs. "City council proposes tax hike for new stadium? What about it?"

"Above that. The nail salon robberies. Mother committed those."

"I doubt it," Gretchen said, skimming the article. "These are strong arm jobs. She's a con woman."

"Mother pulled a gun on us," Axel said. "She's not one kind of criminal. Said it herself. She sees opportunity and acts on it."

"One suspect had a handlebar mustache and a Bob Ross afro," Gretchen said.

"Fritzy," Axel said. "He must have left the monocle at home."

"You're reaching."

"No, I'm not. I wrote these. Planned them. For fun or whatever. Mother read them."

"You still do that?" Gretchen asked. "Write plans for crimes that you aren't going to do?"

"I find it soothing," Axel said. "Mother told me they wouldn't work, but that was obviously bull. I knew they were good. Great, actually."

"Are these the exact plans?" Gretchen said.

"Some changes were made. More like lateral moves than improvements. They're my targets. Doesn't matter. The important thing is that my plan worked."

"That's not important at all," Gretchen said.

"It is to me."

"It doesn't sound like this was exactly your plan. Could be a coincidence."

"I showed Mother and Fritzy two plans. The nail salons and a downtown marijuana-dispensary slash armored-truck gig. She has my notebook, but I know that plan by heart. It only works on a Friday. I don't know which Friday, but she'll attempt it. And I know her first move."

"What's that?"

"Past is prologue," Axel said. "If our experience is any indication, she'll sucker someone else to take the fall. And I know who those suckers will be."

Gretchen didn't bother to go home. She was already prepped for a stakeout.

She parked in front of Stanley Pruitt's house in Santee. The armored car driver lived in a stucco ranch-style house with an immaculate lawn and a garden gnome painted to look like Donald Trump. One of those Southern California buildings that could be found on every block and was built out of ugly in one of three colors: sun-blinding white, three-day-old salmon, and suicide beige.

As the senior Jackson Armored employee, Stanley would be the point of contact for Mother. According to Axel's old research, Stanley lived in a loveless marriage, received boat catalogs in the mail but didn't own a boat, and was desperate for a last shot at happiness. The kind of happiness that money could buy.

While Gretchen watched Stanley, Axel had eyes on partner Steven McCrary's place. Axel only gave a one-in-six chance that Mother would approach Steven, but best to cover their bases.

The Mississippi Cataclysm had been a wake-up call for Gretchen. Most people would have taken the close call to rethink their life of crime. She doubled down. There would always be more money to steal. If crime was a stir-fry, money was the rice. It was always part of the dish. The bigger disappointment was the betrayal. Like crossing the finish line of a marathon and then having your coach punch you in the face. She wanted to believe in honor among thieves.

Gretchen watched Stanley putter around the yard and get some edging done on his day off. She had always considered a well-maintained lawn to be the product of an uncreative life.

When her phone rang, she picked up immediately. She didn't even care if it was a sales call. She was ready for some human interaction.

"Hey, you," Stephanie said on the other end.

"I didn't think they allowed phones at Hippie Camp."

"They don't. I told my aspiration facilitator that it was an emergency. If anyone asks, you're my Aunt Honig and your goiter is acting up."

"It's great to hear your voice."

"You, too. What are you up to?"

"Watching an armored car driver put his gardening equipment into a garage."

"Just say you're watching porn. I don't need an elaborate euphemism."

"We have a potential lead on Mother," Gretchen said.

"If you need my help, let me know," Stephanie said. "My heart really isn't in this retreat. I only went because the deposit was nonrefundable."

Stanley closed his garage door and got in his mid-1990s Pontiac Grand Am.

"Sorry, Steph," Gretchen said. "Got to go. My guy is on the move."

"Toggle between a two-car and four-car distance. Mind your gaps."

"You say the most romantic things," Gretchen said. "Love you."

"Love you, too."

The Pontiac drove the six blocks to the on-ramp and jumped onto the freeway. Gretchen didn't take any of her girlfriend's advice and stayed right on his tail. She didn't want to lose him. Once on the freeway, she passed the Pontiac and got in front of him. She would have plenty of time to get over if the car looked like it was going to exit. The Pontiac Grand Am was not known for its quick handling. It was mostly known for its hideousness.

"Stanley's on the move," Gretchen said as soon as Axel answered the phone.

"Steven's getting in his car now," Axel said. "This could be it."

Gretchen hung up to concentrate on Stanley's car. When she passed the exit for National City, she had a good guess where Stanley was headed.

"Kurty," Gretchen said into her phone. "How quick can you get down to Tijuana?"

"If I leave now, I can be at the border in about a half hour."

"Head south. I'll text you the location when I get to wherever I'm going."

"Stay out of trouble until I get there," Kurt said. "I got your back, sis."

"I know you do."

CHAPTER 34

Kurt parked four blocks from the address. He was worried that Mother might spot the van, until he noticed that it was one of four on that block with a giant Jesus-esque illustration painted on the side. For those keeping score, there were also two Virgin Marys to balance out the Jesuses.

"I'm still not completely comfortable with you here, L," Kurt said to Louder, who sat in the passenger seat. "Something bad could happen."

Louder adjusted her blond wig and checked her dark eye shadow in the rearview mirror. "I'm inconspicuous as shit. They'll spot you in a heartbeat."

"Mother's met you," Kurt said. "Pepe would have been better. He's Mexican. We're in Mexico."

"Pepe can't remember his middle name," Louder said. "I'm in a badass disguise. Don't make me dick-punch you. I'm doing this."

"I want you to be careful," Kurt said. "And it's Carlos. Pepe's middle name is Carlos."

"I know. He's the one that doesn't."

They got out of the van and walked toward Gretchen's car. When they passed a group of four young toughs hanging out in the doorway of a closed tire shop, Kurt felt his spine straighten. They didn't say anything, but their eyes tracked Kurt and Louder unblinkingly.

Louder took Kurt's hand. She had never done that before. At first, he assumed that it was because of the Mexican dudes, but then he couldn't figure out why she was still holding his hand a block later. It felt nice. He wasn't complaining.

He felt like he should say something. Before he could think of what to say, he spotted Gretchen's car. Kurt released his hand from Louder's to point at it. They climbed into the back seat.

"Thanks for coming, Louder," Gretchen said.

"Beats any form of entertainment in Warm Springs," Louder said. "Kurt asks for help, I help."

Gretchen turned in the seat and gave Kurt a wink and moved her eyebrows up and down quickly.

"Are you making a Kurt-and-Louder-sitting-in-a-tree face?" Louder asked.

"You two make a cute couple."

"We're not a—" Kurt looked at Louder.

"We do make a cute couple," Louder said.

"We do?"

"We do."

"Are we?"

Louder smiled and took his hand. "We are."

Kurt opened his mouth to say something but only held it open. He turned to Louder, then away, and back to her.

"Are you okay?" Louder said. "Are you having a stroke?"

"I'm good," Kurt said, the smile on his face broadening until it hurt.

"That was a-door-a-bull," Gretchen said.

"Shut up," Kurt and Louder said together, and then "Jinx, ten, you owe me a Coke. Double jinx."

"Cuteness aside," Gretchen said. "Stanley's been in that bar for the better part of a half hour. Steven showed up a few minutes ago. Axel should be around here somewhere."

"You want me to go in there and observe and report?" Louder said.

"We need eyes and ears," Gretchen said. "Mother's only seen you a few times. The disguise should work."

Louder checked herself in the mirror one last time. "What could happen? This is Mexico. The crime rate is extremely low. Nobody ever gets in trouble in Mexico."

"Uh," Kurt said.

"Who are you going to believe, me or the fake news? What does your guy look like?"

"I'll send a photo to your phone," Gretchen said. "Fritzy's the one you'll have to look out for. He likes disguises."

"I'll look for the guy in a disguise," Louder said.

"The place looks like a local hangout," Kurt said. "Not exactly Señor Frog's. A single white woman might be suspicious."

"If anyone asks, I'll tell them I'm meeting my heroin dealer."

"I can't tell when you're joking."

"That's what makes me so good at this." Louder gave Kurt a hard kiss on the mouth, got out of the car, waited for the traffic to thin, crossed the street, and entered the bar.

"You guys have been dating for twenty years," Gretchen said. "Congratulations on finding out. I can't believe that was your first kiss."

"That wasn't our first kiss," Kurt said. They had kissed on a dare when they were both ten years old. He had also eaten cat food and put his finger in a mousetrap on subsequent dares, but the kiss still counted. It got boring in the desert.

"She's—I can't do this." Gretchen grabbed the back of her neck. "Get in the front seat. My neck is getting jacked."

Kurt opened the back door and got out of the car to switch seats. He immediately dropped to his hands and knees. A block away Mother approached the bar. No sign of Fritzy.

From the ducked position, Kurt opened the passenger door and awkwardly slid inside, attempting to keep his head below dashboard level.

"What are you doing?" Gretchen asked.

"Mother," Kurt said, pointing. "Mother."

Gretchen dropped her seat back to get out of sight. "Got to give it to Axel. Every once in a while, he gets something right."

A few minutes later, Louder texted Kurt.

Louder: Bar way cool. Skeevy. Filthy. Jukebox mostly Mex, but Iron Maiden ACDC too \m/ \m/

Kurt: What about the guys? Mother? What they doing?

L: Mother doing all the talking!!! Operation Dumbo Drop is a go!

K: Can you hear them?

L: Bits. I'll get closer.

K: Be careful.

L: Careful is my middle

K: Louder, you okay? You there?

K: Louder!

K: If you don't text back in the next minute, I'm coming in there.

K: That's it. I'm coming in.

L: name.

K: What happened?

L: Guy hit me.

K: Someone hit you?!?!?!

L: Sorry. Hit ON me. Told him I had boyfriend. LOL

K: Was he good looking?

L: He told me was nominated for Pushcart Prize. What that?

K: And Mother?

L: Talk, talk, talk.

L: Steven looks like Billy Graham. Real swole.

K: Rev. Billy Graham not swole.

L: Superstar Billy Graham, dummy. He's yoked.

L: Talking money. Numbers. It's a vegetation.

K: Vegetation?

L: Negotiation. @#$%! autocorrect!

L: Got plan. No texts for bit. Don't panic.

After five minutes of radio silence, Kurt became concerned. After another five minutes, he got in and out of the car at least three times, panicking. He never took more than two steps before climbing back in the Honda. When Axel jumped in the back seat, Kurt may or may not have sharted.

"You scared the crap out of me," Kurt said, not meaning to be so literal.

"Sorry," Axel said. "How's she doing? Anything good?"

"Haven't heard from her in ten minutes," Kurt said.

"He's extra worried," Gretchen said. "They're boyfriend/girlfriend now." She followed her statement with some grade-school kissy sounds.

"Good for you, Kurt," Axel said.

"Mother pulled a gun on us in Mississippi," Kurt said. "We got no idea what she's capable of."

"Different situation," Axel said. "No reason to come to this meeting armed. Louder will be fine."

"I've only had a girlfriend for about a half hour. Is worrying a big part of it?"

"Most of it," Gretchen and Axel said at the same time. They both laughed, then caught themselves, trying to stay angry.

"Mother," Kurt said.

Mother walked out of the bar, smiling. When the two security guards left the bar, they talked for a little bit, high-fived, and headed toward their cars.

"Where's Louder?" Kurt said. "Where is she? I don't see her. Where is she?"

"Easy, Kurty," Gretchen said.

"I'm going in."

"There she is."

Across the street Louder fast-walked out of the bar. She made a beeline toward the car, got in the back seat with Axel, and ducked. A Mexican man walked out the door and looked around, his hands on his hips.

"What's going on?" Kurt asked.

"We should go," Louder said. "Can we go?"

"Did that guy threaten you or something?" Kurt asked.

"Nothing like that," Louder said. "I promised to blow him, then welshed on the offer. Nobody likes an Indian giver that gyps a guy out of fellatio."

"Did you purposely mean to offend three different ethnic groups?" Kurt asked. "Impressive, but that's not what an Indian giver is. If you had been an Indian giver, that would mean that you gave him mouth sex but then asked for it back."

"Mouth sex?" Louder said. "We need to go."

"That dude looks pissed," Gretchen said.

The man kicked an empty beer can, adjusted his crotch, and walked back into the bar.

"Is anyone going to ask me why I promised to blow the bartender?" Louder asked.

"It was about to come up," Kurt said. "Don't think I'd let that go."

"I had the horndog put my phone behind the bar where the meeting was going down," Louder said. "I recorded their entire conversation."

CHAPTER 35

Axel, Gretchen, and Kurt sat on the edge of the hole that used to be their home. Home, hole. A one-letter slide to the left in the alphabet. More of a crater than a hole, to be accurate. The concrete foundation had been jackhammered into rubble. The lawn had been disced thoroughly. Nothing but dirt and bits.

"All this work," Gretchen said. "All this trouble. Do you really think there's hidden money or jewels?"

"Mother thought so," Axel said. "Enough to do all this."

"It sure as shit ain't here," Gretchen said.

"It's just money," Kurt said. "Who chooses money over family?"

"More people than you'd think," Gretchen said.

"Whatever happens tomorrow," Kurt said, "can that be the end of it? Can we go back to being us? A family? Or you know, whatever we are?"

"Some of that depends on Gretchen," Axel said.

"And you," Gretchen said, "but I'll do it for you, Kurty."

"This is an opportunity," Kurt said. "It brought us together. We can keep it going. Be in each other's lives. Not just do this one thing and then go our separate ways and not see each other for years."

"If you're saying you want to pull more jobs," Gretchen said, "you know I'm all over that."

"Despite all the felonies I've committed, I'm not a criminal," Kurt said. "I was thinking normal family things."

"Like what?" Axel asked. "Go to Walley World together?"

"Lunch," Kurt said. "A weekly lunch. Don't make a big deal out of it."

"I'm in," Axel said, turning to Gretchen. "I want to try."

"As long as it's Mexican food," Gretchen said.

"I have one condition," Kurt said.

"Now who's making a big deal out of it?" Gretchen said.

"It sounds like you don't trust us," Axel said.

"I don't have to," Kurt said. "That's what conditions are for. If one of us doesn't show up, that person owes the other two a hundred bucks each."

"The hell," Gretchen said. "What if I go on vacation? What if I'm sick? What if I just don't want to?"

"Vacation from your not-job?" Kurt said. "Sorry, I don't make the rules."

"You literally made the rules as we were talking," Gretchen said.

"You miss a lunch, you pay a bunch," Kurt said. "It rhymes, which makes it law."

"I like a challenge. I'm in," Axel said, standing up and patting the dirt off his pants.

"Ax's hundos are going to feel good in my pocket," Gretchen said. "Taco money."

The three of them walked back to their cars. Without their house, the road looked unfamiliar.

"You all know what to do?" Axel asked. "What the plan is, right? Do we need to go over it again?"

"The fifteenth time did the trick," Gretchen said. "I was fuzzy about some things the fourteenth time, but I'm good now."

"Hilarious," Axel said. "You'll thank me later for my thoroughness."

Stephanie and Louder approached from town on foot. They both ate Dilly Bars, the evening heat forcing them to work at them to avoid ice cream dripping down their arms. Stephanie tossed a bag to Axel. He opened it. More Dilly Bars. He handed everyone one. Now that was how you planned some larceny in style.

"Give me enough Dilly Bars," Axel said, "and I might one day forgive you."

"Standing around your cars," Stephanie said, "planning to heist somebody else's heist. You three look like you're auditioning for a *Fast and the Furious* movie."

"Dibs on being Vin Diesel," Kurt said.

"More like a no-budget Albanian remake," Louder said, "where everyone drives a fifteen-year-old Tercel and they're trying to steal a prized milk cow."

"*The Relatively Fleet of Foot and the Slightly Perturbed,*" Kurt said.

Stephanie walked to Gretchen and gave her a hip bump. Louder gave Kurt a big squeeze in the middle. Axel stood completely still with no one next to him.

"So much has changed," Kurt said. "You found Stephanie. Me and Louder—oh yeah. Rats. Sorry, Ax. That probably stings. What with what happened with Virginia and all."

"Yeah, Kurt," Axel said. "It does."

"I feel bad that you don't have a date for the heist," Gretchen said.

"Still time to run an ad on Craigslist," Stephanie said.

"I'm going to be single for a while," Axel said. "I have some things to think about romance-wise. Axel needs to work on Axel."

"Is part of that process talking about yourself in the third person?" Gretchen asked.

"Axel thought Axel would try it out," Axel said. "Axel now realizes that Axel sounds like a douchebag."

"You should go to Esalen," Stephanie said. "It's like being inside a TED Talk. But with hot springs and nudity. There's a workshop called 'Romance 2.0: A Soul Initiation' that would be great for you."

"I don't know if you're joking," Axel said. "If you aren't, send me the info."

"Bring it in," Kurt said, stepping into the empty space between them. Axel and Gretchen joined him, and the three of them held one another for a long moment. Stephanie and Louder looked at each other, shook their heads, and stayed back.

"The last time we held each other like this was when Mom died," Kurt said.

"Then this one is for Dad," Gretchen said. "Let's take back what got took."

"And then some," Axel said.

"See you all when it's over," Kurt said.

The Little Grass Shack hadn't changed in the months since Axel had last seen it. A nondescript facade with a green neon cross above the door and the word "Cannabis" frosted in big, loopy letters on the window, a small marijuana leaf dotting the *i*.

Across the street, Axel dropped more change in the meter and got back into the car he had boosted from the Del Mar racetrack lot that morning. The last thing he needed was a meter maid to run the plates. With his luck, the stolen car had fifteen unpaid parking tickets on it.

Gretchen and Kurt were in position. While Mother might have made alterations to his original plan, Axel was confident that the basic concept would be maintained. He had made them go over the most probable variations enough times to create contingencies. He had tried to think of everything but knew he couldn't have.

Because the armored truck had a GPS signal broadcasting back to the security company's headquarters, it limited any thief's options. If the car deviated from the assigned route or spent too long in one location, it could raise concerns. Which was why Stanley and Steven were so crucial to the plan. They gave Mother considerably more latitude.

The duo had never been on time and often made unnecessary stops. It had become their normal. They weren't just facilitating the robbery, but they had unknowingly established necessary inconsistencies through their incompetence, too.

"The hipsters are heading to the haberdasher," Kurt's voice barked from the long-range walkie-talkie they had dug out of storage. The ones they had played with as desert kids. "Repeat. The hygienically challenged are on the road to Burning Man. Over."

"We don't need elaborate codes," Axel replied.

"Where's the fun in that?" Kurt said. "Moving to the second location."

Axel waited. His heart rate doubled, and his hair itched. Not his scalp, his hair. Nerves were strange things.

Two minutes later, the armored car pulled to the curb. If Axel had any doubt that the heist was happening today, it had vanished the moment he saw Stanley and Steven. They had gone from loose slack to wire taut, visibly nervous and sweating through their shirts. Stanley's head darted in every direction, and he did a full John Belushi 360 pirouette on the sidewalk. Steven moved self-consciously, his arms swinging in strange time to his legs, as if he had recently relearned how to walk.

Axel dipped low in the rental car, then popped back up, realizing how suspicious an action that was. He might as well have had a newspaper with two eyeholes cut out of it. They didn't know him. Mother didn't know he was there. He started the car and drove a block ahead, keeping an eye on the armored car in his rearview. Stanley and Steven came out with the cash a few minutes later. Heavy canvas bags, as usual. They stowed them and got back into the armored car. It was the most efficient Axel had ever seen them.

The armored car drove past him. He waited a count of fifteen and pulled into traffic. He wasn't following a yellow cab in New York. It was the only armored car on the road. He could easily keep a distance.

Besides, he knew where the truck was headed. He knew their route by heart. He wasn't tailing them as much as monitoring for deviation.

Hitting a red light, Axel stopped and waited. His nerves had settled. A glance at the empty passenger seat made him jealous that both Kurt and Gretchen had a Bonnie to their Clyde, or a Bonnie to Gretchen's Bonnie, or a Thelma to her Louise, or whatever.

A car pulled up next to him. Mother Ucker sat in the driver's seat of a black SUV. She hadn't looked over, her eyes on the armored car, as well. Axel faced the other way, pretending to fiddle with his stereo.

"Can't risk it," Axel said to himself. He took a right turn on the red. He grabbed his walkie. "Mother is here. Black Ford Explorer. About a half minute behind the car. Be extra careful. She sees any of us, we're blown."

"We should have worn disguises," Kurt said.

"Don't worry," Gretchen said. "I'm wearing a Michelle Pfeiffer Catwoman costume. She'll never recognize me."

"Why do I bother?" Axel said.

"Jokes don't change things," Kurt said. "Just because we make a funny doesn't mean we don't take a thing seriously."

Axel didn't see Mother's SUV when he reached Johnnie's Diner. To be on the safe side, he stayed two blocks back and found some cover behind a camper that people were obviously living inside. It was that kind of neighborhood, mostly industrial with no pedestrian traffic. No prying eyes. Mostly trucks and motor homes on the street. Lots of trash on the sidewalk.

He couldn't see it, but the armored truck would be in the diner's small parking lot, in the back and not visible from the street. This stop was usually quick. Johnnie didn't like to waste time.

Johnnie's Diner was a legendary greasy spoon that had been there for fifty-three years with the same owner-operator, Johnnie Correia.

Axel had never eaten at Johnnie's, but even he knew Johnnie's reputation. His regulars were treated like royalty. Yelpers, tie wearers, and tourists didn't get nearly the same quality of service. Newcomers thought Johnnie's orneriness was an act. It wasn't. He loved their money just slightly more than he hated them, so he took it while insulting them. He threw people out on a regular basis for small infractions to his unspoken and ever-changing rules.

Johnnie's Diner only accepted cash. In a write-up in the *San Diego Union*, Johnnie had said that he would never take credit cards, because "those rat bastards are nothing more than usurers. The Bible is clear about moneylenders being scum that take advantage of people. Hellbound sons of bitches all."

The breakfast-and-lunch-only restaurant had daily lines out the door, which meant there was a lot of cash at the end of the day. That amount of money had tempted plenty of thieves in the past. Not so much anymore. Johnnie's used to get robbed a lot—or rather, people tried to rob it. Johnnie had shot no fewer than five would-be stickup men in the last decade. While that kind of record never stopped an ambitious person from trying, it had definitely reduced the number of attempts.

Johnnie had used the armored car service for the last two years. He claimed he got tired of shooting people, but he was not willing to admit that his trigger finger may have been slower at eighty-one than it had been at twenty-eight.

Mother had no way of knowing that Johnnie was currently sitting inside his restaurant all alone with a loaded shotgun across his lap. At the end of the day, he sent his employees away to grab beers before they did a final cleanup. He sat alone with Betsy Mae, waiting for Stanley and Steven to arrive.

Axel hadn't included any information about the diner in his plan, as he had dismissed the diner as a possible extraction location. Without that small chunk of intel about Johnnie's brand of Western justice, the off-street parking lot would be too much of a temptation for Mother to resist. This is where Mother would deviate from Axel's plan. Axel would put money on it. And Gretchen was going to have a bird's-eye view of the action.

"What do you see?" Axel said into the walkie.

"Everything," Gretchen said. "It's on like Donkey Kong."

CHAPTER 36

After the family meeting in Warm Springs, Gretchen and Stephanie had driven to Gretchen's place to gear up. Leaving her hometown for what she expected to be the last time, Gretchen only felt hopefulness, not loss. Warm Springs was the past. Stephanie and a lucrative life of crime represented her future. Whenever a door closed, there was always a window that could be jimmied open.

Gretchen was nervous. Not about her part in the plan, but about her apartment, vis-à-vis her housecleaning abilities. She had put Stephanie off from coming over to her place for months. Before she opened the door, she turned to Stephanie. "This is kind of a big deal for me. I don't usually let anyone over."

"I'm pretty protective of my space, too," Stephanie said.

"It's not that. I'm a slob. My place is a disaster."

Stephanie laughed. "I don't care."

"You say that now," Gretchen said. "The weird thing about being a messy person is that there's something wrong with our brains. We don't care enough to clean, but we're still self-conscious about it. Lose-lose."

"I'm sure it's not that bad."

"I've been so busy with the whole—"

"Shut up and open the door."

Gretchen let Stephanie into her studio apartment. One big room with a kitchen nook to one side and a bathroom to the other. A futon sat on the floor. Only a few other furnishings: a TV on a milk crate, a weight bench, and a folding table with two folding chairs. Clothes, DVDs, comic books, a laptop, and free weights lay scattered on various surfaces. Locks, doorknobs, and a small safe sat with a number of tools on the dining room table. Everything smelled like WD-40.

"Were you born in a barn?" Stephanie said.

"I thought you didn't—"

"A joke," Stephanie said. "Let's get the stuff we need and go. Whatever's growing in that pizza box might attack at any moment."

"I told you I was self-conscious."

"Sorry," Stephanie said. "I'm done with the jokes."

Gretchen tossed some clothes aside and found a big duffel bag. "Why are you doing this? Helping me and my family?"

"It's what people do for people they care about."

"I know that you care about me and blah, blah, blah, but I mean specifically tonight. This is a one-person job with all the glamour of taking a late afternoon dump in a carnival porta potty."

"The poetry that comes out of your mouth."

"It's a nothing gig," Gretchen said. "I'm recon."

"That's why I'm coming," Stephanie said. "This job is more dangerous than any of you seem to think. All crimes are. People don't like when you take their stuff. Mother wouldn't still be around if she wasn't ruthless. You've seen only a fraction of what she's capable of. Trust me on that. I'm going to be there to protect you."

"What makes you think I need protecting?"

"The state of this room, for one thing."

Gretchen parked in the darkness between two streetlights three blocks from Johnnie's Diner. The industrial neighborhood showed only glimpses of life, mostly in the loading docks of the warehouse down the street. Panel trucks and semis drove past every five minutes. The flashing blue light of a TV shined in one of the campers.

"It looks dead enough," Gretchen said.

A cat walked out of an alley, stopped in the street, licked its genitals, and continued on its way.

"And you said nothing interesting would happen," Stephanie said. "Dinner and a show."

"Let's go," Gretchen said, reaching for the door handle. But Stephanie grabbed her arm. She pointed out the window at an approaching figure in a hoodie.

They waited for the graffiti artist to tag the rolling door of the linen supply company next to Johnnie's and move on down the street.

"Does that say 'Quinoa'?" Stephanie said.

"Sadly, it does."

Gretchen and Stephanie got out of the car, grabbed their gear from the back seat, and, keeping to the shadows, walked toward Johnnie's.

The narrow driveway that led to the small parking lot was in complete darkness. A dumpster and stacks of flattened cardboard boxes sat against the diner.

Gretchen climbed onto the dumpster, got a foot on top of a window frame, and pushed up enough to get a hand on the edge of the roof. She did a pull-up and rocked until she got her leg over the edge.

"Not exactly *Mission: Impossible*, is it?" Stephanie said.

"You can hum the theme if you want to make it more dramatic," Gretchen said.

Stephanie tossed the two duffel bags onto the dumpster. Gretchen dropped down a rope ladder. Stephanie climbed onto the dumpster, handed the bags up to Gretchen, and in less than a minute, both of them were on the roof of Johnnie's Diner.

The roof was flat, with a small amount of water pooling in one corner. A two-foot wall ran along the entire roof edge—an aesthetic choice, as it served no discernible function. There was no access to the interior from the roof, but they had a good view of the neighborhood and, more specifically, the parking lot.

Stephanie unzipped one of the bags and pulled out a blanket and a bottle of wine. "Find a spot with the least amount of birdshit."

"Wine?" Gretchen said. "Which one of us isn't taking this seriously enough?"

"Wine makes it more serious," Stephanie said. "The chocolate and brie are in the other bag."

The produce trucks woke Gretchen up at four thirty in the morning. Still dark. Gretchen stared up at the night sky and counted the stars. In the distance, men shouted at each other in Spanish. Gretchen turned and watched Stephanie sleep. She pictured the two of them traveling through Europe, stealing jewels from heiresses' bedrooms and running elaborate schemes on people with titles, bilking dukes and earls—maybe even the duke of Earl—out of priceless artworks and treasures.

"Are you staring at me?" Stephanie whispered, her eyes still closed.

"You scare me sometimes," Gretchen said. "Coffee?"

Stephanie opened her eyes and nodded.

Gretchen reached into the bag nearest her and found the thermos. She poured coffee into two plastic mugs. "How'd you sleep?"

"This isn't my first roof snooze," Stephanie said. "I can sleep anywhere. Other than the gravel pattern that is embedded into half my body, I'm good."

"What do you want to do while we wait?"

Stephanie bobbed her eyebrows up and down.

"We would have to be really quiet."

"Yeah, that's not going to happen," Stephanie said. "I brought backgammon."

Criminal activity was similar to Space Mountain at Disneyland. It consisted of long periods of waiting and boredom and nothing and anticipation and stress, followed by three minutes of intense activity, eventually ending in excitement, unease, and a bit of a letdown. Until it started all over again with more waiting and anticipation and stress.

When the armored truck pulled into the parking lot, Gretchen had been drifting off. On her stomach at the edge of the roof, she had a perfect bird's-eye view of the lot from a narrow gap between the roof wall and an old sign. Stephanie took a post on the other side of the roof. Between them they had a 360-degree view.

She hadn't tracked the cars that went in and out of the lot during business hours, but when the armored truck arrived, the parking lot wasn't empty. A silver car that could have been about ten different makes and models—one of those cars that looked like every other car— sat alone in the corner. If pressed, Gretchen would have guessed a mid-1990s Saturn. Johnnie was the only person left in the place, but it wasn't his car. Johnnie drove the hugest-ass car ever made, a 1977 Oldsmobile Delta 88 that would never have made the turn into the driveway. You'd have to airlift that boat in. He always parked right in front.

"What do you see?" Axel's voice in her single earbud made her jump.

"Everything," Gretchen said softly. "It's on like Donkey Kong."

Stanley and Steven got out of the armored car, business as usual. The most noticeable difference from their regular routine was that Fritzy got out of the silver car. He must have been sitting in that car for hours.

Without a word between them, Stanley left the back door open. He and Steven walked into Johnnie's while Uncle Fritzy loaded bag after bag into the trunk of his car.

"That's it?" Gretchen said. "That's the plan?"

Gretchen wrote down the plate number of Fritzy's car and texted it and the description to Axel and Kurt. The car was the money. If they lost that car, they would never see the money or Mother ever again.

After two minutes, Stanley and Steven exited the back of the diner. Not even pretending anymore, they dumped the money from Johnnie's directly into the trunk of Fritzy's car.

"Oh shit," Gretchen said. "This is bad."

Johnnie—who must have developed a sixth sense when it came to robberies—stepped out the back door with his shotgun at his shoulder. "You sons of bitches. You dirty sons of bitches. That money is my money."

Stanley lifted his hands straight in the air. Steven lifted his as high as his overdeveloped lats would allow.

"They have my family hostage," Stanley said. "Please go along with it, or they'll kill my children."

Which was an interesting thing to say, Gretchen thought, considering that Stanley didn't have any children.

"You over there!" Johnnie shouted toward Fritzy. "Move away from the car where I can see you."

Fritzy slowly moved out from behind the open trunk. When he cleared the car, the pistol in his hand became visible. He raised it, but not quickly enough.

Johnnie fired his shotgun, knocking Fritzy backward onto the ground.

"Gretchen!" Axel yelled in her ear. "Gretchen! What was that? What's happening?"

"He shot Fritzy."

"Who? What?"

"Johnnie effing Correia," Gretchen said. "Oh shit. Don't do it."

Steven reached for his sidearm and drew like an Old West gunfighter. He fired, missing by at least fifteen feet. The shot ricocheted off a drum of used cooking oil.

"The hell," Johnnie said, firing at Steven and knocking him to the ground.

"Holy hell! What is happening back there?" Axel shouted into Gretchen's ear.

"Quit yelling in my ear," Gretchen said.

Stanley had no interest in trying anything. Crying into his hands, he sat on the ground with his back to the truck.

Fritzy got to his feet. The side of his face was pocked with dark spots, and his arm was soaked red with blood. He crawled into the driver's side of the car and started it.

"Fritzy's up," Gretchen said. "He's in the car. Get ready. He's going to be in a hurry. The money's in the car."

"Cops are going to be on this," Axel said. "This is all screwed."

"Just follow the damn car," Gretchen said.

"On it," Axel said. "Get off that roof. You can't be there."

The silver whatever-kind-of-car backed out, just missing the approaching Johnnie, who loaded more shells into his shotgun. Scraping against the wall of the neighboring warehouse, the car drove out of the driveway, the trunk still open, the money bags fully visible.

Gretchen ran to where Stephanie watched the action, and made it in time to see the car fishtail onto the street. Johnnie took one last shot as the car drove away, blowing a hole in one of the money bags, sending bills flying into the air. Johnnie watched the car for a second, spit on the ground, and walked back to the diner.

"I hope I'm that cool when I'm eighty-one," Gretchen said.

"You Uckers know how to party," Stephanie said.

"Time to make like a horse cock and hit the road," Gretchen said.

"It's your classiness that I'm most drawn to."

"Classy as fuck."

CHAPTER 37

The silver Saturn crossed the intersection in front of Kurt. He counted slowly in his head just like Fritzy had taught him. He let his foot off the brake, and the car idled forward. He braked abruptly.

"Hey," Louder said, both hands on the dashboard to stop her forward momentum.

The Saturn had stopped. The driver's side door swung open. Fritzy hobbled out, one hand holding his bloody shoulder. His face looked like it had caught on fire and someone had tried to put it out with a fork. Using the car for balance, he stumbled to the open trunk, slammed it shut, picked a few loose bills off the ground, shoved them into his pockets, and got back in the car.

"He's a mess," Kurt said. "Should we forget the plan and help him?"

The Saturn drove away slowly.

"As long as he's driving," Louder said, "he's not dead."

"That's cold," Kurt said.

"You going to go?"

"Patience, grasshopper."

"He ain't looking around," Louder said. "You see him? His eyes were zombied out."

"If he sees me, I don't know if I have the skills to stay on him. He taught me."

"The student has become the teacher," Louder said. "You got skills, K. Mad skills."

Kurt smiled and pulled out onto the empty street. They were the only two cars on that stretch of road, but Kurt stayed seventy-five yards back. When Fritzy turned onto the main road out of view, Kurt closed the gap.

"We're on Fritzy," Louder said into the walkie. "He's heading west."

"Stay on him," Axel said. "That car is the money."

"Saw it," Louder said. "Trunk looked full."

"Tell Ax I need him or Gretch here now," Kurt said. "We need to tag team."

Louder relayed the message.

Gretchen's voice came over the walkie. "Steph and me, we're on our way. Three, four minutes depending."

"I'm staying back," Axel said. "Mother is somewhere close. I want to find her. If you absolutely need me, I'm there. But otherwise . . ."

The Saturn took the next turn really wide, showing a loss of control. One of those one-handed turns you make when you're holding a cup of coffee and have your phone in the crook of your neck. Fritzy's injury was affecting his usual precision.

"He turned onto Hilltop, then headed south," Louder said into the walkie. "Drive toward Chula Vista. If he changes course, I'll let you know."

"Got it," Gretchen replied.

Kurt turned onto Hilltop. Fritzy's car drove two blocks ahead, weaving out of its lane, correcting too much, and darting into the other lane.

"I'm worried about him," Kurt said. "It looked like a lot of blood."

"He pulled a gun on us in Mississippi," Louder said. "Don't forget that."

"That doesn't mean he's a bad guy. He's a tough old dude, but not invulnerable. Hope he makes it easy. Pulls over. We can get the money and call an ambulance. I don't want him to die or nothing."

"Whoa," Louder said.

The Saturn drifted across two lanes, forcing a panel van to slam on the brakes. The van rode its horn. Fritzy's window rolled down. The old man's bloody arm held a middle finger aloft.

"Tough all right," Louder said. "Got to give him that."

The Saturn accelerated through a yellow light, forcing Kurt to stop at the red. No longer attempting to be inconspicuous, the car didn't slow down when it crossed the intersection.

"Bullspit," Kurt said. "Either he saw us or thinks he's close to passing out."

The wait for the green light was excruciating. Kurt idled into the crosswalk. The moment the light turned green, Kurt gunned it. The Saturn was no longer in sight. They were almost a half minute behind—an eternity in car tailing. Making matters worse, Kurt got boxed in between two trucks.

"Monkey flunker," Kurt said, swerving into the oncoming lane and passing the truck to the sound of horns from every car in a one-block radius.

"Whoa, whoa, whoa," Louder said, pumping a nonexistent brake on the floor of the passenger side.

"I got it," Kurt said, sliding back into the lane and accelerating up the street.

"I can't believe you'll pull into oncoming traffic but you won't swear."

"The Bible doesn't say anything about pulling into oncoming traffic."

"You're going to get hit."

"By a car, or by you?"

"Both."

"You see him?" Kurt said.

Louder lowered her window and scoonched herself onto the window frame. Kurt reflexively grabbed her calf and held on to it. After fifteen seconds, she shifted back into her seat.

"He's still up ahead," Louder said. "About six blocks. It's him. Unless there's another really drunk guy driving a similar car."

Without any abrupt motion, Kurt eased through traffic, passing cars on the right and left. The moment he had the Saturn back in sight, Fritzy took a hard left, forcing oncoming traffic to skid to a stop. Taking the turn too wide, the Saturn bounced off a parked car. The car alarm blared as Fritzy continued on his way.

Kurt waited for a gap in the oncoming traffic and then took the turn. On the dead end street, there were no cars on the road. None of the parked cars were silver or Saturns. With no visible outlet, Fritzy had to have pulled into one of the buildings. Kurt parked, leaving the engine running.

Louder reported the street address into the walkie.

"Still five minutes at least," Gretchen said. "Traffic. Some cop activity."

Louder set the walkie down. "What do you want to do?"

Kurt opened his door. "Let's poke our heads in some windows."

"Should one of us stay in the car?" Louder said.

"Probably," Kurt said, "but I'm worried about Fritzy. He's hurt bad. Let's see what we can see."

"You're the criminal mastermind," Louder said. "I'll take this side of the street. You take that one."

Kurt wiped grime from a window and squinted through the smeared glass. Streaks of sun lit parts of the tap-and-die facility inside, but there were more shadows than light. It didn't appear that anything had moved in the space for a century.

The sounds coming from the neighboring building indicated that it was a working factory. The blacked-out windows gave him nothing, but there was nothing suspicious about the modest sign over the door that read: "Silicone Zone: Rubber Molding. Since 1979."

The door opened and Kurt jumped. Out walked a man with a loupe in one eye inspecting a large rubber penis. He walked to a patch of sunlight, not even noticing Kurt. Focused on quality control, he ran his finger over a latex vein.

Louder whistled behind him and waved Kurt across the street while she pointed at the building in front of her. She made other hand gestures that made no sense to him.

Kurt shrugged and took three steps toward her, but she only looked at a nearby window and immediately waved to him to get back.

"What is—?" Kurt said, but he was interrupted by the garage door next to her opening and an International Scout roaring out of the building and jumping the curb near Kurt.

The dildo inspector hit the deck and protectively clutched the rubber wang like a small baby.

As the Scout turned onto the road, Kurt and Fritzy made eye contact with each other for a moment. Fritzy gave him a wink and a finger gun. Kurt checked on the man on the ground.

"Are you okay?"

"I'm fine," the man said. "And thankfully so is the prototype."

"K!" Louder shouted, running back to the car.

"He saw me," Kurt said, reaching the car at the same time as Louder.

"No more Mr. Nice Guy," Louder said. "You're going to have to knock his ass off the road."

"Buckle up."

Kurt made a two-point turn in time to see Fritzy turn onto the street back in the direction they had come. A second later, Gretchen and Stephanie appeared at the same intersection.

Kurt tossed the walkie-talkie into Louder's lap as he passed Gretchen. "Tell her what's going on."

"Fritzy saw Kurt," Louder said. "That was him in the Scout you just passed. We're going to nail his ass."

"Go, go, go," Gretchen said. "Right behind you. Don't lose him."

"I don't plan to." Kurt turned onto the road. He fishtailed and corrected, only a couple blocks behind Fritzy. Fritzy's driving hadn't gotten any less erratic. He was swerving and overadjusting all over the road. Blood loss was not conducive to concentration or reaction time.

Kurt heard sirens somewhere. It was hard to tell which direction they were coming from. It's not like the situation wasn't already urgent. He did his best to ignore the sirens and focus on the Scout.

Fritzy took a left and slid onto the sidewalk, missing a fire hydrant by inches. When Kurt caught up, he saw the Scout making a quick right. Kurt knew Fritzy's tactics. He was attempting a Dixie Shuffle, but Kurt wouldn't bite.

Kurt gunned it and made the next turn. His car slammed directly into the back end of the Scout. Kurt jerked forward, his neck burning immediately. With a yelp, Louder slid under her seat belt and onto the floorboard.

Fritzy had fooled him. It wasn't a Dixie Shuffle. It was a Rusty Sheriff's Badge. The Scout took off again but stopped at the end of the block. No steam from the radiator. Kurt rolled forward a little. The car didn't appear damaged.

"You okay?" Kurt asked.

"I'm all tangled," Louder said, fighting the seat belt to get back into a sitting position. "What's going on?"

"I don't know," Kurt said.

The car door opened, and Fritzy got out. He leaned against the car and held a pistol loosely in one hand. The blood on his bad arm had dried at the edges but still gleamed wet toward the shoulder.

"Dang," Louder said. "Did we have a plan for when we caught up to him?"

Kurt rolled the car forward, stopping twenty yards away from Fritzy. He turned off the engine.

"What stupid thing are you going to do?" Louder said.

"I'm going to talk to him," Kurt said.

"He's got a gun."

"I'm not a threat." Kurt got out of the car but stayed behind the open door.

"You're hurt!" Kurt yelled to Fritzy. "You need to go to a hospital."

"This? It's nothing," Fritzy said. "Scattergun swiss cheesed me. Hurts like road rash. How's my face look?"

"One of your eyebrows fell off."

"That happens a lot." Fritzy felt his face where the missing eyebrow should have been. He peeled off the other one and let it fall to the ground. "Some good driving back there, kid."

"I had a good teacher."

Fritzy smiled. "People would now refer to this situation as a Latinx standoff."

"Very PC of you."

"You taught me a few things, too," Fritzy said. "I got nothing against Mexicans. In character, I threw around casual racisms. Makes people think I'm dumb. Makes them underestimate me. A good position to be in."

"I never underestimated you," Kurt said.

"So here we are," Fritzy said.

The screech of tires made Fritzy raise the gun and Kurt turn. Gretchen's car tore around the corner and came to a stop behind Kurt's.

"The gang's all here," Fritzy said, lowering the gun again.

Gretchen and Stephanie got out and joined Kurt. Louder got out of the car and joined them, as well. Kurt gave her a look.

"What?" Louder said. "I'm not going to be the only one waiting in the car."

Fritzy leaned on the top of the door for balance. "There may be four of you, but three of you are ladies and I got a gun."

"You aren't going to shoot any of us," Kurt said. "You wouldn't shoot family."

"Hate to break it to you," Fritzy said, "but I'm not your family. Not your father's brother. I'm your aunt's boyfriend. Hooked up with her a couple years back. We've been running some rackets together."

There was a long silence. Fritzy looked away. Only for a moment. It wasn't much, but it held meaning. Maybe regret and maybe guilt.

"It don't matter," Fritzy said, tossing the gun into the Scout and walking away. "She's done with me. Should have seen it. I was always eventually going to take the fall for something."

"What?" Kurt said. "What are you talking about?"

Fritzy tripped, tried to gain his balance on the wall of a building, but he let his body slide to the ground. He sat there.

Kurt and Gretchen ran to him.

"Things have been rocky," Fritzy said. "I wanted to retire. She wants to keep at this shit. Makes me deadweight. I wouldn't be surprised if she tipped off the diner guy."

"She wouldn't do that," Kurt said. "I'm sure she loves you."

"You got a good heart, kid, but you're dumb as shit." Fritzy laughed and fell over onto his side, unconscious. Kurt felt for a pulse. It was faint, but the old man was still kicking.

"Call an ambulance," Kurt said.

"I'm on it," Louder said, punching the number into her phone.

Stephanie popped the back hatch of the Scout. "Uh, guys. Come here. Right now."

Kurt and Gretchen rushed to the back of the car. They stared at the empty vehicle. Well, not completely empty. There was a spare tire, a jack, and a gas can. But no money—that was for sure.

CHAPTER 38

An International Scout coming from the other direction blew past Axel. He caught sight of Fritzy behind the wheel. Ten seconds later, Kurt's car followed, and then Gretchen's.

Any subtlety to the operation had been abandoned. A car chase drew attention. The police would be a problem soon. If they didn't catch Fritzy in the next two minutes, they would need to abort. Not that it mattered. Axel knew that Fritzy didn't have the money.

If he had learned anything about how Mother operated, the money wouldn't be with Fritzy. Mother buffered herself from risk. Fritzy was her new patsy. While Kurt and Gretchen did their job, Axel would do his.

He headed to the location of the building where Fritzy had swapped vehicles, where he expected to find the money. And Mother.

She was the perfect candidate to transport the stolen money. She wouldn't fit any description involving the crime. She looked like the opposite of an armored car thief. She hadn't been at the scene. She wasn't driving erratically. She looked guilty of eating too much chocolate pie, not stealing thousands of dollars.

He turned down the chatter of the walkie-talkie—Louder and Gretchen shouting street names to each other.

What had Mother said? Opportunity and willingness. Were those really the only two things that separated a criminal from a citizen—identifying the opportunity and possessing the willingness to execute?

Mother had double-crossed them in Mississippi, but they had created the opportunity for her. She had warned them not to trust her, but they chose to ignore her. Instead, they had given her the benefit of the doubt that they had never gotten themselves. It stung. Just because a person warned you they were going to kick you in the balls didn't mean it hurt less.

Axel parked across the street from the address. On the sidewalk, a man holding an enormous dildo smoked a cigarette with a shaking hand. Axel gave him a head nod. The man smiled.

Crossing the street, Axel reached into his pocket like he was digging for his keys. He pulled his lockpicks and casually opened the warehouse door.

"Hey!" the man shouted.

Axel turned around, smiling even wider.

"Are you the owner?" the man said.

Axel shook his head. "No. I just work here."

"Do you know someone that drives a big, older SUV?"

"Yeah," Axel said. "Probably Fritzy."

"If you see him, do me a big favor and tell him he's a shit eater that eats shit. He's going to kill someone the way he drives."

"Shit eater. Eats shit. Got it," Axel said, entering the building and closing the door behind him.

The expansive space had the faint smell of motor oil. Large machinery lined one wall, its function a mystery to Axel. The center of the large room was mostly empty, with scattered tables and smaller equipment. In the far corner was a car that someone had sloppily tried to cover with a tarp. One bloodstained corner of the tarp had slid off the hood of the silver Saturn.

Not knowing if he was alone, Axel stayed along the perimeter. He made his way to the car slowly. Hearing a noise, he stopped and closed his eyes. The air in the room felt dead and still. A hum came in from the street, as did dull, fart-like noises from the rubber molding factory.

Axel opened his eyes and continued his slow creep. He reached the car and pulled off the tarp. Small holes pockmarked the side panel. A smear of blood ran down the door. The driver's side seat was soaked dark.

His lockpicks were getting more mileage than they had in years. He popped the trunk. The canvas sacks from the armored car filled it, one of them ripped open and exposing its contents. If he had to estimate the amount, Axel would calculate that it was a bunch. A bunch of money.

Axel whistled, because not whistling would have been wrong. He texted Gretchen and Kurt, told them to forget Fritzy and come there. He looked around the room, eventually spotting a big wheeled trash can, the kind you rolled to the curb on garbage day. Not bothering to empty the layer of trash at the bottom, he transferred the money from the trunk into the can.

When he was done, he tilted the trash can and rolled it toward the exit, only to see Mother blocking his path.

"Where're you going with my money?" Mother stepped toward him.

"You robbed my robbery," Axel said. "I'm robbing your robbery."

"I admire your moxie."

"A plagiarized robbery, by the way," Axel said. "You used my plan."

"I rescind my admiration of your moxie," Mother said. "It may have been your target, but the plan was garbage. All paste and glitter. Too many moving parts. A great opportunity, but you assed up the execution. I simplified it and reduced the risk."

"Your plan was way more risky."

"I meant the risk to myself." Mother smiled. "There's a point one reaches in life when you no longer do any heavy lifting. Stanley and Steven were underused in your scenario."

"And Fritzy."

"Friendly fire."

"No different from what you did to us in Mississippi."

"If something works, you don't futz with it."

"How did you convince Stanley and Steven that they wouldn't be implicated when it was over?"

"I didn't have to. They're idiots. They were focused on how much money they would make. They never thought that far."

"I'm assuming you're armed," Axel said.

Mother nodded. "I'm surprised you're not. Fool me once, you know?"

"I don't like guns. Not since Dad."

"So long as we're on the same page, it'll stay in the purse."

"There wasn't any good reason to double-cross us in Mississippi. It was free money for you."

"I saw an opportunity to make more," Mother said. "Have I answered all your questions? Because it's time for you to wheel that garbage can out to my car. And to show you there are no hard feelings, I'll give you—let's say—two random bags as your cut. You can share with your brother and sister or keep it for yourself. I don't care. Think of it as a 'story by' credit on the robbery."

"That's supposed to make us square?"

"Grudges are bad business," Mother said. "Fairness isn't a thing. You kids are going to be pissed at me no matter what, but you can't buy lessons like the ones I taught you."

"I'm supposed to forget that you came to the funeral of my mother and saw it as an opportunity to not only steal from me and my siblings, but to get us to commit crimes for you. A fake will. You leveled our house. You made us think our own mother betrayed us. And those are the things that I can think of off the top of my head."

"You were enthusiastic enough," Mother said.

"Are you the devil?"

"No, I'm an Ucker."

"You forgot one thing," Axel said.

"What's that?"

"So am I." Axel picked up the gas can from the trunk, unscrewed the cap, and poured its contents into the trash container.

Mother drew her gun. "Don't do something stupid. That's money. Take it for yourself or let me have it, but don't invent an option that makes no sense."

"It's the only option I have," Axel said. "If I take all of it, you'll try to get it back. Or, at the very least, find a way to screw up my life even more. If you take the money, then you win. And I can't stomach that. But if I burn it, you lose and there's no reason for you to be in my life."

"What about revenge?" Mother said. "Maybe I'll get revenge?"

"Grudges are bad business."

"Do it, Ax," Gretchen said, standing by the door with Kurt. "Light that mother up."

"You got here quick," Axel said.

"We were on our way back when you texted," Gretchen said.

"Did Fritzy get away?" Mother asked.

Kurt shook his head. "Stephanie and Louder are taking him to the hospital."

"Tough break," Mother said.

"It's a gunshot wound," Gretchen said. "It won't take long for the cops to put two and two together. Especially with witnesses. He wasn't happy with you."

"He won't talk," Mother said.

"Normal people would ask how bad he's hurt," Kurt said.

Mother nodded and looked down at the gun in her hand. "Normal people probably would."

"So here we are," Axel said.

"I'll call your bluff," Mother said. "Let's see what a bunch of money looks like on fire."

Axel reached into his pocket. And then into the other one. He looked in the trunk and patted his hand around the carpeted interior.

"What is it?" Gretchen asked. "What's wrong?"

"I thought I had matches," Axel said. "I don't have a light."

Mother laughed and walked toward Axel. Axel closed the lid of the garbage can and attempted to roll it away from her, but he couldn't get any speed with its weight. Mother was faster than she looked—which wasn't saying a whole lot. She caught up to Axel and knocked him to the ground with a hard push.

Mother put a hand on the lid of the can and held the gun on Axel. She gulped air. "You made me run. I've shot other relatives for less."

Axel didn't see the arc of the butterfly knife. From his perspective it appeared out of nowhere. First, Mother's arm had no knife sticking in it. And then, presto, knife.

Mother yelped and dropped the pistol. Axel slid on the ground and picked it up. Gretchen and Kurt ran over to them. Gretchen had Fritzy's gun in her hand.

"Nice throw," Axel said.

"You get pretty good when you're stuck in a hotel room in Mississippi," Gretchen said. "I just hope they don't take the pictures off the wall, or they're going to find some holes."

"Let me take a look at your wound," Kurt said, reaching for Mother.

"Stay away from me," Mother said. Grimacing, she pulled the knife out of her arm.

"Damn," Gretchen said.

Holding the knife, Mother seemed to consider something for a moment, but then dropped it. She grabbed the handkerchief that Kurt held out for her and held it to the wound. "I'll be interested to find out what you think is going to happen next. You going to kill me?"

"We're not you," Kurt said.

"Are you sure?" Mother said. "Uckers are as Uckers do."

"There's no such thing as bad blood."

"You're wrong," Mother said. "Blood is everything."

"Blood and family mean nothing to you," Gretchen said. "You wanted the money. It wasn't any more than that."

"It's naive to think that family is supposed to arbitrarily help each other," Mother said. "What have you done for me?"

"A family is what you make of it," Kurt said. "It only takes a little bit of effort. Fritzy was better family to me than you, and he was lying to me and trying to steal from me, too."

"We need to get out of here," Axel said. "There's a guy with a dildo outside that I don't like the looks of."

"Him?" Kurt said. "Naw, he's cool."

"We should get going anyway," Gretchen said. "It's going to take a few hours to get everyone together."

"Everyone?" Mother asked. "Who is everyone?"

"Your family," Axel said. "The other Uckers."

CHAPTER 39

The Skinrippermobile—returned to its former gory glory by Pepe—pulled into the massive parking lot of Hofbräuhaus. Kurt drove. Gretchen sat in the passenger seat. Axel kept an eye on Mother in the back, her hands bound in front of her.

"You didn't have to tie me up," Mother said.

"I know," Axel said.

"We wanted you to know what it feels like," Gretchen said as she got out of the van. "Hurts, don't it?"

"You think I ain't never been tied up?" Mother said. "Handcuffs, rope, zip ties, phone cords. And that's just recreationally."

"Not a picture I want in my head," Kurt said.

Mother looked out the windshield. "Appropriate place to leave my body, I suppose."

"I told you, we're not going to kill you," Gretchen said. "I don't think we are. Are we?"

"I'm not. I don't know about them," Axel said, gesturing toward the restaurant entrance.

Standing at the front door, a group of five men and three women waited.

Gretchen and Axel helped Mother out of the van. Kurt shook hands and hugged the people gathered. As Mother walked past her relatives into the restaurant, she said, "Be careful, kids. These are bad folks."

Kurt had been the only sibling who had fully embraced the family reunion that first introduced them to the rest of the Ucker family. While Mother sequestered and recruited Axel and Gretchen that night, he mingled and made relationships with aunts, uncles, and cousins.

Gretchen didn't know if Mother had seen Kurt as simple or a nonthreat, but she had underestimated him. He was all about family, something that had eluded him to that point. He had created ongoing correspondence and social media friendships (under pseudonyms) with a half dozen relatives. That led him to contact a few incarcerated Uckers whom he hadn't met in person, members of the family eager to connect with anyone.

The subsequent correspondences that arose from that single meeting helped Kurt create bonds. He wrote a few of his relatives once or twice a week. Everyone remained cagey about discussing any criminal activity, but there was still plenty to talk about. He mostly traded book and movie suggestions, jokes, and recipes. He played Words with Friends. And found a cousin who was more of an aficionado of Viking metal than he was. Friendships had been formed from far less, especially within the arbitrary bond of family.

After Axel pitched his plan to catch Mother in the act of robbing the armored car, they knew they needed to do more than just get the money from her. It wouldn't end there with Mother. They needed a path that wouldn't create a never-ending back-and-forth between them and Mother. Kurt suggested he reach out to the other Uckers.

He sent a simple message to his contact list: "I need some help. Will you help me?" No context. No backstory. No scale to the amount of help. Did he need help moving an old refrigerator or to bury a body?

Not a single Ucker answered with equivocation. No "Depends." No "First you have to tell mes." The overwhelming response was "Whatever you need. Give me a time and place. I'll be there." Kurt brought that kind of loyalty out in people.

"Let it be known on this day herewith that the official tribunal of Mathilda "Mother" Ucker took place in San Diego, California, for the purpose of determining violations in the Ucker family code."

"Shut up, DJ," Mother said. "There's no code."

Dolphus Ucker Jr. laughed. "Where's your sense of humor, Matty?"

Mother sat at the end of the table, with Kurt and Gretchen on either side of her. The rest of the family sat or stood throughout the room.

Axel wheeled in the trash can filled with money. It had been easier to just put the whole thing in one of the cars than to load and unload the bags of cash. He left the trash can near the table and found a seat.

"When did you get out of Club Fed?" Mother asked Dolphus Jr.

"A couple weeks ago," he said. "If you get the chance, Lompoc is nice. Knocked a couple strokes off my handicap. I would've stayed longer, but the more money you steal, the less time you do. Nobody is impressed if you steal a hundred bucks, but try to steal a few million, the jury is so impressed, they want to let you off."

"You still angry with me about that thing in Manitoba?"

"You threw me off a moving train," Dolphus Jr. said. "I broke my leg and got arrested. Luckily we were in Canada, so it wasn't like real jail."

"That was fifteen years ago."

"Yeah, you're right," Dolphus Jr. said. "That makes all the difference."

Mother turned to Kurt. "Every single person at this table is worse than me." She pointed around the table. "She ran a fraud scam after that hurricane in Texas. He bilked senior citizens out of their retirements. DJ shot a man in Reno. Not to watch him die, but because he's the worst shot on the planet."

"That may be," Gretchen said, "but they didn't screw us over. They didn't turn us against our dead mother, destroy our home, use us, and then throw us away."

"Matty is good at that," Uma Ucker said. "The bag you're left holding is always empty."

"I don't want to be a prima donna," Mother said, "but can we put the gasoline-soaked money somewhere else? I was getting light-headed in the van, and I'm still smelling it."

Nods and grunts from the room seconded the motion.

"She's right," Dolphus Jr. said. "It's a strong odor."

"Sorry," Axel said, getting up and rolling the trash can to the far end of the room.

"Thanks," Mother said. "That's better."

"Kurt explained to us what happened," Dolphus Jr. said. "Pretty bad, even for you. Especially to family. We've worked together and bilked each other, to be sure, but this is different. They weren't born into the life. You should have shepherded them. The preacher thing was your normal MO, but the will and the house—that was over the line. You destroyed the house they grew up in. Not so happy you used Pop's name either."

"Henry held my half of our scores. I never got that money. Henry owed me. When he died, the family inherited his debt."

The Uckers, except for Mother, all performed the sign of the cross.

"What about my money?" Mother asked.

"A write-off," Dolphus Jr. said. "These kids are Uckers. They are family. They owe no debt to you, but now, you owe them."

"Let them take the armored car money," Mother said. "We'll call it even."

"That money is not yours to give. They stole that money from you fair and square. You owe them for the house. Damages. Pain and suffering."

"We don't want anything," Axel said. "Other than for it to be over. The things she took, we can't have back. Money don't matter. She can walk away, but we need to know she won't show back up in our lives."

"That's where you were after Mississippi," Mother said. "You didn't need to do any of this for that to happen. If you had gone home, licked your wounds, and left me alone, I would have stayed out of your hair."

"That was on your terms," Gretchen said. "This is on ours. You don't get to beat us."

"Which is where we are," Dolphus Jr. said. "We need your assurance that you'll stay out of their lives. We're here to make it official."

"Or else what, DJ?" Mother asked. "You've been acting the big shot since we were kids."

"First off, there's the matter of Fred Kramer."

"Who?" Axel said.

"Fritzy," Dolphus Jr. said. "He's been arrested and charged. He might keep quiet out of love or loyalty or tradition or whatever reason. Sounds like a stand-up guy. But the lawyer we sent to talk to him suggested to me that he was open to giving up his associate."

"He wouldn't do that," Mother said, but the confidence waned in her voice.

"He has the distinct impression that you were done with him and even if he hadn't gotten caught that you would have probably double-crossed him at some point very soon. You have a habit of swapping out boyfriends."

"I'll be honest," Mother said. "I was getting a little tired of him."

"You are a piece of work," Gretchen said.

"No matter which way the wind blows," Dolphus Jr. continued, "keep in mind that your condo in Rosarito isn't a secret and Mexico extradites."

"I'm getting the picture," Mother said.

"Also." Jeremiah Ucker, a young man in a suit, pulled out a piece of paper. "I've done some research and dug up your account in the

Caymans, your other account in Costa Rica, safety deposit boxes in Panorama City, Irvine, Palm Desert, and Yuma, and some other assets that every Ucker will consider to be in play if you don't take the deal. I've distributed the list to everyone. You'll get hit on all sides."

"That's a very good 'or else,'" Mother said.

Waiting for Mother's Uber, Kurt checked the bandage on her arm. "You should get this looked at. The cut is clean but pretty deep. Infections can be serious."

"You're a good kid," Mother said. "Too good for this family."

"You're wrong," Kurt said. "I'm as much a part of this family as anyone here. I just don't believe that the last name I was born with defines me, limits me, or tells me who I can be."

"For what it's worth, I'm sorry about some stuff," Mother said.

"It doesn't really matter," Kurt said. "You're going to have to go away knowing that we could have been family. A real family. That you could have enjoyed my love and loyalty and been a part of the lives of two great human beings, Axel and Gretchen. You blew it. You chose money you didn't need. You were given an opportunity, but you weren't willing to accept it. I feel sorry for you."

Axel and Gretchen stood near but didn't add anything. When the Uber arrived, Kurt gave Mother a hug, careful not to hurt her arm. "Goodbye, Mathilda."

Mother turned and got in the car. It drove away.

Kurt put his arm around Axel and Gretchen. "It's over."

"Did we win?" Gretchen asked. "I don't even know anymore. I'm just exhausted."

"I think we won," Axel said. "We got away with everything. We're free and clear of the police and Mother. And we got the money."

"Yeah, about the money," Dolphus Jr. said.

CHAPTER 40

Kurt flipped the grilled cheese sandwich in the pan. He started the slow count to 117, his scientifically tested method to get to golden brown.

Louder walked into the kitchen. "How many of those are you going to make?"

"I figured two dozen," Kurt said. "If I cut them diagonally, that makes forty-eight individual servings. The warmer is almost full."

"There's only six people. Total. Us and four other people."

"You need to count Pepe twice."

"Let's call that one in the pan the last one."

"You want it?" Kurt asked.

"Hell yeah," Louder said. "Slip some jalapeños in it. Burn some parmesan on the outside." She gave him a kiss and went into the living room.

Kurt wanted his first housewarming party to be perfect. It was like christening a ship. If the bottle didn't break, it was bad luck. If he ran out of food, that was an ill omen. He wasn't only celebrating the new apartment or moving away from Warm Springs, but also the fact that Louder had moved there with him. They were going to try their hand at living together. He was scared and excited and scared. He was also scared.

One more grilled cheese. Just in case.

The final tally for Axel, Gretchen, and Kurt's foray into criminality came to $4,762. That included their non-cut of the Stephanie Holm and Brother Floom jobs and their paltry take from the armored car deal. The rest of the armored car money would end up going to Fred "Fritzy" Kramer for his legal team and continued silence. He deserved it as much as anyone.

They split the money five ways, having decided that Stephanie and Louder deserved a share. For the months of work, they had each earned $952. Axel, Gretchen, and Stephanie gave their shares to Kurt and Louder to help cover their first, last, and deposit.

Axel put the monstrosity of a house on Xanadu Lane on the market. His new real estate agent, Ingrid Moreland, felt confident that a number of single men would find the house to be both a good investment and a nice place to raise a family. The handwritten messages that she sent each potential buyer still looked computer generated to Axel.

The day after the armored car heist, the siblings met at their mother's and father's graves. They thought it would be profound, but they ended up just staring at the names. There wasn't much to say or do. They stayed for ten minutes, then went on their ways.

Stanley Pruitt and Steven McCrary convinced juries that they were coerced and threatened to participate in the robberies. They were let go from Jackson Armored but found jobs as mall security guards. Axel checked in on them every once in a while. From a distance, they looked happier to him.

Axel called Virginia Floom one last time, but the number had been changed. He embraced bachelorhood in the same way that someone on a desert island embraced solitude. He hoped someone saved him soon.

The three Uckers hadn't discussed their futures, but they all showed up to their weekly lunch meetings. Nobody had had to pay the fine yet.

"I like what you've done with the place," Gretchen said, handing Kurt a present. "I think I saw that Iron Maiden poster on Martha Stewart."

"Don't listen to her," Stephanie said, offering Kurt a gift of her own. "*Number of the Beast* is timeless. You can open my gift later. When you and Louder are alone. It's a sexy sex gift."

"Thanks." Kurt felt his face get hot. He tried to use his mind to stop from blushing, but that's not how biology works.

"You guys are great together," Stephanie said. "Gretchen told me that you and Amanda have known each other since grade school. That's awesome. You know the good stuff and the bad, and you still want to be with each other. It doesn't get better than that."

For a moment, Kurt couldn't figure out who Amanda was, but context reminded him that was Louder's real name. It was a pretty name. He'd ask her later if she wanted to be called Amanda. Or maybe he would surprise her. No, probably better if he asked.

"There's food and stuff to drink in the living room. Pepe's already here. He has weed if you want some, but you'll have to answer three riddles."

Gretchen and Stephanie laughed.

Kurt shook his head. "I'm not kidding. He has a riddle book he stole from the junior high school library. He had a vision quest or something and wants people to call him the Sphinx now. It's a thing."

"You people are the weirdest people I've ever met," Stephanie said. "I feel right at home."

Axel knocked on the door and walked in at the same time. "It's me."

"Hey, Ax," Kurt said. "Come on in."

Axel gave Stephanie a head nod. "'Sup?"

"'Sup with you?" Stephanie asked.

"I'm proud of you two," Gretchen said. "You're making headway. Pretty soon you'll be besties. Come on, Steph, let's see how good you are at riddles."

Axel held out a potted succulent to Kurt. "I didn't know what to get you. A plant is traditional. It's like a practice puppy. Or I suppose a taxidermied puppy would be a practice puppy, but a creepy gift."

"Thanks, Ax," Kurt said, pulling Axel into a bear hug. The spines of the aloe plant cut into his midsection, forcing him to back up.

"You can name him Stabby," Axel said.

Full of bread and cheese and wine and beer, Kurt sat on the floor. The beanbags were for guests. Louder, stretched out next to him, used his belly for a pillow. The content smile on her face filled Kurt with happiness.

"A plane crashed," Pepe said. "Every single person died. Who survived?"

"Sphinx," Gretchen said.

"*The* Sphinx," Pepe corrected her.

"My mistake, the Sphinx," Gretchen said. "What happened to 'What's brown and sticky?' Easy riddles?"

"The riddles got to be hard," Pepe said. "Pepe was too generous. He handed out weed like it was free. The Sphinx is a whole different person. But it's a party and you called me Sphinx, so you only got to answer the one riddle."

"Just give it to them," Louder said.

"The Sphinx has spoken," Pepe said.

"I got it," Stephanie said. "If every single person died, the married people survived."

"That's it," Pepe said.

"Booyah," Gretchen said.

"I'll pretend like you didn't just say 'booyah,'" Stephanie said.

"While you drug up," Kurt said, "I'm going to open your present, Gretch."

"It's not—If you don't want it," Gretchen said. "I didn't know what to do with it."

Kurt tore at the wrapping paper. It was the family portrait that had hung in their hall. The one taken just months before their father's death. Mother, father, and children smiling back at him. "I thought you wanted this?"

"I did then," Gretchen said. "I don't know about now. Maybe I'm loaning it. I like the way the future looks. I don't need anything that's about the past. If that makes sense."

"Get up," Kurt said, tapping Louder's shoulder softly. "Everyone get up. We're going to take a new family picture."

The grunts that rose weren't protests, but pain from eating too much melted cheese. Axel looked like a turtle on its shell, rolling back and forth in an effort to rise.

"My foot is asleep," Pepe said.

"Here. Over here." Kurt pointed to one side of the room as he dug through a pile of stuff next to his computer. He found a small tripod. "Everyone. You, too, Stephanie. The Sphinx. All of us. This is our family now."

Everyone lined up. Kurt set the timer, hit the button, and ran to join them. He put a hand around Louder and smiled. They waited.

"How long is the timer?" Gretchen asked, a frozen smile on her face.

"It's taking a long-ass time," Louder said.

"We're set to pop here, honey," Kurt said.

"Great reference," Louder said.

The flash blinded them. The camera clicked. A keeper.

"Let's crack another bottle of wine," Gretchen said, "and really warm this house." Taking a step toward the kitchen, she brushed against the framed portrait on the table. It fell to the floor, causing the glass to crack and the wooden frame to split at one corner.

"You okay, Gretch?" Kurt said.

"I'm fine," Gretchen said. "Luckily this isn't one of those weird 'no shoes' houses."

"It's not weird," Stephanie said. "It preserves the wood floors. We'll discuss it later."

Kurt gently picked up the portrait. He walked it over to the trash can in the kitchen and slid the glass into the bin. He carefully plucked out the remaining glass.

"Sorry, Kurty," Gretchen said, coming up behind him. "Maybe it was an unconscious rebellion. More fodder for the therapist I don't have."

"It's just the glass and frame," Kurt said. "The picture is fine."

He flipped it over and bent the points to take out the backboard. He dropped that in the trash, as well.

"What's that?" Gretchen asked.

Some folded pieces of paper rested behind the photo. Kurt handed them to Gretchen. They were the August and September pages of a wall calendar from 2003. Cursive, sloppy and quickly written, filled both months.

"Holy shit," Gretchen said, reading as she walked into the living room.

"What?" Kurt said. "What is it?"

"Mom wrote this," Gretchen said. "It's a letter to us."

Axel walked to Gretchen. "When was it written? What does it say?"

Without taking her eyes off the letter, Gretchen reached behind her to find a chair. She sat down and read.

"To my beloved children," Gretchen said. "I leave the future and the truth and my own well-being, as everything in my life, in God's hand. If He so chooses that you find this message, then God meant it to be. If it remains hidden, then that, too, will be God's will. He knows the when and the why. Like us all, I will be judged for my sins when it is my time."

"Sounds like a confession," Axel said.

Kurt shushed him.

Gretchen continued. "I loved Henry. I took the marriage vows from our wedding day as an oath to both him and God. He fought his past, his blood. He saw his sins as the only way to help me, his wife, and you, his children. By doing so, he broke a promise to me and a solemn vow to God. Henry let the Devil in his heart. He failed you and me and God. He meant well, his motivation was compassionate, but his actions were unforgivable." Gretchen stopped. "I can't do this. Axel, can you read the rest?"

Axel took the pages. He found where Gretchen had left off.

"There is no healing a child's loss of their father nor the pain of his sins. You are the innocents. While the fruits of Henry's labors were obtained through the worst of his deeds, he did it for you. It is yours. His legacy. I can't deny that. If God so wills, He will lead you to this message. And ultimately lead you to everything that Henry worked hard to obtain. It must have a purpose, a value. It destroyed him. And in the same moment, me.

"If by God's grace this message falls into the hands of my children, know that you were loved. By both your parents. Loved beyond expression or imagination. And that God loves you, too. And that all we ever wanted to do was protect you. Love, Mom."

"Why leave that note and not just tell us?" Kurt said.

"There's a final message at the bottom," Axel said. "Henry's ill-gotten gains weren't his, but once taken, they weren't the previous owner's. Companies and insurance and lifeless institutions. He sinned for the future of his children. If the stolen goods are anyone's, they are yours, my children.

"If this message falls into the hands of a stranger or thief or another Ucker, then I implore you to find my children so they can understand, just as I implore you to find Jesus so that you may walk a better path."

Axel turned over the calendar page. A crude map was drawn over the image of a French bulldog chewing on a rawhide bone.

"You recognize anything on it?" Kurt asked.

"Yeah," Axel said. "Kitchen Creek. There's Buttcrack Rock."

"I named that." Gretchen turned to Stephanie and Louder. "We used to camp at Kitchen Creek. Same spot. We called it Ucker Hill. Buttcrack Rock was at the top. Haven't thought about it in years, but I could take you there wearing a blindfold."

"I don't mean to be flip during a somber moment," Stephanie said, "but are we going on a treasure hunt?"

The question only brought silence. There was no manual on what to do in the situation. Everyone found a piece of wall to stare at, until Gretchen finally spoke.

"Not tonight," Gretchen said. "Tonight we're celebrating family."

"This has been hidden for more than a decade," Axel said. "It can wait. Tonight is about Kurt and Louder and their new digs."

"Let's get that wine going, then," Stephanie said.

Kurt filled everyone's glasses. He toasted. "To Mom and Dad and—you know what?—here's to Mother Ucker. Without any of them, it never would have led us to now. It might have taken all of that chaos to force us together, but I wouldn't want anyone but you weirdos as my family. Huzzah."

"Huzzah," everyone repeated. Drinking and laughter followed.

Looking around the room, Kurt smiled. Whatever they found in the mountains didn't matter. In that moment, he had what he wanted. Everything that mattered to him was in that apartment, because everyone who mattered to him was there.

Although, to be fair, Kurt was pretty excited about the thought of finding buried treasure. It made him feel like a pirate.

ACKNOWLEDGMENTS

As this is my sixth novel to be published by Thomas & Mercer, I need to thank everyone past and present at T&M for their hard work. The time put in by such talented and capable individuals has been integral to any success I've had in my writing life.

For this book, in particular, I have to call out Gracie Doyle and Jessica Tribble, who have shepherded the book and given me the creative freedom and latitude to play. At the same time, their feedback and guidance kept me from going completely off the rails. Big thanks.

When I started writing crime novels, I had no idea what other novelists were like. The inclusivity and support of the crime fiction community exceeded my expectations. Consisting of more than just writers, but readers, editors, reviewers, and more, they have welcomed me into their family. Too many people to name, but you know who you are. I love you all.

Author Bart Lessard is the only person I often willingly give half a manuscript to for feedback. The only person I'll talk to about the book midway through the process. There's no one I'd rather talk story with. Everyone should read his books. Thanks to a great writer, a great person, and a great friend.

A huge thanks to Pinkie and Rich Drew, whose generosity and support throughout my life and career have been amazing. I appreciate and love you.

Some days I can't believe how amazing it is that I get to spend the rest of my life with my wife, Roxanne. As we travel the world together, work on our creative projects, and find joy in the simplest moments, I know it wouldn't be half as interesting, challenging, or fun without her. Looking forward to another twenty-four years of love, laughter, and adventure. I've got a few more harebrained schemes up my sleeve.

ABOUT THE AUTHOR

Illustration © 2012 Roxanne Patruznick

Johnny Shaw is the author of the award-winning Jimmy Veeder Fiasco series, including the books *Dove Season*, *Plaster City*, and *Imperial Valley*, as well as the stand-alone novels *Floodgate* and *Big Maria*. He has won the Spotted Owl and Anthony Awards and was the Grand Marshal of the 69th Annual Carrot Festival Parade. Johnny lives nomadically.

22406143R00180

Printed in Great Britain
by Amazon